"Colonel, we h
breach at the waterline."

"Patch it," Bolan ordered. "I'm coming down." He stepped forward and grabbed one of the ropes leading through the hole the demolitions team had blown into the deck.

"Indigo Phantom Wing, did you copy?"

"Affirmative, Colonel. I got your starboard side."

The helicopters came with a sudden wave of thunder, little more than fifty yards above the ocean's surface, the CH-53Es looking like giant insects.

With unerring accuracy, the combat choppers unleashed everything at their disposal. Twenty-millimeter cannon, chain guns and rocket pods lit up the night with an incendiary display of total destruction.

Two of the powerboats were destroyed before the Executioner gripped the rope and slid down into the hold.

MACK BOLAN ®
The Executioner

#167 Double Action
#168 Blood Price
#169 White Heat
#170 Baja Blitz
#171 Deadly Force
#172 Fast Strike
#173 Capitol Hit
#174 Battle Plan
#175 Battle Ground
#176 Ransom Run
#177 Evil Code
#178 Black Hand
#179 War Hammer
#180 Force Down
#181 Shifting Target
#182 Lethal Agent
#183 Clean Sweep
#184 Death Warrant
#185 Sudden Fury
#186 Fire Burst
#187 Cleansing Flame
#188 War Paint
#189 Wellfire
#190 Killing Range
#191 Extreme Force
#192 Maximum Impact
#193 Hostile Action
#194 Deadly Contest
#195 Select Fire
#196 Triburst
#197 Armed Force
#198 Shoot Down
#199 Rogue Agent
#200 Crisis Point
#201 Prime Target
#202 Combat Zone

#203 Hard Contact
#204 Rescue Run
#205 Hell Road
#206 Hunting Cry
#207 Freedom Strike
#208 Death Whisper
#209 Asian Crucible
#210 Fire Lash
#211 Steel Claws
#212 Ride the Beast
#213 Blood Harvest
#214 Fission Fury
#215 Fire Hammer
#216 Death Force
#217 Fight or Die
#218 End Game
#219 Terror Intent
#220 Tiger Stalk
#221 Blood and Fire
#222 Patriot Gambit
#223 Hour of Conflict
#224 Call to Arms
#225 Body Armor
#226 Red Horse
#227 Blood Circle
#228 Terminal Option
#229 Zero Tolerance
#230 Deep Attack
#231 Slaughter Squad
#232 Jackal Hunt
#233 Tough Justice
#234 Target Command
#235 Plague Wind
#236 Vengeance Rising
#237 Hellfire Trigger
#238 Crimson Tide

DON PENDLETON'S
THE EXECUTIONER®
CRIMSON TIDE

A GOLD EAGLE BOOK FROM
WORLDWIDE®

TORONTO • NEW YORK • LONDON
AMSTERDAM • PARIS • SYDNEY • HAMBURG
STOCKHOLM • ATHENS • TOKYO • MILAN
MADRID • WARSAW • BUDAPEST • AUCKLAND

First edition October 1998
ISBN 0-373-64238-5

Special thanks and acknowledgment to
Mel Odom for his contribution to this work.

CRIMSON TIDE

Let no guilty man escape, if it can be avoided. No personnel considerations should stand in the way of performing...duty.

—Ulysses S. Grant
1822-1885

I intend to hold the line against the predators of the world, those who threaten to consume civilized man. And if I have to, I'll draw the line in the predators' blood.

—Mack Bolan

To the dedicated men and women of the United
States armed forces, both past and present.
God keep.

PROLOGUE

Fire Dolphin Island, the Caribbean

"I know you're a rich man. Even before the money you are going to get from this deal. You can afford a little black-mail."

Lyndon Palfrey stared at the man standing across from him. He kept his aplomb with effort. Emotions were a weak-ness in most of his businesses.

The hot, midday Caribbean sun beat down on them as they stood on the small plateau overlooking the construction area a few hundred yards away. Palfrey's ranch house was on the other side of the island, almost a mile away, but the peaked roof was still visible against the sea of verdant trop-ical vegetation.

"What is it exactly you think you have to blackmail me with, Señor Ruiz?" Palfrey was a tall man in his early for-ties, with a lantern jaw and big bone structure, but he kept it leaned out through exercise, stripping fat from his body through hard work and focus that rivaled the surgical pre-cision of the big yellow earth-movers working in the valley below them. His blond hair was so pale it was almost col-orless against his dark red tan.

Gustavo Ruiz shrugged his beefy shoulders. Perspiration clung to his face in fat drops and his thick black hair hung in sweaty clumps from being under the hard hat. He was heavy, but not obese; his mustache, cut short and neatly trimmed, was out of place on his round face. He wore olive slacks that showed white salt scars and tucked them into calf-high mud-encrusted work boots. The khaki shirt had the sleeves hacked off unevenly at the shoulder.

"This place," the construction boss said, indicating the site with a wave of his hand.

"What about this place?"

"Well, *señor,* first you have us dig this fine, big hole in the ground, to construct an underground bunker for your exercise camp—"

"Paramilitary camp," Palfrey interjected. "If you're going to blackmail a man, at least get it right."

Ruiz had grown up in Cuba, according to the background check Palfrey had gotten on the man, and had only fled Communist rule eight years ago. He still carried peasant ways even though he was apparently integrating himself with capitalistic ideals with a piggish zest.

The construction worker bowed his head slightly. "Of course, *señor.* Your paramilitary camp. You told me you were going to train men here, men who would be willing to pay for your expertise in fighting. I've been told you were a highly decorated officer in Special Forces."

Palfrey stared at the man without saying anything.

"I know some of the people on the neighboring islands didn't like that idea," Ruiz continued, "but you told them it was your island and you'd do anything you damn well pleased with it." He smiled broadly. "Me, I like a man who stands up and tells the world to kiss his ass. It takes a brave hombre to do this."

Palfrey raised an eyebrow with interest. Ruiz was trying to take the sting out of the bite now by being complimentary. If the construction worker had been given a little more time, not been in such a rush to grab as much as he could get, he could have done well for himself. The islands were full of illicit business these days.

"So tell me why I'm not telling you to kiss my ass right now?" Palfrey asked.

"Because I know about the Japanese man." Ruiz reached

into his pocket and took out a matchbook. His lips moved as he attempted to sound out the name there. When he pronounced it, he got it wrong.

Knowledge of the name wouldn't have mattered anyway, because it was a false one. But the connection to the Japanese had to be kept quiet.

Ruiz put the damp matchbook back in his shirt pocket. "See, when you were very first advertising for this job, I was told that maybe your money was not so fat."

It wasn't, which was why Palfrey had set up the deal with Shotozumi and the Yakuza. This was the first time he'd let business touch the island.

"So I was a little surprised when you had your payroll here on the island on time. The banks told me there might be some problem."

"The banks told you that?"

"*Sí.* My brother's wife works for one of the banks where you keep accounts." Ruiz shrugged. "It is a natural thing for a man to check up on his employer."

Palfrey took a handkerchief from his pocket and mopped the perspiration from his neck. He scanned the jungle around them. Down at the dig, the deep basso roars of the diesel engines continued. A cement mixer poured a thick, gray soup into molds on one side of the excavation. "You'll still be paid. The deal falling through doesn't affect your payroll."

"I know." Ruiz nodded happily and ran a finger alongside his big nose. "The other men on the crew are happy to know this. But this made me curious, as well. Knowing as I did that you didn't have enough money for this project on your own, I wondered who your backers might be. My brother's wife did some checking, and she found out about the Japanese corporation. I think to myself, Gustavo, does it make sense for Señor Palfrey to use Japanese money to build a...paramilitary camp to train wealthy Americans who want to learn how to fight?"

Palfrey watched the man working the unloading gate of

the cement mixer pull away the trough after the mold had been filled. Pies of the liquid gray mix, ranging in size from silver dollars to pizzas, stood out against the fresh-turned earth.

"I was puzzled," Ruiz admitted. "Even more so when you told us yesterday that we weren't going to finish the bunker we were building."

"The money fell through," Palfrey said.

"My sister-in-law looked into that as well. She says there's much more money in your account."

"But not enough to buy the guns and other needed equipment. I'll have to give that money back, as well as make up the money I spent." He glanced at his watch. It was 11:55. He wasn't worried. This little deviation in his time schedule could be easily caught up.

"That's what you say," Ruiz went on. He paced over to the observation point with Palfrey. "You had us build a few shooting ranges on this side of the island to make it look like we were putting in a bunker for your camp. Now, poof! No camp." He grinned. "But you still have this big hole in the ground when you could have us cover it up."

"What if the financing should come through later?" Palfrey asked, amused at how much thinking the man had been doing. "I'd have to pay for the same work all over again."

Ruiz shrugged. "I think you've already got what you wanted. I see this Japanese man come around. I ask my cousin's son at the airport in Kingston about Japanese arrivals. Presto! He tells me this name, then checks with a friend of his to find out that, *sí*, this man has chartered a helicopter to come see you."

"Presto," Palfrey repeated with mocking enthusiasm.

"*Sí.*" Ruiz nodded contentedly. "I know about the money. I know about the Japanese. The only thing I don't know is what you're going to stick in that big hole. But I'm wagering that you'll pay me not to discuss what I do know with anyone."

"I see." Palfrey turned to the man with a cordial smile. "Well, Gustavo, I'll admit, you're a canny son of a bitch."

His easy demeanor made the Cuban nervous. "Don't go getting any ideas about trying to do anything with me," Ruiz said. "I've told Manolo and Tadeo, as well. Should anything happen to me, they'll make sure the Jamaican police look into my death."

"Oh, I wouldn't expect you to needlessly expose yourself to any risk," Palfrey said. "You're a smart man." He glanced at his watch again. It was noon.

A moment later, the lunch whistle for the construction workers went off. The shrill keening startled a flock of gulls from the beach only a hundred yards away, and they leaped into the air with a great beating of long, white wings.

Palfrey took his flat-brimmed hat from his head and slipped the Raven Arms .25 automatic pistol from inside the headband. He spun with it in his fist, taking advantage of the blowing whistle to cover the noise of his shots. Sunlight sparked off the stubby barrel as he emptied the 6-round clip into Ruiz's face.

Blood spattered onto the thin grass growing defiantly in the sand around them. The big Cuban crashed to the ground, quivered for just a moment and lay still.

Palfrey calmly knelt and picked up the loose brass, then put a fresh magazine into the little pistol. The whistle finished blowing only seconds before he finished. Standing back up, he jiggled the hot brass and gazed at the work site. No one was looking in his direction.

He walked back to the gleaming Land Rover parked under the trees and took a cellular phone from the passenger seat. He punched in a number for the house and slid over behind the steering wheel. "Crispus, I want you to fire up the big helicopter and drop down on our friends at the construction site. Then make the hop to Kingston with them. Take them to Antonio's and tell them lunch is on me. Tell them Mr. Ruiz will be finalizing the separation wages with me." He glanced at the workers milling around the stalled machines. "Hurry up, man, those people are hungry."

He punched the End button and started the Land Rover. Smoothly he drove over the corpse. Minutes later, the big-bodied Bell workhorse landed near the construction site, sweeping sand in all directions with its rotors. It didn't take the workers long to get the idea and they jumped aboard, yelling to one another.

When it took off, Palfrey waved. They could see him, but there was no way they could see the dead man. After the helicopter vanished in the distance, he backed the Land Rover off the corpse. It took some work and he was dripping sweat when he finished, but he loosened Ruiz's belt and looped it over the 4WD's trailer hitch. He didn't want blood inside his vehicle.

He drove slowly, dragging the body back to the construction site. When he arrived, he got out, unhooked Ruiz's body and dragged it over to the poured concrete. Without ceremony, he dropped it in, jumping back in time to keep the splatters from getting on his hiking boots.

The body vanished without a trace, sinking into the ooze. It was only the first secret that would be hidden there.

Climbing back into the Land Rover, Palfrey drove toward the main house. He wanted a shower and a cool drink. He scooped up the cellular phone and dialed an international number.

The person who answered spoke in Japanese.

"I'd like to speak with Mr. Shotozumi," Palfrey said. "There is a small problem requiring his attention." He waited while the call was forwarded. Manolo and Tadeo would regret ever having been called friend by Ruiz. Friends were for losers.

But business partners, that was another thing. He'd never done business with the Yakuza before, but he admired its efficiency.

1

Kingston, Jamaica

Mack Bolan sauntered casually toward the Chrysler sedan parked in the shadow of the hurricane fence protecting the dock area. The Beretta 93-R rode in a paddle holster at his back, hidden by the lightweight sports coat he wore. Dressed in charcoal slacks, a turquoise-and-black short-sleeved shirt and loafers, he didn't draw any attention from most of Kingston. Jamaica's late-evening tourist crowd was still making the circuit among the gaily lit bars near the beach.

The gazes from the two men in the Chrysler felt as intense as crosshairs from a sniper scope. The Executioner knew they could be every bit as deadly.

The guy sitting behind the wheel was in his late twenties. His face was hard and lean, with deep-set dark eyes. He had a full head of wiry red hair the color of dark rust, and it was carefully cut to look professional. He wore a summer-weight dark suit that, like the Chrysler, didn't draw a lot of attention.

The car shifted on its springs as the big man on the passenger seat climbed out and glared at Bolan across the top. He was walking muscle, boosted by steroids and kept mean by natural inclination. Bolan gave him ten years on the man behind the wheel, and his sunburned face bore the stamp of hard time spent outdoors recently. His windbreaker advertised a jai alai team on a shoulder patch and gapped open enough that Bolan could see the pistol tucked in the holster under his left arm.

"You need directions or something, pal?" the big man demanded.

"No," Bolan said. He didn't stop walking toward the car.

"Maybe you need to back off then, if you know what's good for you. This here's a private party."

"Well," Bolan said, "then, we're going to take a look at all the invites." He ignored the big man and looked at the driver. "I've got a card in my pocket."

The driver nodded. "Slow and easy. My associate tends to get somewhat overly enthusiastic."

"You the headcock pulling the freight on this op?" Bolan asked. He pushed the card against the windshield, face outward.

The driver reached out and took it. He pulled a penflash from his shirt pocket and played it over the card. "You're buying into this personally?"

Bolan regarded the man with a level gaze. "As of this minute, I own it."

"What the hell is he talking about?" the muscle asked.

"Here, Bobby," the driver said, handing the card out the window to him. "You ever seen one of these?"

Bobby took the card and stared at it, turning to catch the surface in the moonlight. "The Ace of Spades." His mouth tightened as he glanced at Bolan. "I don't know you."

The Executioner nodded. "That's right. And after tonight, you won't know me either. I'm comfortable with that. How about you?"

The hardman shrugged and tried to look relaxed. He didn't come across that way. "Sure."

"Why don't you take a walk and let me talk to your friend here," Bolan suggested.

A belligerent look filled the big man's eyes.

The driver spoke from inside the car, never looking away from Bolan. "Breeze, Bobby. Stay around. You'll know if I need you."

"Sure, kid." Reluctantly the hardman wandered off to

another car about fifty yards back and stood outside talking to the men inside.

"Like to sit?" the driver asked.

Bolan walked around to the other side and climbed into the car. He glanced around the beach area, knowing they'd fallen under the scrutiny of at least a dozen local undercover cops and the embassy agents working liaison for U.S. interests. If things had broken the other way, he might have been in that camp tonight.

"What do I call you?" the driver asked. A 9 mm SIG-Sauer P226 pistol lay on his left thigh within easy reach of his fingers. It was matte black and wouldn't easily be seen in the night.

"LaMancha."

A slight smile twisted the driver's lips. "Well-read, I see." He glanced at Bolan. "Unless that's your real name."

Despite the situation and the fact that the man sitting across from him was mafioso, Bolan found himself warming to the guy. Still, he kept his distance. "Who're you?"

"Gabriel Syxx. How did you get into this?"

"I was asked in."

"By whom?"

Bolan looked out at the dark water. Boats moved out in the bay with their running lights on, looking festive. Buoys lit up the restricted areas where a few swimmers still braved the cooling winds. "By Mr. Catalano."

Syxx lifted the cellular phone mounted on the dash. "You don't mind me checking that out?"

"No." Bolan recited the number as the mafioso punched it in, surprising the other man. It was Catalano's personal number—the one he would be at until news of his daughter's ransom reached him.

The conversation was short. The soldier knew it would be. The fix had been put in by Leo Turrin, who was still deeply connected to mob affairs despite pulling a double life as a semiretired mob member and holding down a desk in the Justice Department in Washington, D.C., as a liaison for blacklight State Department operations.

Bolan had stepped into the high-stakes game with an ante of his own, using the cover of a Black Ace. As an Ace, he had anonymity and power within Mafia ranks. Aces were allowed to cap a boss in front of his own Family if acting on orders from La Commissione. It was a role the hellfire warrior had used many times to strike against his enemies. This night, he hoped to use it to save innocent lives.

The ransom payoff had become complicated.

Syxx punched the phone off and cradled it. "Okay, you're legit. Now what? I'm supposed to follow your lead."

"Tell me what you've got," Bolan directed.

"You know about the kidnappings?" Syxx asked.

"Mr. Catalano's daughter and two other women." Bolan knew about the string of kidnappings leading up to the latest one. They'd been in the news for the past seven months. Cruise lines in the Caribbean were being selectively targeted by a group of modern-day pirates.

None of the law-enforcement agencies involved had a line yet on who was behind the kidnappings. The general consensus was that the group was from the islands. They used only stolen boats and outfitted them with a variety of military ordnance. Two of the pirates had turned up dead in unexpected gunplay during the kidnapping of Devon Catalano four days earlier from the *Foambreaker,* but running their fingerprints through National Criminal Intelligence Center had turned up nothing. Paper was circulating through the islands now, looking for a match with a local police department, but it would take time.

The Executioner's interest had been captured by the pirates' foray before the one that got the mobster's daughter. Almost two weeks earlier, the pirates had approached a small cruise ship based in the Caymans and ordered it to drop anchor. Faced with at least two minicannons, the captain had had no choice.

The pirates had boarded, searching for a Hollywood film

star who was rumored to have been on the ship. They hadn't found him, but what they did find was a small tactical unit of Grand Cayman police waiting for their arrival. Island police had been tipped about the possible interception.

The gun battle had been pitched and bloody. In the end, the pirates had placed charges aboard the cruise ship and blown out the stern. Fourteen people had died before rescue ships could arrive, even though they'd been standing by. As far as anyone knew, the pirates didn't lose anyone.

"These people are fast and they're good," Syxx commented. "Like a good special ops team. Nothing fancy, nothing complicated, and they keep it all to simple in-and-out. They sink the boats they use to attack the cruise ships with. Some of them have turned up in follow-up search-and-rescue maneuvers, but nothing's ever been found to tie anyone to them."

Bolan scanned the marina. He could sense the tension building. "What time's the pickup?"

Syxx glanced at the readout on the clock radio. "Nine-fifteen. Within the next four minutes."

"Who's picking up the money?"

"Local guy named Mestipen Seid." Syxx shifted restlessly in his seat. "Works as a part-time private eye from what we've been able to find out." He grinned without mirth. "As you might guess, our connections here on the island are limited. Catalano doesn't handle any drug action, but the Rastafarians know who he is just the same. Anybody with an Italian name is suspect to them."

"How'd you get a name like Syxx?" Bolan asked.

"My grandfather came over from the old country in the forties. Chicago. People figured he was looking to hook up with Capone, the Purple Gang, those guys. He bastardized his name to Syxx, made it legal somewhere in there. Back then, it wasn't too hard." Syxx started the Chrysler's engine and pulled on his seat belt. "He was a cop, a good cop. Busted my dad a couple times for making book. They'd always loved the Sox, but the gambling made it rough for them to enjoy a game together later.'' He reached into a ready-file and pulled out an eight-by-ten picture.

Bolan looked at it. The picture was printed on good stock and in color. The moonlight washed out most of the hues, but he figured he'd know the man if he saw him. "This Seid?''

"The very guy,'' Syxx answered, gazing up the road winding to the beach.

Mestipen Seid was black and wore gold rings in both ears. His hair was razored close to the scalp and looked like stubble. In the picture, he was smiling, confident. An attached sheet gave his other stats: six-two, one-eighty, hazel eyes.

"So what does he do when he's not being a private eye?'' Bolan asked as he passed the picture back.

A five-year-old Subaru Brat with flames painted on the sides topped the hill of the road leading down to the beach. It pulled into a spot in the public parking area and a man got out alone.

Bolan took out a compact pair of IR binoculars and looked at the man.

The guy was black and lean, and dressed in a jacket over casual jeans and a sports shirt. He kicked sand with his open-toed sandals, looking around as if he were waiting for someone.

"Hey,'' Syxx said suddenly, straightening in his seat. "That's not Seid.''

"No,'' Bolan agreed, "but it looks a lot like him. Hopefully anyone who knows him personally will be fooled, too.'' He swept the night glasses over the area, charting the movement by the police and State Department teams.

"What's going on?'' Syxx demanded.

A small powerboat thudded to a stop against one of the long wooden docks protruding into the bay. Three men hustled off and walked toward the private eye's double. One of them carried a fat valise while the other two fell into flanking positions around him. Short, stubby barrels glinted in their fists.

"Change in plans," Bolan said. "Start the engine. When the wheels come off this thing, hang back and don't get involved. We're not getting caught up in it."

"You got a ringer for Seid?" Syxx demanded.

"Yeah. What did you think you were going to do with all the local heat if they decided to interfere?"

"They're not supposed to. Our people were going to score the cash to Seid and he'd vanish."

"Taking an entire posse with him." Bolan moved the glasses back to the impostor as the three men came closer. "Senator Gladsdale wants his daughter back, too. Those law-enforcement people aren't going to back off."

The media hadn't missed that tidbit in their coverage. Although Catalano was based in Boston and Gladsdale was a congressman from Arizona specializing in environmental issues, several of the sensational magazines were already hinting at possible illegal dealings between them. From what Bolan had found out from Hal Brognola, the Stony Man liaison with the White House, the women didn't even know each other.

"If push came to shove, I figured we could push harder," Syxx answered. "Mr. Catalano doesn't want anything to happen to his daughter."

The three men had converged on the Seid look-alike. Bolan knew the couriers didn't know much about the man they were meeting except the kind of car he was driving and where he would be. It was the same information that had leaked back to the Jamaican police and the State Department people.

"Things will go better," the Executioner said, "if we don't start shoving early."

"So where's Seid?"

"Getting his money from the real couriers."

The valise was passed and the black man climbed back into the Subaru. The cars surrounding the area started their engines, the low rumble of concealed horsepower combating the sound of the low breakers coming in from the ocean and the undertone of calypso music belting out of the bars. No one switched on their lights except the Subaru.

"What if he gives us the slip?" Syxx asked.

"He won't." Bolan didn't elaborate. Shadows on top of one of the buildings caught his attention. It was possible they belonged to the police department or State agents.

Without warning, thin light beams jetted across the intervening distance from the cars to the buildings. It took the Executioner only a heartbeat to recognize them as laser sights turned green in the IR binoculars. Then one of them splashed across the Chrysler's windshield, leaving a glowing dot against the glass.

"Sniper!" Bolan warned, drawing the Beretta in one smooth motion and shoving his arm through the window. The 9 mm pistol rocked against his palm as he squeezed off shots at the shadow lying across a two-story warehouse fifty yards away. Although the pistol was silenced, it didn't take people long to figure out what was going on when they spotted the muzzle flashes.

Gunfire broke out, rolling in like a sudden summer squall. The Chrysler's windshield shattered inward.

"Go!" Bolan ordered.

The sniper on the rooftop rolled over the edge and dropped onto a tattered awning defiantly sticking out from the front of the warehouse. Some of the other cars had already taken hits. Less than thirty feet back of their position, Bolan watched through the back glass as one of the Mafia hardmen stumbled from the car holding his face as blood ran down his arms and stained his brightly colored T-shirt.

The Chrysler was hit repeatedly. More of the windows imploded, and the headrest was ripped from the passenger seat.

Syxx yanked the transmission in gear and shoved the accelerator to the floor. The tires spun on the layer of sand that had blown onto the asphalt during the day.

The drivers of two of the island police undercover cars switched on spotlights and swept them across the buildings and boats. One of the lights exploded almost immediately as a high-powered rifle bullet took it out.

"Get clear," Bolan said, watching as two older cars raced toward the fleeing Subaru. A flatbed truck roared across the access road behind it and cut off possible pursuit.

"I'm going for it," Syxx warned.

"Do it." Bolan leaned out the passenger side again. He dropped the Beretta's sights over the face of a man shoving a machine pistol through the truck's side window. Bullets chopped at the Chrysler, and the Executioner flamed a 3-round burst.

The gunner's head snapped back, and blood covered the truck's windshield on the inside.

Syxx steered hard, fighting the wheel. "Hold on." He stayed close to the truck as it stopped, aiming for the gap. The truck's reverse lights flared white as the driver worked the transmission.

Bolan stitched a half-dozen shots across the back glass, shattering it into gleaming shards that showered into the truck cab. The driver hesitated just long enough.

The Chrysler roared through the gap, scraping long scars down the side of the body and rocking as it fought against the truck's greater weight. Then they were past. Metal pinged as the battered fenders hammered against the tires.

Bolan reloaded the Beretta. Ahead of them, the two cars had the Subaru shouldered over to the side of the road. Five dreadlocked men brandishing guns jumped out of the two pursuit vehicles and charged the small 4WD.

The guy who looked like Mestipen Seid shoved the valise out the door and showed them his open palms as he sank to his knees.

"Rastafarians," Syxx said. He freed the SIG-Sauer from under his leg and kept driving. "Like everybody else on this goddamned island, they must have heard about the ransom delivery, too. Five million bucks was too much to pass on. Looks like they decided to cut themselves in on the deal."

"Keep driving," Bolan said.

A Rastafarian wearing a silver eye patch over his right eye grabbed the driver's hair and yanked viciously, pulling him into an even more vulnerable position. He shoved his pistol muzzle to the man's forehead.

"They're going to kill him."

Less than fifty yards separated the Chrysler from the Rastafarians.

Bolan knew it, but the driver had known going in that the assignment wasn't a safe one. He'd been culled from the island's shadows as well, living life in the shadows. Still, the big man didn't like the idea of leaving the driver behind.

Sighting carefully, staring into the Rastafarian's face as the Chrysler closed on him, Bolan said, "Hold it steady."

"You got it." Syxx kept a firm grip on the wheel.

The other Rastafarians turned on the approaching car, using their own vehicles as shields. They opened fire without hesitation.

Calm inside, as in tune with his weapon as the sight, Bolan loosed two rounds. One caught the Rastafarian in the silver eye patch and the other took off the top of his head. The corpse collapsed to the ground like a puppet with its strings cut. The driver was in motion at once, throwing himself over the Subaru and scrambling for cover amid the trees and bushes scabbing the sandy hills coming up from the beach.

Bullets thudded into the Chrysler as it passed the stalled cars. Glass shattered and spun, glittering in the moonlight. A piece kissed Bolan's cheek and he felt the warmth of fresh blood.

"Where to?" Syxx asked.

"Windward Road," Bolan said. "Take it south, to where it links up with Marcus Garvey Drive. We head east to Linda Street across the railroad tracks. I've got a car waiting."

"Man, those directions don't mean jackshit to me," the Mafia hardman said. "This isn't my island." He was coming up to an intersection.

"Left," Bolan said. "Now."

Syxx nodded and made the turn, shooting through the red light and across a staggered lane of oncoming traffic. "You know where Seid's going with the money?"

"I will." The Executioner glanced through the back window. The night was lit up with neon for the late beach traffic and carousers, but the unmistakable glow of official and emergency lights was mixed with it now. Sirens screamed from approaching vehicles, and a police chopper whizzed past overhead, a search beam probing the ground ahead of it.

Syxx reached for the cellular phone.

"Don't," Bolan advised.

"I was just going to call the rest of the team, let them know where to meet us."

"There's no us," the Executioner said. "The guys who didn't make it out of the snare back there can keep attention from the police as well as whatever eyes and ears the pirates have open to them tonight."

Syxx glanced at him. "Do you think Seid is really going to get Catalano's daughter back?"

"If the money's there," Bolan said. Of the eleven other hostages taken for ransom, six of them were paid for. The other five were killed. One of them hadn't been who the pirates thought they had, and with all the confusion in the wake of the abduction, the family hadn't been notified until the hostage had turned up dead.

"The money's there," Syxx said. Then he looked at Bolan. "It is, isn't it?"

"Yeah. The Rastafarians got a case of paper bills. Take another left." The soldier had memorized his escape route earlier.

Syxx pulled the car around in a tight turn, not bothering with the speed limits. If they were noticed in the shape the car was in, they'd be pulled over anyhow. "So the rescue squad is me and you."

Bolan looked at the man and gave him a wintry smile. "The way I figure it, that's all it's going to take."

"YOU SERVED in the military," Bolan said as he unlocked the back of the Jeep Cherokee. He'd parked in an alley near a small canning operation near the Railway Corporation line that serviced the shipping interest of the island and ran northwest to Montego Bay.

"Marines," Syxx replied.

Bags in the back held armament the Executioner had scavenged from the local black market. With money no object, he'd outfitted himself well. As a port of trade, even with the Kingston law-enforcement teams cracking down on drugs and weapons, weapons were readily available—just expensive.

"I was told you saw action," Bolan said, taking out a duffel and tossing it to the younger man.

Syxx caught the bag easily, surprise showing on his face when he realized how heavy it was. "You heard a lot."

"I do my homework." Bolan shouldered his own duffel and moved to the front of the Cherokee. He laid the Beretta on the hood and started to strip. The alley was deserted except for a handful of rats working the garbage containers. He left the clothes where they fell and pulled on a combat blacksuit.

"Desert Storm," Syxx said. "One of the first in." After only a moment, he started to strip on the other side of the vehicle.

"You'll find an M-16/M-203 combo in that bag," Bolan said. "Should be familiar."

"Oh, yeah." Syxx pulled on a combat blacksuit too. "I take it a ransom run isn't exactly what Mr. Catalano has in mind for tonight."

"No." Bolan opened the door and slid behind the wheel. "The guys who've been hitting the cruise lines just hit the endangered species list. Are you up for it?"

"I got a choice?" Syxx pulled himself into the Cherokee.

"Yeah. This is a volunteer assignment." The soldier put the transmission in reverse and backed out into the street, turning the lights on after he was rolling.

"And if I say no?"

"Pick a street corner." Bolan swept the lanes with his gaze. They'd left the Chrysler blocks back, and he didn't expect anyone to connect them to it now. He glanced at his watch. It was 9:28 p.m. Seid should have been rolling for thirteen minutes. He put his foot down on the accelerator. It was time he'd have to make up.

His Intel on the operation was limited at the moment. Tonight had been designed as a soft probe into the defenses. He planned on rattling the cages and seeing what struck back out of the dark.

"Then you're on your own?" Syxx asked.

Bolan nodded. "I've been there before."

"Not tonight, buddy." Syxx pulled on one of the hiking boots from the bag. "Hey, the shoes fit."

Skating through an intersection on a yellow light, Bolan nodded. "Mr. Catalano said there was a certain lady in one of his Little Italy offices that would probably know your sizes. When I called back, he had the sizes."

"He knows about Gina?" Syxx laced the shoe.

"He didn't give me a name."

"He act pissed?"

Bolan glanced at the rearview mirror. "Should he?"

"Mr. Catalano doesn't like us fraternizing with the straight help. Brings heat to the wrong places."

"My advice?" Bolan offered, making the left turn onto Spanish Town Road.

"Sure." The hardman put the extra magazines for his pistol into the pockets of the blacksuit.

"Keep your head low and your nose clean."

"Terrific." Finished suiting up, Syxx glanced at the highway ahead of them. "You got a plan for finding Seid and the guys who took Devon?"

"Better." Bolan reached down between the seats when he hit the straightaway. He lifted a small bag, unzipped it and revealed the notebook PC. "Instant Intel. Hold the wheel."

Syxx did.

Working swiftly, the soldier plugged the PC's AC-adapter cord into the cigarette lighter's outlet and powered it up. While the system came online, he took a cellular phone from the glove compartment and hooked it up to the PC's modem. After punching in a local number that connected with an Internet service, he handed the setup to Syxx.

"I'm the wrong guy for this," the Mafia man said. "I'm still trying to figure out Windows 95."

"I've got a friend who keeps it simple for me," Bolan said. He glanced at his watch again. "There's an icon called TRACK."

"Found it."

"Light it up."

A second later, Syxx said, "Done. I'll be damned."

Glancing over from the wheel, Bolan saw the coastline of Kingston Harbour reproduced in colored lines on the computer screen. "Press F1."

"Got it."

In response, a glowing red blip showed up on the screen, sailing down Spanish Town Road.

"That's Seid?" Syxx asked.

Bolan nodded. "Push F2 next."

The hardman did, and a blue blip showed up behind the red one, less than two inches away. The map cycled through, feeding in new information and changing as the location changed.

"GPS?" Syxx asked.

"Yeah." Global positioning satellites had been relied on heavily during the Gulf War.

"The red blip's Seid and we're the blue?"

"Yeah. We're running on borrowed space in an American weather satellite monitoring the Caribbean and using two radio stations to triangulate the speed and distance."

"You're getting speed and distance information too?"

"Alt P. For pace."

Syxx keyed it in, amazed. "Sixty-three miles an hour, and

we're less than five miles away.'' He glanced up. ''I figure you're using the phone frequency as one signature to ID our location, but what's broadcasting in the money Seid was given? Guy probably didn't take the container that was brought to him. Did he?''

''It wouldn't have mattered,'' Bolan replied. ''The bug wasn't in the container. It was in the money.''

''How?''

''It was a thin transmitter. About the size and shape of a one-hundred-dollar bill, and made up to look just like one.''

''You always go high-tech?'' Syxx asked.

''It's just a resource,'' the Executioner said. ''What's going to get those women out of there tonight is whatever skills we've got between us. That computer's just going to get us closer to the target.''

''Looks like we're getting closer now,'' the Mafia man said. ''Seid just took a left.'' A window opened up on the screen, momentarily exploding the section of the map.

Bolan read the street listing printed neatly in the space provided: Washington Boulevard. He knew from the maps he'd referenced getting ready for the campaign that it was only six miles to Spanish Town, Jamaica's former capital. Along the way, though, were a number of small roads that led into the tropical jungles.

Death was waiting somewhere up ahead, not far off. And the Executioner was closing the distance.

SANTIAGO CROWE TOOK the pocket watch from his shirt pocket and glanced at the time. It was 10:07, and the moon was full above them where they'd tied up off one of the small inlets coming in from Great Salt Pond.

Seid was late.

For a moment, he listened to the tune the pocket watch played. The music came a little slower these days and struck the occasional false note, but he wouldn't have gotten rid of the watch even if it quit altogether. He took it from the third man he ever killed. His first kill was out of self-preservation, and the second from fear. But the third was purely for profit.

He was fifteen, and the man was a tourist staggering out of a bar with a local working girl. At first, the girl was angry. She thought she'd lost her meal ticket—until Crowe gave her the money he stole from the tourist.

The girl, five years older than Crowe though she claimed to be the same age, showed her appreciation physically most of the night. The next morning, when she heard on the radio that the tourist was a pro-football scout taking a vacation in the off-season and that police were going to make every effort to find his killers, the girl became angry at him all over again. Crowe didn't understand. Done was done and they did not get caught. Life was like that.

She became even more irate when she found the watch in his shoes. She accused him of trying to cheat her. He couldn't believe it, and had to hit her to calm her down and make her listen to reason. By then the hotel manager was banging on the door, and Crowe was forced to make a hasty retreat.

Crowe now rubbed the surface of the watch and grinned in spite of the tension around him. That had been almost thirty years ago.

"Santiago."

Crowe snapped the watch closed and turned to face the man.

Domingo Krauss was half-islander and half-German. His mother had been an Olympic swimmer who'd unexpectedly gotten pregnant while on vacation, then hung around long enough to have the baby and abandon it to her lover's family.

"What?" Crowe demanded.

"The man is late," Krauss said. His mixed blood had softened his skin hue and put it beyond the darkening process of the Caribbean sun. It was the color of café au lait, but in some ways fit perfectly with his strawberry blond hair and blue-hazel eyes.

"He'll be here," Crowe said. "The Mafia man is going to pay for the return of his daughter." In contrast to his second-in-command, Crowe was six and a half feet tall, with skin burned ebony. His body was sculpted muscle overlaying thick bone, weathered by the sea and honed by a life of violence. A scar, turned white with age, overlaid his flat, broad nose and curved around to the left corner of his mouth.

He wore jeans he'd hacked off at the knees, and sandals. A Colt .45 pistol was shoved in his back pocket, and a thick-bladed machete hung from his left wrist by a leather thong. Bleached white regularly, a tiny baby's skull hung from a beaded necklace around his throat. He didn't especially like it, but it had added to the appearance and the stories some told about him.

"I just want to be for certain, man, that's all." Slender and rakish, Krauss could easily dress in slacks and a dress shirt instead of the short-cropped island pants and sleeveless tunic he wore now, and fit in at most of the tourist places. "I feel exposed here, you know. Don't like these swaps."

Crowe stared down the hill. From his vantage point he could see the overgrown rut that led from the rough highway more than two miles away. The trees and brush were thick around them, and he knew it offered threat as well as protection. Below, the three women sat huddled together in one of the four outboards they were using for the ransom.

The women didn't talk. They'd been in captivity for days, and he hadn't kept the men from them. Their lives were ransomed back to their families, not their physical well-being nor their virginity.

Bedraggled and dressed in the dirty rags that remained of the clothing they'd been captured in four days earlier, Crowe wouldn't have paid ten dollars for any of them. Luckily he hadn't had to pay, and he always got any place in the line that he wanted.

"That girl, Erin, you never hear from her family, eh?" Krauss asked.

"No," Crowe replied.

"So what we going to do?" Krauss drew a forefinger across his throat and raised his eyebrows inquiringly.

"Yes," Crowe replied. "We need to leave the others a warning."

"We give Seid the gangster-man's daughter?"

"For five million dollars," Crowe said, laughing. "Of course we do. We have to show our customers that we follow through." He liked thinking of them as customers. This line of pirating wasn't new. People had told him about it from days of old. He'd grown up with stories around the islands about Blackbeard and other Europeans. The islands had their own dark stories, too.

"And the senator's daughter?" Krauss asked.

"Something special for her," Crowe said. "After all, the bastard nearly cost us Seid."

Down below, the men had shown renewed interest in the women. They laughed and joked and made rude comments about events over the past few days. As they pulled and pushed at them, making the women flinch, the boats rocked in the water and the lapping noises filled the small cove.

"Keep an eye on those dogs," Crowe said. "I don't want to have to pull them off that Italian bitch when we give her to Seid."

"Man, I tell you the truth. I don't want to see her go either. After four days—four days, man—she still fights like it's her first time. Going to miss that." Krauss stroked his chin absently. "Something else you should think of. How long you think we going to be able to pull off this ransom gig? That time in the Caymans, I thought they were going to tear us a new ass before it's over."

"I'll let you know," Crowe said. But he liked the fast action and the money.

"A greedy man," Krauss said, "now he sees where there's money to be made pretty easy. But a greedy *dead* one, man, he don't get to spend none of it. That's what I'm telling you."

"I'll keep that in mind. Go take care of that bullshit below before it gets any more out of hand."

Krauss went, bellowing names and touching the pearled handle of the pistol in his hip holster. He'd killed men under him before, and all of the band knew it. They quieted in short order.

Lights sweeping through the trees drew Crowe's attention. "Look sharp. We got company coming." He moved to take cover in the sheltering dark. If anything was going to go wrong with the buyback, now was the time.

2

Bolan made his way over the rough tropical terrain as fast as was feasible. Gabriel Syxx was at his heels, not having much trouble matching the frantic pace.

After seeing Seid's last change in direction, the soldier had known where the bagman was headed. The Great Salt Pond was on the terrain maps he had, with an almost guaranteed passage from there out into Green Bay and the Caribbean beyond.

Seid had a roundabout approach to where the road ended next to a cove. The geography software Aaron Kurtzman, Stony Man Farm's resident cybernetics genius, had downloaded onto the notebook PC over an Internet connection had reported the physical layout of the land in detail.

Bolan had left the Cherokee at the side of the road, pulled well back in a copse of trees that would keep it from being seen by a casual observer. Judging from the map, Seid had roughly two and a half miles to cover in his car while Bolan and Syxx made a five-hundred-yard jog.

He breathed easily, responding to the exercise. He carried the Beretta 93-R in shoulder leather, counterbalanced by the heavier .44 Magnum Desert Eagle on his right hip. Webbing and ammo pouches supported extra magazines for his weapons, as well as other ordnance. The M-16/M-203 assault rifle/40 mm grenade launcher he carried in both hands was a solid, comforting weight. A Second Chance armored vest covered his chest. Syxx hadn't complained when he'd put his on.

The Executioner's face was camou-striped in night black to lessen chance of reflection. A black, lightweight watch cap covered his head.

The ground started a gradual slope toward the sea, becoming marshy and soft underfoot. By the time they'd reached their target area, the soldier was covered in sweat that had soaked through his clothing. The silhouettes of the boats were low in the water, but he made out the women sitting in one of them.

Four men stood around them in a semicircle on the shore, taunting them. Occasionally their rough voices reached Bolan.

The Executioner dropped into position behind a thick rosewood tree. The scent of the cedars was strong in the air, almost blotting out the briny smell of the sea.

The sound of a struggling engine drew his attention back to the left. The headlights of a dark blue 4WD Silverado pickup slashed through the trees. The transmission whined as the driver forced his way through the underbrush as close as he could get. When he could go no farther, he switched off the engine, left the lights on and got out. Bolan recognized him as Seid.

Two men came out to meet the go-between. One was an ebony giant who had a machete hanging from his hand. The other was fairer, with blondish hair. Behind them, shadows ranged the hill.

"Did you get a count?" Bolan asked.

"Twelve," Syxx replied. "Maybe fifteen. Could be a few more lost in the shadows."

"It's not going to be easy," Bolan said. He took out the night glasses and scanned the hillside. He found two more men. "How are you at long range?"

"I can hit what I'm shooting at," the Mafia man said.

"Even when they're not shooting back?" It was a legitimate question and Bolan knew it. Snipers weren't made, they were born. Not many could do the job without the adrenaline flow and the instinct for self-preservation kicking in to take away the doubt and hesitation. The Executioner had made his peace with his own actions years ago. His bullets took out fights that didn't have to be fought by people who would have gotten hurt even if they'd won.

"I've never done it before," Syxx admitted. His dark eyes were hard. "But I can see how those girls have been treated even from here, without binoculars. I won't have a problem."

"I'll be counting on you." Bolan scanned the meeting between Seid and the two men. The Kingston private investigator was opening a suitcase he'd taken from the passenger side of the pickup. "Cover me. When I give the signal, take down as many of those people as you can."

"What signal?"

"You'll know it," Bolan said. "If I can, I'm going to keep the women clear of the area. Fall back to the shoreline if I manage to get a boat. If I don't, I'll try to get them up the hill and manage a line of demarcation while you head them back to the Jeep."

"You got it." Syxx settled himself in behind the trees.

Bolan moved into the shadows, taking advantage of the land and brush. He reached the water unseen and crept in. It felt cold and oily. Close to the surface of the bay, the sound was amplified and distorted. He avoided the plants shooting up in clumps, using them for cover but not getting near enough to ruffle them.

The chest-high water swirled around him as he walked toward the boats. Eight yards away, he ran out of cover.

Devon Catalano was slim and dark, her face framed by black hair cut off at the shoulders. Her sundress was torn and disheveled, one strap hanging broken from a scratched shoulder. Still, she managed a defiant attitude.

Janet Gladsdale looked like a child hanging on to Devon Catalano. Her eyes were wide, and tears leaked down her abraded face, framed by dirty, blond hair going wild.

The third woman had close-cropped chestnut-colored hair and a sharp, angular face. She was easily ten years older than the other women. Ignoring the jibes, she held her head in her hands.

Bolan's Intel had pegged her as Clarissa Thomasson, one of the cruise liner's personnel who'd been taken while off duty. She'd evidently started up a shipboard friendship with Janet Gladsdale, according to investigators' reports that Brognola had gotten access to.

On top of the hill, the men were laughing, talking about the violence that had broken out back in Kingston. Seid's words left no doubt about whose camp he was in.

"After those Mafia bastards called me, man, and suggested the changes so I wouldn't be picked up by the island police working on Gladsdale's orders," the Jamaican private eye said, "I tipped off a group of Rastafarians I do a little ganja business with on the side. There's a Hollywood film crew on the island doing one of those sci-fi shows for television. I hung around long enough to watch some of the fireworks, then got the hell out of there. Man, if I'd been there, I'd have been locked up by now and you'd still be here waiting on your money."

"It was your choice to come yourself instead of using another the way we have in the past."

Bolan guessed that the deep, rumbling voice came from the big man. He checked up the hill and shifted, trying to find a shot that would let him take the man down during the rescue attempt. Trees blocked his way, and the flashlights they held and moved made the illumination more uncertain than the moonlight.

"Couldn't pass this up, man," Seid replied. "This is our biggest take yet. I didn't want anybody getting any cut of this. And it's too much money to trust with most of the people I know. Five million dollars, man, that would have made a bastard confused for a moment, make him think he was invulnerable and fast as the wind."

"Kind of sounds like the thought crossed your mind too, man," another voice suggested.

"No shit. I'd be lying to you, Krauss, if I said it didn't

cross my mind a half-dozen times on the way here. But if I pulled a fade, I'd have you and the Mafia looking for me. I don't think either one of you would give up.''

"The American gangsters," the deep voice stated, "may be asking questions of you anyway."

"Let them ask. I'll bring the boss's daughter back when all the rest of them think she's probably dead. If anything, I should be a goddamn hero to that man."

Bolan shouldered his weapon, sighting through the forked branch in front of the big man's face. His finger was curling around the trigger, taking up slack, when a scream sounded to his right. The sound of tearing clothing and the impact of flesh on flesh followed.

The big man moved, disappearing again.

"Bitch!" one of the men yelled at Clarissa Thomasson. He pulled back and put a hand to his mouth, then checked his palm for blood.

The woman sat in a defensive crouch aboard the long metal outboard. The boat rocked wildly in the water. "You stay away from me, asshole!" she yelled at her attacker.

The other pirates were laughing at the injured man.

"Didn't have to be doing that, bitch," the guy said. "I already taken some of what you got. A little more, that's just play. But now, I'm going to cut you. Dead or alive, isn't going to make no difference to me as long as you're still warm." He yanked a knife from his belt and advanced on her.

Swiveling, the Executioner put the M-16's sights between the man's eyes and stroked the trigger. The 3-round burst caught the man in the left eye and tracked up. The impacts shuddered through the corpse and sprawled it backward onto the swampland at the edge of the water.

Bolan managed to pick up another target with two sweeping bursts that stitched the guy from right hipbone to left shoulder and spun him. The dead man dropped into the water.

Syxx opened up with his own assault rifle next, firing

deliberate shots that pealed through the chaos that now ripped through the bay. Two of the shadows at the top of the hill stumbled and went down in loose, disjointed rolls.

The other two men by the boats went to ground. Bolan thought he might have nicked one of them, but he wasn't sure. Charging forward, the M-16/M-203 in his hands, he readied a grenade and yelled at the women, "Get down and stay there!"

Thomasson and Catalano took cover at once. Catalano had to reach back up to bring Gladsdale down with them.

The water slowed Bolan's passage. Bullets smacked into the water around him, and two rounds stopped dead against the armored vest. He raised the rifle and fired a grenade toward the top of the hill.

The 40 mm warhead was high explosive, designed to take out whatever it hit and leave confusion in its wake. The HE detonated against a tree and blasted the trunk to bits, killing the three men around it as they tried to return fire. The bright flash threw a sheet of white light over the surface of the water.

Another short burst from the M-16 knocked down the third man behind a thick, moss-covered log that had been washed up on shore.

The Executioner drew his Ka-bar fighting knife and slashed through the rope anchoring the outboard to the shoreline. Grabbing the prow, he used his body weight and every bit of leverage he could dig against the mud to propel it out into the deeper water.

He pulled himself aboard, having to fight for balance as the prow bobbed and shifted under him. Fire from the shoreline drew sparks from the metal ribs of the boat and hammered holes through it. Puddles had already started to form along the bottom of the boat.

Janet Gladsdale was screaming and struggling to get out of the boat. Devon Catalano threw herself on top of the other woman, screaming at Thomasson to help. A second later, the older woman wrapped an arm around the kicking girl's legs.

Raking the shoreline with fire, Bolan ran the rest of the M-16's clip empty as he stepped across the tangle of women to the outboard motor. He dropped the assault rifle next to him as he reached for the controls. The ignition key was tied to a safety line on the engine. He shoved it in and turned it as another of Syxx's grenades tore a hole into the hill.

Even though there were only the two of them, Bolan hoped the cross fire would hold down the pirate crew until they were able to outflank their attackers. The soldier yanked the pull cord and the engine turned over sluggishly, but caught.

The high-pitched whine of the two-cycle engine drowned out much of the other sounds of the firefight. Bolan twisted the accelerator and shoved on the tiller handle. He drew the Desert Eagle while the outboard sped along the shoreline, cresting the incoming waves at an angle. They moved like a stone skipping across a pond, becoming an even more difficult target for the pirates.

Settling beside the engine, Bolan looked at the women. Janet Gladsdale was still struggling, still screaming, lost to terrors in her mind that were only triggered by the events going on around her.

"Keep her down," Bolan said in a steady voice. "We'll be clear of this in just a few minutes now."

"Are you a cop?" Clarissa Thomasson asked.

Bolan shook his head. "I'm just here to help."

"You're from my father," Devon Catalano stated.

Slapping noises around them, followed by the crack of gunfire, let the Executioner know they were still being fired on. He moved the tiller, scooting around an outcrop that would have dashed the long outboard to bits.

"Yeah." The lie was told partly to reassure the woman, and partly to protect Turrin's cover.

"Did he send the money?" Her voice was doubtful.

"He sent it, Devon."

"I didn't know if he would. We haven't been on the best of terms." She continued to hold Janet Gladsdale, who'd given up screaming and fighting, and was trying to curl into a fetal ball.

Bolan glanced over his shoulder. Despite the barrage of fire Syxx was maintaining, the pirates had broken and sprinted down the hill.

The men cast off the lines and started the engines. In seconds they were in pursuit. Muzzle-flashes cracked intermittently, gaining in number as more of them brought their weapons to bear.

Bolan stayed low, racing only a few yards from the shoreline. The load his boat carried was less than the two boats behind him, so it would help some. What was going to count most, though, was maintaining his lead.

The outboard crested the next wave, coming up out of the water at a bad angle, then slamming back down. Spray splashed over the hellfire warrior's face and stung his eyes. Recovering the boat, he opened up the outboard motor even more. One way or another, the next few seconds would be telling.

"SORRY TO HAVE to detain you," the Kingston police officer said, handing Lyndon Palfrey's ID back to him, "but with the confusion of the past few moments, we wanted to check everyone out."

"Sure," Palfrey replied, accepting the plastic rectangle. He'd been known by some of the higher-ranked police officers, which had helped cut the time of the investigation. He'd already gotten the story about the ransom demand that had gone awry.

He stood in front of the club and surveyed the damage. Several of the windows had been shot out, leaving gaping holes in the glass. The sea turtle framed with green neon tubing standing in a neon lavender top hat with pink monocle that had decorated the club's main entrance had been shattered to pieces by repeated hits.

Fire trucks had arrived and were organizing the evacuation of the buildings. Emergency medical teams circulated among the wounded, assessing the damage. Already some of the dead had been dragged out into the street, and news photographers were jockeying for position to capture the tablecloth-covered images on prints and tape. The police barricade was going up slowly. The island didn't have a metropolitan attitude of noninvolvement. Everybody in a neighborhood generally felt well-disposed toward their peers even if they didn't know them. The police helicopter hovered overhead and raked the alleys with the searchlight.

Palfrey took off his Panama hat and wiped his forehead. It was a shame, actually. The club had been a favorite of his because of the martinis. Spotting Hideo Shotozumi being detained by one of the female police officers at the corner of the building, he reseated his hat and crossed over to the man.

The Yakuza lieutenant was tall for a Japanese, standing just over six feet. His back and shoulders were broad, tapering to an unusually small waist. His hair was cut short. He smiled politely at the police officer, his thick, callused hands clasped in front of him, as he listened attentively.

"Is there a problem?" Palfrey inquired politely.

"Not if you mind your own business," the female cop told him. She was petite and black, with her cap squared off on her head perfectly.

"I'm afraid Mr. Haganura is my business," Palfrey said.

The woman glared up at him from her notepad. "Do I know you?"

"No, but Captain Swaby does." Palfrey pointed at the big, dark man in a worsted suit shouting orders at different patrolmen.

"I'm supposed to be impressed, right?"

Palfrey read her name badge, posted below her shield. "No, Officer Rochester, but you might ask him if he'll vouch for me while I vouch for Mr. Haganura. We have

business, and the sooner we can get to it, the better it'll be."
He handed her his ID.

"What's this?"

"If you take a look, you'll see the address he gave you
is mine. Makes it more permanent than someone who's just
going to move out in the dead of night, don't you think?"

Rochester looked at Palfrey. "If I have any questions, I'm
going to come knocking on your door."

Palfrey smiled. "Call ahead. It would be a pleasure to
have you. I've always liked women in uniform."

The police officer jerked a thumb over her shoulder.
"Grab some air before you make me angry." She glanced
at Shotozumi. "You can go with him."

"Thank you, Officer." Shotozumi bowed his head in
deference.

Palfrey led the way along the boarded sidewalk and toward the marina where his yacht was tied up. He kept a slip
at Kingston Harbour for his convenience. The island was a
rare treat these days. Crime was often bloody and violent
there, not exactly his cup of tea. He wasn't afraid of the
violence, but he'd generally found higher stakes could just
as easily be blood-free.

"These men doing the kidnappings are getting dangerous," Shotozumi commented as they walked the length of
the floating pier stabbing out into the bay.

"Actually," Palfrey said, "if you don't mind all the killing, it's not a bad racket. I wouldn't touch it, though." He
shoved his hands into his pockets. "Myself, I prefer the quiet
game of cat-and-mouse, of acting the part of a ne'er-do-well
to someone who's willing to take advantage of me." He
grinned at the Japanese. "Or at least, of the me I present to
them."

"Do you know the people behind the kidnappings?"

Palfrey shook his head. On the whole, he liked the Japanese, even liked his company. Shotozumi was street edu-
cated, but had picked up books and classes and contacts over
his forty-plus years to enhance an already keen intellect. In

many ways he reminded Palfrey of himself: self-made and savvy, and searching for his own goals and means, without the restraints and complications of conscience forced on them by others.

"They're island trash," Palfrey commented. "The ransom they demanded from the Mafia was a pretty generous score, but they'll have that squandered in due time."

With the amount of cash involved in the transaction, he'd sent out feelers for the group. They'd need someone to convert the cash, in case it was marked in some way, and they'd lose half the street value or more in that bit of business alone. By the time expenses were paid, as well as the crew involved, he was certain the group would be looking to make another hit again soon.

"After tonight," Shotozumi said, "it is possible no one will try to double-cross them again."

"Those were Rastafarians back there," Palfrey said, "not the people who took down the passengers off the liners. Your basic bottom of the pond feeders looking to go big. They died hard tonight, and for what? The news reporters are talking about the bundles of paper that were inside that bag they took. They got exactly zip. Personally I think somebody saved the pirates' asses tonight. That should have been them dead in the street, not the ganja boys."

"Still, it gives me pause to think they might be out there when we are putting our deal together."

Palfrey put on his best con man's smile. "They hit cruise ships, my friend. Not freighters. We're even more invisible with this going on. It's a bonus cover we hadn't counted on. The law-enforcement agencies in the area are going to be doubling up trying to provide security for the tourists and civilians and letting more of the trade ships through with less fuss." He turned at the juncture that led down to his yacht. Strings of lights hung from poles and lit up the area. "These people are going to get caught because they don't know when to back off. But it won't be till after tomorrow. By then, we'll have accomplished our transaction."

"I hope you're right."

"I know I am." Palfrey clapped the other man on the back. Physical touching on the part of the Japanese wasn't an accepted behavior, but transgressing personal barriers was a specialty of Palfrey's. Before he'd been brought into the blue-chip con games by Vance Tillage, he'd gotten by living off older women with money and itchy libidos. There were still plenty of them out there, but lately he'd found they had counterparts in their early twenties, women totally hipped on careers and ownership of businesses. They didn't have time for affairs, but flings with them could be pleasant diversions.

However, flings didn't keep a roof over his head or pay for the other things in life that he desired. Events had conspired against him for the past few years and plunged Palfrey in more dire straits than he'd seen in the past seventeen years. But it was nothing he couldn't extricate himself from.

Shotozumi and his boss had come to him as a result of a bit of business in Hong Kong during the mass exodus resulting from the return of the area to China. The Yakuza had been staking out some territory Palfrey had already been working. He and his team had settled for a smaller score and left everything intact for the Japanese Mafia. They weren't known for their generosity, but they were always looking for people who knew what they were about.

Plus, they'd done their research on him quietly, without letting him know they were around, and found out about Fire Dolphin Island. The deal couldn't have come at a better time.

He didn't relish the thought of hiding the freighter's deadly cargo on the island, but the money was right. At the moment, that was all that really mattered.

Palfrey took out his cellular phone, then slid it back into his pocket. "You know, I was going to call Crispus and have him meet us at the yacht, but I think I'm going to buy you a drink first."

"I'll let you," Shotozumi said. "I find myself in need of one, I think."

When Palfrey put a foot on the yacht, he knew something was wrong. He'd spent months at a time on that boat and knew every vibration and quiver she made. He'd gained intimacy with the engines while mentally working out the kinks of other plays he was setting up.

The shiver that ran through her now was different and all wrong. People walking—the crew, the guests—all left their own marks. For the first time he felt as though the yacht had been invaded.

Then he noticed the door leading belowdecks was waving gently with the action of the water. It should have been secured. Only he and Crispus had keys to it. The low-wattage security light that stayed on beside it was also dark.

Palfrey slid a hand into his boot, acting as if he were tying it preparatory to boarding. He palmed the Beretta automatic pistol from the small holster inside and flipped off the safety.

"Problem?" Shotozumi asked. He'd noticed the gun and slowly turned into a profile stance, his arms loose at his sides.

"Nothing we can't handle," Palfrey replied quietly. He pushed himself over the low railing and stepped onto the rear deck of the yacht. With the small automatic slightly ahead of him and held at waist level, he went forward. If Crispus had been aboard, he would have waited above deck.

Before Palfrey could step to the door, a flurry of movement ripped free of the shadows and raced forward. Shudders vibrated the length of the yacht, echoed by the quick slapping of bare feet running across the deck.

Using the adrenaline that filled him, Palfrey pushed away from the door and twisted around the corner, throwing the pistol up in front of him. Just because he preferred not to deal with aggressive violence from others didn't mean he wasn't able to handle it.

Two figures ran across the deck. One was thin and slender and hinted at curves. The other was broad-shouldered.

Palfrey took off in pursuit at once. He kept jewelry, bearer bonds and cash in five different currencies in a safe built into the yacht. There were also at least three identities he hadn't used yet. Usually he didn't let any of his various enterprises touch his personal holdings. Having Shotozumi aboard was an exception to that rule.

Palfrey broke cover and sprinted after the fleeing figures. Shotozumi was a ghost at his side, apparently moving with little effort. They were two paces behind the last figure when the two vaulted from the yacht onto a neighboring houseboat.

Not breaking stride, Palfrey threw himself after the figures. He recognized them now, a man and a woman. Both were young and swarthy-skinned, maybe Cuban. An ill thought formed in Palfrey's mind as he leaped to the docking area. For a moment he teetered off balance, on the verge of dropping into the water. Then he got his feet under him again.

His breath whistled in his ears. He didn't cry out. If someone stopped the burglars for him, he didn't want them found with documents that would incriminate him, or leave them with valuables he wouldn't be able to claim.

His longer stride made a difference, and he closed quickly as they hit the straightaway.

The man, lagging behind the woman, stopped suddenly and yelled to her in an accented voice that hinted at Hispanic without the island intonations, "Keep going!"

"Tilo!" the woman cried, slowing for just a moment.

Tilo didn't have time to reply because Palfrey was on top of him. They went down on the rough wood in a tangling flail of arms and legs. Tilo was little more than a boy. His face was round and smooth, with only a few stray hairs shading it. At most, he was nineteen or twenty. He was dressed in black slacks and a black T-shirt that bore the logo of a local reggae band.

The young man threw a fist at Palfrey's face.

Palfrey blocked it easily with an elbow, then reached down to lay a hand over Tilo's face. He shoved the Beretta's snout under the young man's chin. "Don't try that again, asshole, or I'm going to shoot you through the head."

Eyes blazing but his lip trembling, Tilo spread his hands out beside his head, palms facing outward.

Palfrey glanced up and saw the woman's silhouette disappear into the darkness. So far, though, no one appeared to have noticed them. He pushed himself off Tilo and stood, holding the man's shirt bunched in one fist and the pistol screwed into his throat tightly. "Get up," Palfrey ordered.

Awkwardly Tilo stood, keeping his arms up. "You killed Uncle Gustavo."

Palfrey looked at him, searching the dark face. "Gustavo Ruiz?"

The young man nodded.

Yanking on his prisoner, Palfrey pushed him into the shadows against a houseboat. Tilo was moved by the boat's listing on the waves. "What did you think you were going to do?" Palfrey patted him down, turning up a switchblade that gleamed with fresh oil.

Shotozumi stood nearby, watching the other boats. Light spilled across the docks and water in gleaming shards. Music, voices and the sound of motors in the distance created an auditory mosaic. Most of the marina crowd was still down at the bar watching the police action.

"I don't know," Tilo replied. "I got scared. Gustavo was Natacha's uncle. She was determined to come to your boat and find out about her uncle."

Palfrey doubted that. Ruiz may have had family in the area, but the man hadn't been familially disposed. He twisted Tilo around and leveraged his arm up behind him, then Palfrey pushed him ahead of him toward the waiting yacht. His heart still beat fast as he checked over the boat. It was entirely possible that the two had holed it, intending to let it sink.

He shoved his captive down the companionway and sent him sprawling in the living quarters belowdecks. Tilo started to get up, blood leaking from the corner of his mouth.

"Stay down," Palfrey commanded. He gazed around the room as Shotozumi locked the door behind them. Everything was in disarray. The sofa cushions had been slashed, and stuffing leaked out. Pots and pans had been scattered around the galley, their shiny surfaces looking like coins in the darkness in the room.

The search through the room looked totally unprofessional. There had been no rhyme or reason as to procedure. He was certain, however, that the two hadn't been there just to find out what had happened to Ruiz.

Keeping the pistol on Tilo, Palfrey walked through the debris, kicking part of it and shifting part of it by hand. It took him a moment to realize his day organizer was gone from the small rolltop desk built into the wall. Some of his other personal papers were missing too, but nothing as damning as the loss of the organizer. Information about the *Jilly St. Agnes* was among those cards.

Palfrey turned to his captive. Without showing any sign of what he was going to do, he backhanded Tilo, sending the younger man to his knees with a yelp of pain.

When Tilo looked up, more blood was smeared across his lower face.

Smiling coldly, Palfrey knelt on a level with Tilo. He took the switchblade from his pocket and popped it open with a practiced gesture. "You're going to tell me who the woman is," he said softly, "and you're going to tell me where I can find her."

Before Tilo could respond, his eyes already showing his reluctance, Palfrey stabbed the switchblade through Tilo's hand. Palfrey twisted the knife viciously and held it for a moment, then yanked it away.

Tilo screamed, a full-throated howl of pained anguish, and cradled his injured hand to his chest.

"It won't matter if you scream," Palfrey said in a calm voice. "The cabin's soundproofed. Scream all you want. But the longer you take, the worse I can make it. Trust me." He readied the knife again.

3

Fighting against the incoming tide surging up the muddy shoreline, Mack Bolan threw the outboard motor into neutral and cut the tiller sharply. The boat slapped through the choppy waves and butted against the muddy bank.

Devon Catalano and Clarissa Thomasson still lay on top of Janet Gladsdale. Bullets ricocheted off the metallic hull of the boat and drilled into the muddy bank.

The soldier dropped the empty magazine from the M-16, then reloaded from the spares he carried in the webbing. The two pirate boats were closing in, their engines whining like angry bees.

The boat came up hard against the shore and splatted against the mud as the waves forced it out of the water. Gabriel Syxx broke cover at a dead run. Rounds tore bark from tree trunks around him and branches overhead, leaving hard white scars against the dark wood.

Bolan shoved one of his remaining four 40 mm warheads into the grenade launcher's breech and closed it. He sighted on the lead boat as Syxx climbed into the outboard. As soon as he thought he had the wind and trajectory in line, he squeezed the trigger.

Arcing a little in its line of flight, the grenade impacted against the lead boat. The explosion was just above the water line on the starboard side and caught the boat with its full force. The outboard acted as though it had hit a brick wall, then split open and sank as pieces of it sailed into the air with the corpses of the men who had been aboard.

"Devon?" Syxx said, sitting in the prow and reaching out to the young woman. "Do you know me?" He had to talk loud to be heard over the motor's roar as Bolan twisted the accelerator again.

The woman nodded but didn't say anything.

"Damn," Syxx growled. His features hardened as he looked at the women.

Bolan knew how Syxx felt. No matter how quickly they'd come, despite saving at least three lives, they'd arrived too late to save the women completely. He steered the boat out to sea again. The waves were higher there and offered momentary cover as well as an uncertain target.

The outboard had taken on enough water that it was turning sluggish. Bolan knew they'd have no choice but to abandon it soon. He ran with the waves, closing the distance to the shoreline again. More than two hundred yards lay behind them. His best guess told him they were almost parallel to the point where he and Syxx had left the Cherokee.

The soldier caught Syxx's attention. "Hand me the spare fuel container."

The Mafia hardman reached under the wooden bench seat, hauled out the red plastic five-gallon container and handed it across to the Executioner.

Bolan locked the tiller with his leg and slipped his Kabar free of its sheath. With quick strokes, he ran slashes down the sides of the container. The gasoline and oil mixture poured out, but before much had spilled, he tossed it overboard. The fuel container plopped into the water and twirled for a moment, then maintained a loose equilibrium.

The remaining pirate boat came straight for the Executioner, muzzle-flashes punching holes in the night in deadly flickers.

Bolan stayed low and kept an eye on the bobbing fuel container. Even with the waves coming in, he figured most of the gasoline would stay together. Being lighter than the water, it would also stay on the surface.

When the boat full of pirates got within the circle he

guessed had spread from the sinking container, the Executioner straightened and fired a sustained burst into the water. The bullets slapped into the water only a few feet in front of the boat. Every third round was a tracer, and the burning phosphorus ignited the gasoline.

Flames jumped across the water and wrapped around the boatload of pirates. Even though the craft powered through the wreath of fire, flames clung to it as it emerged. With the fire blazing behind it, the vessel and its crew looked like two-dimensional shadows. Some of them caught fire as well and leaped from the boat, shouting in agony.

"Burn, you bastards!" Clarissa Thomasson yelled. Her face was drawn and tight, but tears glittered in her eyes. There was no mercy in her expression.

Out of control, the boat caught an incoming wave and overturned. The motor sounded like a buzz saw as the propeller came free of the water. An instant later, the flames reached the motor's fuel tank and exploded in a fiery display of orange and yellow.

Turning his attention to the shoreline, Bolan made sure no one was waiting in the jungle, then cut the boat toward land. He choked the engine a couple of feet from the shoreline and let the waves push them onto the sandy area.

Syxx jumped out of the boat with the line in his hand. He pulled and guided the prow, yanking it onto land.

Bolan stepped over the back and helped to push. The outboard ran up onto the beach over halfway. The soldier changed magazines again and recharged the grenade launcher. "Let's go," he said to the women. "We've got a car waiting only a short distance away. A few more minutes, and you can start putting all of this behind you."

Catalano and Thomasson pulled at the senator's daughter. Janet Gladsdale was tightly curled up in the bottom of the outboard, chewing on the back of her hand hard enough to draw blood.

"It's no use," Catalano said. "She's not going to get out of the boat."

"We're going to have company in a few more minutes," Syxx warned. "They haven't given up yet."

Bolan stared through the trees and brush and saw the flashlight beams in the hands of their pursuers. The head start they had was already being cut down. With as many men as he and Syxx had killed, and with the way the operations against the cruise liners had gone down, he knew the pirate base was larger than he'd been expecting.

Curses from the approaching pirates echoed in the jungle. The crack of gunfire interspersed with the sound of bullets ricocheting off stones and trees.

Bolan reached into the boat and pulled out Janet Gladsdale. The woman started to struggle and scream at once. She drummed her fists against Bolan's face and chest. The soldier shifted her, trying to keep her from hurting him or herself.

Syxx stepped in without hesitation and punched her on the jaw. The meaty impact shivered through the woman and she collapsed.

"If we get out of here alive," the Mafia hardman said, "I'll feel bad about that later."

Bolan nodded. He hoisted the woman's deadweight over his shoulder and moved off at a trot, keeping the M-16 fisted in one hand. "You've got drag," he told Syxx.

"I'm there."

The Executioner scrambled through the brush, using his night sight to clear most of the tangles and fallen trees. Bullets chopped at branches over their heads as they headed up the incline leading back to the Jeep.

Catalano and Thomasson followed close behind him, urged on by Syxx. When they fell or got caught in the debris, they shoved themselves free and kept moving.

Going up the incline was hard. Bolan's breath burned in his lungs as he reached the top. He was slick with perspiration under the blacksuit, and it felt warmer than the chill from the wet clothes.

He opened the rear door of the Cherokee and quickly

belted the unconscious woman into the seat. "Go around," he told the other women. "Get in back and stay low."

The sounds of the pirates thrashing through the brush grew louder, and more of the rounds were getting closer to their target.

Bolan slipped behind the steering wheel as Syxx threw himself into the passenger seat. The engine caught on the first try. The soldier pulled out into the path as a hail of bullets punched out the back glass. He put his foot hard on the accelerator. The 4WD grabbed traction and sent the Cherokee surging forward. Small trees and brush went down under the front bumper.

Rounds beat into the Jeep's body and ripped off the passenger-side mirror, but none of them touched the tires.

Bolan steered hard, targeting a shadow that crept in front of them. There was an instant of blazing gunfire that lit up the man's scarred features. The autofire sparked across the 4WD's nose and a white fog from the radiator hissed. Before the man could get away, the Executioner caught him with the Jeep's fender and sent him flying into the jungle.

The soldier shifted into a higher gear, hoping that the engine wouldn't overheat until they made it out of the jungle. He glanced in the rearview mirror. The fragmented back glass remained in the frame and diffused the weak moonlight. Muzzle-flashes created pockets of illumination behind them, but the next curve erased them from sight and took away the threat they presented.

He glanced at the gauge. So far the temperature was holding steady. He looked at Syxx. "You've got a team standing by?"

The Mafia hardman nodded, wiping at a stream of blood coming from his temple. "With a Marine chopper that's already been cleared through Jamaican air traffic. You say where, we can disappear in minutes."

"Have them meet us at the highway," Bolan replied.

"Can do." Syxx took his cellular phone from the belongings at his feet and made the call.

Bolan flicked on the lights as he continued along the rutted path. The women would need medical assistance as soon as possible, and he needed to get clear of the picture before the law-enforcement teams arrived. The cover he had in place to arrive in the country didn't account for his involvement with the Mafia or the pirates. And he didn't want to stop the impetus on the strike he'd already gathered.

He stared through the dark night, then glanced in the rearview mirror at the terror-stricken faces of the two conscious women, and the slack features of the unconscious one. Justice had yet to be served to those who deserved it. Someone out there, somewhere, still had the money. As long as they did, with the transmitter in place, he could find them. And the big warrior had that next on his agenda.

OUT PAST the southernmost point of Port Royal, Lyndon Palfrey dragged the corpse onto the deck while Shotozumi walked behind him. The Yakuza representative had remained implacable throughout the interrogation, despite the lengths Palfrey had taken to arrive at the truth.

Tilo's clothing was drenched in blood. In many places it was torn to tatters. The young man had tried to lie at first, but Palfrey had known it was because he hadn't truly believed Palfrey would hurt him. Tilo had expected to be hit and slapped. Those actions weren't any different from anything else he'd been exposed to working the docks and living a life steeped in the black market that ran through Jamaica.

But when Palfrey had used the switchblade and hacked off the first two fingers of the young man's right hand while standing on his arm, Tilo had known. The truth had come quickly. The girl's name was Natacha Liberto. Her mother was Gustavo Ruiz's sister.

Palfrey vaguely remembered the Liberto name from mention by the police team who came to question him about Ruiz's disappearance. The questioning hadn't taken long. Palfrey's reputation on the islands was good, and he was also linked to several successful people in Kingston, including one of the more senior detectives. After assuring the men that Ruiz had left shortly after the work crew on the day in question, the matter had been dropped. After all, Palfrey's tax money paid a lot more salaries than a missing Cuban who wasn't above working with slum lords and was already under investigation on other claims.

Palfrey's own clothes were stained with blood as well. He hated the waste. Good clothes were meant to be well kept. However, Tilo's terror had been immediate and he'd needed to keep that edge before the man had succumbed to his body's natural defenses against pain.

He didn't worry about the yacht's crew seeing the dead man. It wasn't the first. There was already a bucket of chum waiting.

Palfrey pulled the body to a rest against the back gunwale. "Cut the engines," he roared to the skipper.

The black man was dressed in crisp whites. He gave a brief salute, then switched off the twin diesels. They rumbled fitfully and died away.

Gently, pushing the water now instead of cutting through it, the yacht slowed to a stop. Palfrey took the bucket of chum and scattered it across the ocean's surface. Only a few minutes passed before the blood of the fish attracted the sharks.

The sinewy bodies arced through the water, pale gray shadows under the dark sheet of the sea. The pieces of chum disappeared rapidly, vanquished by serrated teeth.

"How did you know they would be here?" Shotozumi asked. He stood at the boat railing and peered into the ocean.

"I feed them here," Palfrey said, hoisting Tilo's body, then shoving it over the side. The corpse hit the water with a splash that washed up on deck. "I guess I keep them on retainer, you might say."

"Yes." Shotozumi nodded in approval. "I like working with a man who keeps options open to him."

The corpse floated for a moment, serene and splayed beneath the waves. Then it jerked suddenly, twisting and turning like a live man drowning. The body was hit repeatedly by the sharks as they attacked, and they dragged it more deeply into the water until it vanished.

Palfrey reached into his pocket and removed the two fingers, ear and part of the nose he'd sliced from Tilo during questioning. He flung them into the water, and they barely made ripples against the waves before they were lost from sight. Stripping to his underwear, he threw his clothes in, too. Enough blood had soaked into them that he knew the sharks would make short work of them, as well.

"Crispus," Palfrey said.

"Yes, sir." The man stood a few feet away.

"Have one of the crew remove the plastic tarp from belowdecks and destroy it."

"Yes, sir." Crispus turned and bellowed orders to the crew.

Palfrey stood in the chill breeze swirling in from the ocean and gazed at his newest partner. Despite the chaos that had struck, he wanted the Yakuza lieutenant to know he was capable of dealing with the situation. "I can handle this," he said. "*We* can handle this."

"The girl will have to be found," Shotozumi stated.

"Crispus," Palfrey said.

"I think we've got her, Mr. Palfrey," Crispus replied. "Our sources indicate that Natacha Liberto has been in trouble with the law. She's not going to run to them very quickly." While the interrogation had taken place, he'd been using the ship-to-shore telephone.

"What kind of trouble?" Palfrey accepted one of the guest robes kept aboard the yacht from one of the crew members who'd been belowdecks.

"Prostitution and drugs."

"Did you get an address for her?" Palfrey belted the robe and accepted a cigarette from Crispus. He ducked down to light it from the flame the other man held in his cupped palms.

"There are at least three that she's given over the last year. I have a man sorting through them now."

Palfrey nodded and exhaled smoke. He maintained a deep throat within the Kingston Police Department that thought he was working for someone else. Drug money bought some of the cops on the force. "Can we find her?"

"Given time," Crispus said, "yes."

"See that it's done."

Crispus bowed his head. "Of course, sir."

"This girl," Shotozumi said after the other man had departed, "could be very dangerous to us."

"Not for long."

"It is imperative that the cargo aboard the *Jilly St. Agnes* not be tracked back to Minoru Corporation," Shotozumi said. "The corporation is vulnerable to retaliation at this point."

Palfrey understood the meaning to be that Minoru Corporation had its fingers in more mud pies than merely trafficking toxic waste. He shivered, thinking about the barrels of dangerous chemicals and substances that would be offloaded at sea tomorrow evening and sailed into the bunker he'd built on his island. If he hadn't been so desperate for cash, he'd never have allowed it.

The earthquake that had hit and destroyed Kobe, Japan, had left behind a number of problems. It was more than the rebuilding of structures and highways, and the reorganization and refinancing of businesses. The question of what was to be done with the toxic waste left over from the disaster had headed the lists of several corporations. They'd already tried to farm out the waste to the Caribbean dump sites, but countries in the area, and more powerful nations with vested interests like the U.S., France and Great Britain, had flatly refused to allow it. If the containers broke open and spilled into the sea, all kinds of havoc would be unleashed on the ecological structure of the islands. Most Japanese corporations were looking for ways to cut their losses, and dump sites—even illegal ones—were at a premium.

The Yakuza had stepped in, offering to dispose of the waste through whatever means possible—for a price. Palfrey knew from the cut he was getting that the cost was exorbitant. But the amount was only a fraction of what it would have been to dispose of the waste legally or break it back down into inert components.

"Even if the police or DEA boarded the freighter," Palfrey stated, "and opened the containers, they wouldn't know what they had their hands on."

"Possibly," Shotozumi said, "but we can't take that chance."

"We won't," Palfrey assured him. "My people can find the girl. Trust me. It won't take long. At most, she knows of my interest in the *Jilly St. Agnes,* and has no hint at all as to what the cargo is." He flipped the cigarette butt out to sea, and it arced like a falling orange comet until it extinguished in the water. Nothing remained of the corpse. "She'll be dead by morning."

GABRIEL SYXX LIT a cigarette and handed it to Devon Catalano. "Feel like talking?" They sat in the Cherokee less than a mile south of Highway 1A. Kingston was six miles east.

The woman took the cigarette and drew a deep breath into her lungs. "No," she said as she exhaled.

"I'll take one of those," Clarissa Thomasson said. She sat beside Janet Gladsdale. The senator's daughter was unconscious in the seat-belt harness. One of the blankets was pulled up to her chin to keep her warm. It had taken long and vigorous shaking to get most of the broken glass out of the blanket's weave.

Syxx passed over another cigarette.

Mack Bolan listened to the conversation as he leaned under the open hood of the 4WD and examined the damage left by the barrage of bullets. One of them had ripped through the top radiator hose, and the vehicle had lost almost a gallon of water and coolant. He repaired the hose by wrapping a piece of vinyl cut from one of the Jeep's seats and securing it with ordnance tape. The fan blades were chopped up and had been making scraping noises toward the end, but he'd bent them back into a semblance of shape. Fresh scars shone against the dirt-streaked engine and wheel hubs. Nothing else had been damaged. Several of the radiator vanes had been holed, but the tubing was intact.

"Can you give me a name, Devon?" Syxx asked.

"Damn it, Gabe," the young woman said, "I can give you a lot of names. Okay? But I don't know who the guy was who was calling the shots. They were careful around us. I heard him called Santa-something a couple times, but the guys who slipped got reminded real damn quick to watch what they said. When those guys got around me, conversation wasn't exactly on their minds, you know." Her voice took on a brittle edge.

"Okay," Syxx replied. "I'm sorry, Devon. It's just your father's going to want to know is all."

"Then he should have been here asking questions. Is he even down here?"

Syxx hesitated before answering. "No. He stayed in Boston. He told me to get you on the first plane headed back stateside."

There was silence for a short time, then the door creaked open. Bolan was slicing through the windshield-wiper dispenser hose with his Swiss Army knife when Syxx came around the Cherokee.

"Damn," the Mafia hardman said in a quiet, hoarse voice. He dropped his cigarette into the sand and crushed it underfoot. His eyes were hard when he looked at the Executioner. "Meaning no disrespect, but Don Catalano should have been here."

"I agree," Bolan said. He shoved the windshield-wiper hose into the open radiator. "Trouble is, he's not."

"He's going to want to know about these guys that did this to Devon."

"You're here," Bolan said. "He's not. Do what you and she can live with."

"Christ, I know. He's not going to be happy about that five million dollars disappearing, either." Syxx scanned the dark sky. "How about you? Are you out of the deal now?"

"No," Bolan answered.

"I didn't think so." Syxx regarded him. "I'm supposed to stay with Devon, make sure she gets medical attention and get her back to Boston. You think maybe you could call Catalano and tell him you need a hand?"

The soldier looked at the man. "Gabe, you pulled your freight tonight. If you hadn't been there, maybe none of these women would have gotten out alive."

"Yeah, but this isn't finished."

"Not by a long shot," Bolan agreed. "Your part of it is. Get Devon home safe. That's what you've got to do now."

"I know. I just wish there was more I could do."

"For Devon?"

"Yeah."

Bolan straightened and met the hardman's level gaze. "Tracking down the guys who did this isn't going to help her. She's going to need a friend. It doesn't sound like the home life is going to do it for her."

"You got that right. What do you know about Catalano?"

Bolan shrugged. Turrin had filled him in enough to let the soldier know Catalano hadn't cared as much for his daughter's welfare as he had for his reputation of being someone to leave alone.

"Guy's a hard man," Syxx said. "Devon and him don't exactly get along these days. Her mother ended up in a sweatshop for recovering alcoholics a couple years ago. Not by choice. While she was there, she couldn't quite get around the habit. One night she hung herself with an electrical cord."

"Devon's going to need someone to talk to."

Syxx nodded. "I got a lady friend I used to be close to.

She's an insurance investigator. Ex-cop and worked rape crisis intervention. I figure we could start there.''

Bolan nodded. ''In my line of work, I don't often get to see what happens to good people who got chewed up in the cross fire. It's nice to know Devon's got someone to look after her.''

''Yeah, well, she's got you to thank for that. With all that law enforcement around tonight, the payoff wouldn't have been made and she'd have ended up with her throat cut.''

Helicopter rotors slapped against the air, growing louder as they approached. Bolan glanced up at the dark sky and saw the running lights of the chopper getting closer. He stepped away from the Cherokee and put his hand along his thigh near the Desert Eagle.

Syxx used his cellular phone and talked briefly. ''Our guys,'' he said.

Bolan nodded.

The Huey helicopter settled to a gentle landing less than fifty yards away. Sand whipped around them, stinging, raining blinding pellets against the Cherokee's metallic hide like a snare-drum solo.

Squinting through the haze, Bolan saw four armed men peel out of the big cargo aircraft, dressed in dark clothes. Syxx went forward to meet them. The conversation was short. Syxx kept them moving the whole time. Two men used a collapsible gurney to take Janet Gladsdale from the Cherokee. She moaned for a moment before one of the men stuck her with a hypodermic.

''Sedative,'' Syxx said. ''We're going to keep her down for a while until we get her to a hospital. I cut a deal with some of the law enforcement and State Department people. In exchange for passage out of Jamaica on a private jet we've got waiting, they get the senator's daughter without the paparazzi getting candid pictures of her that would show up on every tabloid in the States for months. Seemed like a useful bit of blackmail to get us clear.''

The two men took up the gurney and hustled Janet Gladsdale toward the waiting helicopter.

"The island police are already on their way here," Syxx went on. "Guy I got monitoring the Kingston cop bands said the call went in about the action down at Great Salt Pond only a few minutes ago. Some of the locals went to investigate and didn't have a hard time putting it together. They're going to be looking."

Bolan nodded. "I'll find my way clear of them."

A half-smile twisted the Mafia hardman's lips. "I think you will." He offered his hand.

The soldier took it. No matter what side of the law they fell on, they'd been fellow combatants fighting against a predator. Another time, Bolan knew, and they might have been enemies instead of allies.

Devon Catalano made her own way, brushing aside the men who offered to help her. She stood in front of Bolan and tried to speak, but her voice wouldn't cooperate. "Thank you," was all she could manage. But her eyes spoke volumes more.

Her gaze touched the part of the soldier that was Sergeant Mercy. Most had known him as a killing tool, specializing as a behind-the-lines sniper-assassin for special ops, a machine that mowed down targets. But it was the flesh-and-blood man who pushed the muscle-and-bone soldier into doing what needed to be done.

"Work on getting past this," Bolan said, "and you will."

She nodded. "I know," she finally said. "I just wanted to say thanks. My dad couldn't have paid you enough to take the chances you did tonight. I know that." Quietly and with dignity, she turned and walked away, walling herself off from the men around her who tried to help.

"She's young," Clarissa Thomasson said at Bolan's elbow, "but she's got enough mad in her to make it through until she finds something else to hold on to."

The soldier turned to face the remaining woman.

Thomasson had a bruise around her right eye that had

already faded yellow with time, washed out even more by the lights from the idling chopper. She'd done what she could to straighten her clothing and wash some of the accumulated grime off with the package of wet wipes that had been in the medkits.

"How about you?" Bolan asked gently.

"Hell," the woman said, "I'm a survivor. I'm alive right now, and it didn't have to work out that way. I'm not going to forget what's been done, and getting past this isn't going to be easy, but I'll manage." Her bloodshot eyes lingered on his face, and Bolan had the impression she was memorizing every line. "She was right, you know. Not many guys would have stuck the way you and the other man did."

"Maybe more than you think."

She shrugged. "Could be. I've always been a cynic at heart." She wrapped her arms around herself and took another hit from her cigarette. "But not many of them would have been able to wade into a fight like that and walk away."

Bolan didn't say anything.

Thomasson looked up at him speculatively. "I heard you tell him you weren't through with this."

"No," Bolan answered her. "I'm not."

"You're not a policeman?"

"No."

"Do you plan on bringing the animals responsible for this back to stand trial?"

The soldier looked into the pain-filled eyes and gave her an honest answer. "No."

"Good." Thomasson dropped her cigarette butt to the ground and stubbed it out with a broken, mud-encrusted shoe. "These aren't men who'd understand justice except in rudimentary terms. The leader's name is Santiago. I didn't get a last name. They're not a formal bunch." The smile she gave him was wan and hollow, devoid of mirth. "This evening, I heard some of them talking about a bar called The Golden Peacock. I figure you're probably not up on the island geography, but maybe you're a quick study. The Golden Peacock is on the outskirts of Ocho Rios. You know where that is?''

"Yeah," Bolan replied. Ocho Rios was a growing tourist attraction on the north side of the island. The fishing village it had been was giving way to the concrete and glass of an enhanced economy.

"I know of the place," Thomasson said. "Comes from working the cruise lines down here for a few years. They were talking about meeting there after tonight. In case anything happened. I'd say your showing up qualifies."

"I'll look into it," the soldier said.

"Cops won't go there," the woman told him. "That's purely bandido territory. If this Santiago guy is there, it's because he's got a working arrangement with the establishment. He's got a lot of people working for him."

"I appreciate the tip."

"Take care if you decide to check it out. They're not big on strangers up that way. Especially ones who come in asking questions. When the police talk to me later, I'm going to have amnesia about that for twenty-four hours or so. That'll give you some time." Without another word, she turned and walked away from him.

As the helicopter clawed its way into the air, the Executioner slid in behind the wheel of the Cherokee and started the engine. He pushed the windshield wiper fluid button and pumped the container into the radiator in seconds. When it had finished, he capped off the radiator and drove onto the highway.

He peered into the darkness in front of him and pushed away the fatigue. He chose back roads from memory, heading toward Spanish Town. When he'd checked the transmitter's location only a few minutes ago, it had been there.

Reaching over to the notebook computer, he brought it up and quickly attached the cellular phone. In seconds, he was hooked back into the GPS grid Kurtzman had established. The money was on the move, and so was the Executioner.

Gazing through the night glasses, Bolan figured that Mestipen Seid had seen the writing on the wall and had let his
greed get the better of him. Evidently during the confusion
at Great Salt Pond, he'd ended up with the five million in
ransom. The soldier guessed that because the suitcase Seid
had carried to the meet with the pirates was against the wall,
stained with mud streaks.

After everything that had happened in the past two hours,
Seid had to have known police would be looking for him
and the pirates wouldn't trust him anymore, and he would've
tried to cut himself the best deal he knew how. The Kingston
private detective had holed up in a two-bedroom bungalow
in one of Spanish Town's older sections, which hadn't been
shored up by tourist dollars yet. The suitcase holding the
five million dollars never left his sight as he walked restlessly from kitchen to living room. From the way he kept
looking outside, Bolan figured the man was waiting for
someone.

The house was apparently owned or leased by a woman
in her midthirties. Bolan had only had brief glimpses of her,
because Seid was closely monitoring her movement. She
didn't appear happy to see Seid. Short, slender and brunette,
she wore a light cotton robe over an emerald sleeping gown.

In the breakfast nook, dimly visible on the other side of
the heavy curtains in the dark kitchen, the woman sat on
one side of the small, round dinette while Seid kept watch

out the window. He kept a .357 Magnum pistol in his hand the whole time.

The Executioner kept the glasses on the window. He stood next to the corner of the alley and let the shadows mask him from Seid's view. The supplies in the back of the Cherokee had yielded a fresh change of clothing: a black T-shirt and dark jeans, as well as dry boots. The Desert Eagle rode in shoulder leather under the dark shirt he left unbuttoned and untucked outside his pants. Up close, the shirt would never have fooled a cop for a second, but it prevented the casual observer from noticing his weapons. An Ithaca Model 37 Stakeout 12-gauge shotgun hung from his right shoulder from a Whip-it sling under the shirt.

Traffic along the narrow street was sparse. The trouble was going to be the number of dogs kept in backyards. Judging from the lights still on in a few of the surrounding houses, not all of the neighborhood was safely in bed.

Also, Bolan knew he wasn't the only one stalking Seid.

Three men sat in a weather-beaten brown Toyota two blocks down the street, and kept watch over the house. At one point one of them got out and used a pay phone on the corner, talked for a short time, then returned to the car.

Bolan didn't recognize any of them from the earlier action, but one man sported a white bandage through a hole in his jeans at midthigh, and had an as-yet uncoordinated limp. The soldier had been in place for ten minutes. He didn't know how long the observation team had occupied its position. There was no doubt that they'd called for backup.

The numbers on the play were swiftly leaking away. Bolan timed the pickup coming down the street and started out of the alley as it approached. He stepped off the curb as it drew abreast of him, narrowly avoiding the splash of headlights, and walked into its wake. With the passage of light, he knew the watchers would be at a temporary disadvantage seeing him. It wouldn't take much luck for them to believe he was simply a resident returning home late.

It was after two now, and he was going to have to hurry

if he wanted to make the possible meet in Ocho Rios. He didn't glance toward the Toyota, relying on his combat radar to let him know if he was drawing too much attention.

He walked for the home two houses down from Seid's position, then broke into a run. There were two dogs in the backyard, and both noticed the Executioner at the same time. Loosing baying yelps of surprise and inspired ferocity, the mongrels came clawing out of the crate that had been fashioned into a home.

Bolan put a hand on the fence and vaulted over it. His boots thudded into the soft ground and sank a couple inches as the dogs raced for him. He sprinted hard, driving his feet against the ground. The dogs had to alter their course, and he gained a couple steps on them. By the time they turned, he was over the fence on the other side, streaking for the adjoining fence to the house Seid was in. The dogs butted against the wire mesh behind him and howled.

The small light Seid and the woman had been using in the kitchen was suddenly doused. An engine started up on the street, then a transmission whined as it was engaged.

Bolan fell into position beside the rear door of the house. He yanked the sling and freed the slack he'd tied to keep it out of sight. The shotgun dropped down to its full extension, the pistol grip even with the soldier's hand.

The barking dogs covered most of the other surrounding noises. With lights and loud voices, other parts of the neighborhood came awake.

"Goddamn it, Gina," Seid yelled from inside the house, his rough voice muted by the walls, "I thought you said no one was out there!"

"I said I didn't see anyone!" the woman yelled back. Her words carried fear, as well as anger.

The sound of a racing engine closed, followed immediately by the shriek of brakes, then the thump of metal against wood. Gunshots cracked the heaviness of the night. Glass broke and rained on stone in tinkling crescendos.

Bolan wheeled and drove his foot against the door. The

lock tore out of the wood and he moved forward, using his peripheral vision to identify the squared-off shapes of the washer and dryer in the small room. Another door was to his left. He tried the knob and found it unlocked. Without hesitation, he took the two short steps up and through.

The kitchen was set up in an L. The sink was to the soldier's left, while the stove and refrigerator stood against the opposite wall. At the end of the narrow passageway, the room bent into the dogleg, allowing scant room for the breakfast bar and two stools. The dinette where the woman was still seated was just beyond.

Mestipen Seid was taking cover to the right of the bay window. He held the suitcase in one hand and his pistol in the other. Blood leaked from three slashes across his face. Palm-sized sections had been shot out of the glass in the window, jagged cracks connecting them. Shards of broken ceramic pots were scattered everywhere.

As Bolan entered the room, the woman slumped out of her seat and fell to the floor. Crimson threads wrapped around the bone revealed in her smashed temple. One eye was missing, and her face was ruined. Bolan went past her, knowing she was beyond help.

Seid spotted the Executioner and tried to raise his weapon.

Bolan swung the shotgun and caught Seid across his gun wrist. The impact was solid. The pistol went spinning and clattered to the floor.

A face appeared in the window over the squared-off barrel of a Glock 17. Gripping Seid's jacket in his free hand, Bolan yanked the man away. Bullets tore through the plasterboard where he'd been standing. The Executioner brought the shotgun around in a tight arc and fired at the center of the gunner. The weapon boomed in the tight space of the kitchen and jerked in the soldier's hand.

Keeping in a narrow mass, not spreading much over the short distance, the double-aught buck smashed into the man in the window. The pellets took out most of the remaining glass, as well as the gunner.

Bolan racked the shotgun's slide and shoved Seid ahead of him. "Move if you want to live," he said in a graveyard voice.

Seid got his legs working and headed for the back door.

"Try to lose me," Bolan warned, "and I'll cut you down. That's a promise."

Seid grabbed the door frame and hauled himself around it, losing traction for just an instant. "Who are you?"

"Not a friend," the Executioner growled. He paused in the doorway on Seid's heels and scanned the street in front of the house. The Toyota had jumped the curb and smashed against the wooden railing surrounding the front porch. The shattered remains of the roofed trellis that had been to one side of the main entrance lay draped over the Toyota. Terracotta tubs filled with plants and flowers lay over the car and the yard.

Suddenly the Toyota's engine caught life again, and it lurched backward. The tires spun, and the debris from the trellis and plants spilled from it. Only the left headlight was intact. The hot yellow light spread over the front of the house, leaking through the broken windows and creating new patterns of shifting shadows. Someone kicked the front door open, and two men rushed inside.

Bolan fired a round in their direction. The buckshot pattern ripped a cabinet door from the corner, reducing it to a spray of splinters. As he followed Seid outside, he removed two fresh shells from his shirt pocket and thumbed them into the shotgun.

Seid hesitated at the corner of the house.

The Executioner grabbed his jacket and shoved him forward. "Don't stop until I tell you to."

The man panted and shifted the suitcase to his other hand, having trouble with his stride for an instant until he got everything balanced again. The dogs met him at the next fence, snarling and snapping at him.

Bolan fired a round into the air. The sudden blast sent the dogs streaking back to their house for safety. They continued to bark from inside. At the next fence, Seid stumbled and had trouble getting across.

A line of autofire kicked up clods of grassy dirt at their feet.

Swiveling, Bolan brought up the Ithaca and fired at the gunner who'd followed them from inside the house. The first group of pellets hit the man in the shoulder and spun him. The second burst put him down for good.

Bolan gave Seid directions, heading left. Near the front of the house looking out over the street he'd crossed earlier, the soldier grabbed the man's collar and brought him to a halt.

While Seid gagged and choked from the constriction of his throat, the Executioner surveyed the combat zone. He thumbed more shells into the Ithaca to bring the tubular magazine up to its max capacity of five, and found he only had three more. Settling in for a long exchange hadn't been in the plan. It still wasn't.

The Toyota sat in the center of the street facing their direction like a dented gladiator. The passenger door was open, and a man knelt behind it with an assault rifle at the ready.

A black-and-white Bronco outfitted for off-road travel, sporting big tires and a raised suspension, approached at high speed. More armed men were inside. On both sides of the street, the residents extinguished lights, and angry yells challenged the gunners, promising that the authorities had been called.

"You're not with Santiago?" Seid croaked.

"No," Bolan replied.

Men poured out of the Bronco, vanishing like wraiths into the residential area. The driver talked briefly on a walkie-talkie, his face illuminated by the lights of a passing car that hesitated for a moment, then gained speed and turned at the end of the block.

"You a cop?" Seid asked.

"No." Bolan switched the shotgun into his other hand and pulled the Desert Eagle from the leather. "When I say run, take off for the alley across the street. If you fall or I pass you, I'm going to shoot you once through the head and leave your corpse for those men.'' He made his voice cold and hard, letting the man believe he meant every word. "Do you understand me?''

"Yeah. But, hey, running out there…'' Seid shook his head. "That's going to be suicide.''

"No,'' Bolan replied, "not running—that's suicide.'' The Executioner leveled the heavy Israeli .44 Magnum pistol and squeezed off three rounds in the space of a heartbeat.

The 240-grain boattail slugs crashed through the Toyota's windshield at eyeball-level for the driver. The shadow behind the wheel jerked with the impacts, then suddenly slumped forward. The car lurched and immediately died. Then the sound of the horn blared over the neighborhood and drowned out all other sounds, erasing the last of the rolling thunder that had issued from the Desert Eagle.

"Run!'' Bolan ordered.

Seid froze for only an instant, then darted across the street. Shouts followed him, with gunshots ringing out almost at once.

The Executioner moved out into the open and took a Weaver combat stance, lining up the Desert Eagle's sights over his forearm while he held the shotgun. The Bronco was moving forward, but the Toyota was partially blocking the way and providing cover. The soldier chose his targets, watching the way the gunners inside the 4WD leaned out the passenger door and one of the rear doors. He let out half a breath, held it and started to fire.

He put his first round in the upper body of the man leaning out the passenger door. The gunner jerked when the heavy bullet took him, then slid out of sight. The second bullet missed the man farther back on the driver's side, but the third shot caught him in the face. The last two rounds smashed into the driver's side of the glass. Out of control, the Bronco raced forward and slammed into the front end of a parked station wagon up on blocks.

Holstering the Desert Eagle, Bolan ran after Seid. With no one at the wheel, the Toyota was the site of mass confusion. A man stepped out on the passenger side, blood gleaming wetly against the side of his face, and brought up a Colt Commando assault rifle, pointing it in Seid's direction.

The Executioner fired the Ithaca on the run. The shotgun's pattern spread appreciably over the intervening thirty feet. The pellets knocked their target down instantly.

Voices took up the alarm in the houses to Bolan's left and behind. Although the two vehicles were temporarily disposed of, ground pursuit was still active. The soldier caught up to Seid easily.

Seid breathed as loudly as a bellows pump, and his step was beginning to falter. It had been a strenuous night, and exercise obviously wasn't his preference.

"Don't stop," Bolan warned. He let the other man hit the opposite curb first, then followed him into the alley. The car he had waiting was a fourteen-year-old Chevy he'd boosted near the railway station off Bourkes Road. The security around the stored cars at the station had been lax, and he'd been gone in seconds.

The suitcase threw Seid off and slowed him, but they still had enough of a lead to make it to the Chevy. It sat in the darkness against a badly listing wooden fence around the main market area.

"The car," Bolan said. "Get in."

Seid opened the door and dropped into the seat, holding the suitcase across his knees. His chest rose and fell rapidly, and sweat ran in silver streamers down his face and neck.

Bolan slid behind the wheel and scooped up the screwdriver he'd left on the floorboard. He jammed it into the broken ignition switch on the steering column. Sparks jumped out of the hole as shadows sprinted for them from the alley. The engine turned over and caught. The soldier managed to dump the Desert Eagle's empty magazine and replace it with another before the first shots rang out.

He yanked the transmission into drive and put his foot hard on the accelerator, the rear tires spinning as they sought traction. Steering hard right to clear the knot of pursuers, the Executioner kept the .44 at hand. The back end of the Chevy slammed against a stack of trash cans and sent them spinning toward the collection of men chasing after it.

There was a brief barrage of fire, then Bolan cleared the curb and pulled back onto the street. He crossed at the intersection and turned left on Young Street at the next intersection. He was headed north, out of town, looking to score the meet in Ocho Rios. Adrenaline surged within him, keeping him clear-headed and thinking quick.

Reaching under the seat, he pulled out the pair of plastic disposable handcuffs he'd stored there earlier. He kept the Desert Eagle on the wheel as he shoved the cuffs at Seid. "Put those on."

Seid offered no argument at all, but he kept the suitcase on his knees.

Bolan checked the rearview mirror, seeing nothing but streets and light traffic. He kept the accelerator down, running consistently above the speed limit by five or ten miles.

AT 2:45 a.m., Bolan pulled the Chevy over on a side street off Monk in the Ravenswood district and killed the engine. A brief scan of the neighborhood reassured him they would go unnoticed for the next few minutes. He looked at his prisoner. "Who is Santiago?"

Seid glanced at him, his shirt spotted with perspiration. "You're not with the police, man. Why should I be talking to you?"

"I'm not with the police," Bolan said, "and that might be a good thing to remember." He lifted the Desert Eagle and pointed it at the man's head. Although he had no intention of shooting Seid in cold blood, the man wasn't so sure.

A nervous tic started by Seid's left eye. "Crowe," he said. "Man's name is Santiago Crowe. Maybe it's a real name, maybe it's made up. I don't know for sure."

"He's the man behind the kidnappings?" Bolan asked.

"Yeah."

"How did you get involved?"

"He sent a man named Domingo Krauss to see me. Make a deal. Santiago kidnaps people, I set him up with go-betweens to pick up the ransom money. I do a lot of business off the island, so I know some mainland people with connections to talk to the families. I didn't kill nobody."

"The law's not going to see it that way. You do it once, you're accessory after the fact to kidnapping. But you've done it more than once, and people have been killed."

"I didn't kill them. Santiago did. Man, that big bastard is crazy. Wearing that baby skull on a chain around his neck and all that shit. He ain't no one a man would want to fuck with. He sent Krauss to make a deal with me, I didn't have no choice unless I wanted my damn brains blown out. I was as much of a prisoner as any of them people he took."

Bolan dropped the Desert Eagle's muzzle toward the suitcase. "You didn't seem to have any trouble taking the money tonight."

"Santiago thought I set him up, man." Seid clenched his hands into fists, kept close together because of the cuffs. "I didn't run. That crazy man would have killed me for sure. That money, I figured I could run long and hard before he could get me."

"Where can I find Santiago?"

Seid tapped his chest in a show of disbelief that Bolan judged to be totally false. "You think he's going to keep me up with his agenda, man? Bastard tried to kill me twice tonight."

"I don't think he'd keep you up with it," Bolan replied, "but I do think you'd try to find out." He rolled the hammer back on the big .44, and the triple click was ominous to the man trapped inside the car.

"How do I know you're not going to kill me if I tell you anything, man?"

"You don't," the Executioner replied. "You're going to

have to trust me on that. Anyway it plays, you're a dead man if I want it that way.''

"He's going to be up in Ocho Rios, man." Seid had to concentrate to keep from looking at the pistol's barrel. "A place called—"

"The Golden Peacock," Bolan said.

Seid's eyes widened. "Yeah. If you already know that, then why're you leaning on me?"

"To keep you honest." Bolan shifted in the seat. In the distance he could hear the police sirens. "Now tell me something I don't know."

"Like what?"

"What's he doing in Ocho Rios?" the soldier asked. "Is he based there?"

"No. He's setting up another job that's going to take place near there."

"When?"

"Tomorrow," Seid replied.

Bolan considered that. None of the other kidnappings had taken place so quickly. Usually there had been a layover of a few weeks at least. "Why is Santiago moving so fast?"

"The heat, man. Santiago knows everybody in these waters be looking for him. After taking that Mafia man's daughter, he knew he was going to have to lay low for a while. He wanted enough money to do it. That prize he has his heart set on, she promises to bring in another big ransom."

"What cruise line is he after?"

"Sunchaser Cruise Line."

Bolan wasn't familiar with the name, but there were a number of cruises operating in the area. "What's the target?"

"A ship called the *Obsidian Princess*. Her passenger list includes some heavy hitters in financial circles. International bankers, lawyers, politicians. Those kind of people."

"They're going to be well protected," the soldier pointed out.

"Won't matter, man," Seid replied. "Santiago's going in hard on this one. He's got some people already aboard her. Wait staff, passengers. He'll come in guns blazing, take what he wants and make everybody pay big to get their people back. That last time, when the Cayman police tried to take him down, they pissed him off. He wants to show them they can't fuck him about without getting burned. He gets through with his raiding party, he's planning on sinking that liner with all the passengers aboard."

Bolan glanced at his watch. It was almost three. "When is the raid going down on the *Obsidian Princess?*"

"All I know is tomorrow evening, man. He was going to have one of his people e-mail me with the list of people he took from the liner." Nervously Seid shook his head, trying to buddy up to the soldier. "Man's got somebody with a computer, and he still wears a child's skull on a necklace. Doesn't make sense, does it, a man being up with the times and a barbarian at the same instant."

The Executioner had no problem believing it. Predators' motives hadn't changed since the day Cain picked up a rock and smashed Abel's head. Only they didn't have to resort to rocks anymore. "How many people does Crowe have with him?"

"Man, I'd only be guessing."

"Then give me your best guess."

"My best guess? With the way things are in these islands?" Seid hissed angrily. "You're talking about a depressed economy depending on the tourist trade. Hand-to-mouth for a lot of people, and them doting on all these tourists who got no respect for their ways, for their land. Builds up a lot of mad, you know? A lot of guys, they're mad they got to work for the foreigners, but they know that's the way of it. Some, they don't fit in so well as waiters and the like, and they don't like having to cut the bananas or work the docks or fish. I tell you, like as not Santiago, he kicks open his boats and says I need somebody, he's going to have a loaded boat before you can blink your eyes."

The soldier had it figured that way, too. By cutting the head off the serpent, though, he hoped the rest of the body would die instead of growing a new head. "Domingo Krauss is Crowe's second-in-command?"

"Yeah. And a crazier man you'll never see the like of. Krauss will cut a man open and watch him bleed to death on the sand just cause he's bored. Him and Santiago go way back to when they were kids."

"Is there anyone else Crowe depends on?"

"No. Crowe and Krauss, they run the operation. Anybody don't see it their way, they get turned away. Anybody get real objectionable about it, they get killed."

"Where are they based?"

"That I don't know. Crowe moves around a lot. He's got some boats somewhere, maybe they call them home, but looking for and finding them boats ain't no easy thing."

Bolan nodded, then waggled the Desert Eagle slightly. "Get out of the car."

"Get out of the car?" Seid acted as though he didn't believe his ears.

"Yeah."

"You're not going to shoot me here, are you?"

"If you don't start moving, I will."

Reluctantly Seid opened the car door and kept his eyes locked on the Executioner. The tic near his eye had grown worse, almost closing the lids now as it flickered. He kept his hand in the suitcase handle and tried to drag it with him.

"Leave it," Bolan instructed.

"Couldn't we work out some kind of split? I've told you a lot more than I should have."

"You shouldn't have gotten involved with Crowe at all," the soldier replied. "And you never should have taken the money from Crowe."

Seid opened his hand and held it shoulder high as he stepped from the car. Just as he was almost clear of the door, he ducked and took off running, obviously expecting to be shot. He managed four long strides before he stumbled and fell headlong onto the ground. He groaned and cried and bolted immediately for the thin shelter of a row of ferns and flowering plants growing in a garden inside the yard.

Bolan shoved the screwdriver home and started the Chevy. He pulled away fast, and the motion shoved the door shut. Seid was no longer a threat. If the man managed to slip through the police net, Crowe and the pirates were still hunting him for taking their money.

While he drove, Bolan opened the computer and brought it on-line, then added the cellular phone. Once he'd connected to the Internet, he tapped out a quick note.

TO: ELECTRON RIDER@stoneface.com
   CC: STRIKER
   Re: Ransom
   Santiago Crowe?
   Domingo Krauss?
   Terrain: Ocho Rios
   Obsidian Princess, time, agenda

After a quick glance at the note, he tagged it and sent it zooming along, a mass of electrons until it reformed at the other end at Stony Man Farm and caught Aaron Kurtzman's attention. He shut down the phone and the computer and stored them safely. There was one other stop he needed to make before he headed north.

THE CHURCH HAD SEEN better days. Worn and weatherbeaten, the building was tucked up under a copse of mahoe, bulletwood and Spanish elm. The light against the windows came from candles and not electricity.

Bolan pulled the Chevy to a halt against a thick and gnarled Spanish elm, and killed the engine. He'd doused the lights after turning onto the block. Emergency vehicles were still rolling in the combat zone he'd left.

He opened the door and got out, sensing that he'd already

attracted attention. The Desert Eagle was snugged under his arm, and the shotgun was within easy reach between the bucket seats. He reached in and took out the suitcase containing Catalano's money. The marked bill had already been removed and destroyed.

Without hesitation, he started up the stone-laid path that ended at the modest door of the rectory. Light moving in the window alerted him and he stopped.

A heavy-set black man opened the door and stepped out. He wore dark robes that ended high enough to reveal skinny legs that didn't look as if they went with the body. His hair was gray, a mere fringe around his bald pate. Gold-framed glasses enlarged the hazel eyes behind the lenses. He carried an oil lamp in one hand and a rosary in the other.

"May I help you?" he asked in a deep voice.

"Maybe I can help you," Bolan said. "I have a gift." He held the suitcase forward, then knelt and placed it on the ground. The latches gave easily, and he lifted the lid.

The priest lifted his lantern to get a better look. When he saw what was in the suitcase, he redirected his gaze at Bolan. "So much money."

"Yes." Bolan stood.

"Why?"

"Because here it can do some good. If it was returned to its owners, only more evil would come of it."

The priest was cautious and stood his ground. "This money was for the ransom to be paid in Kingston."

"Yes." Bolan didn't want to lie. The money had come from Catalano as bait for Crowe and his band. The Boston Mafia don had been hoping that it would be returned, but if it were, it would only go back into the deep pockets where Catalano kept all his ill-gotten gain and be used to further build his empire. By placing it here, in the hands of the priest, he hoped that it could work some good.

"What of the women?" the priest asked.

"They're safe," the soldier answered.

"Without the money?" The priest lifted an eyebrow.

"It wasn't by choice."

"Will men be looking for this money?"

Bolan nodded. "If they have the time. The kidnappers are being hunted now, but the men who lost this, they'll look."

"And you feel they don't deserve it back."

Bolan looked at the other man and spoke honestly. "All that money in that suitcase can't return to those women what's been taken from them, Father. The one in whose name the money was given, I think she'd be glad to know it's going to help someone instead of simply being returned where it came from." He pointed at the suitcase. "If you spend it judiciously, you won't attract any notice. Hopefully you'll be able to help those who need it."

"Then, on behalf of my church and God, I thank you. What is your name?"

Bolan gave the older man a slight smile. "What's in a name, Father?"

"I see." The priest bent and closed the suitcase, then picked it up. "I will pray for those women, for their deliverance from pain."

Bolan nodded and turned away.

"You're not leaving, then?" the priest asked.

"Not yet," the soldier replied as he slid behind the steering wheel. "I've got unfinished business."

"Then I'll also pray for you, my son," the priest said, "because these men will know you're coming."

The big man had it figured that way, too, because he didn't intend to make a secret of it. He whipped through the town, taking the outside corners of Spanish Town, then caught Highway A1 and headed north. Ocho Rios was less than an hour away.

5

"Pit!" the referee screamed.

Santiago Crowe stood on the sideline of the cockpit and watched as the two handlers unleashed their fighting cocks. The smell of blood was already in the air from the earlier fights, and dark stains roped through the buckets of sand spread across the floor.

The black-and-gray rooster broke high as soon as it neared its opponent. Steel flashed along its spurs as it raked out aggressively. The reddish rooster ducked under the initial cutting, then swung on the gray. It hopped once, then buried one spur deep into the gray's back and another through the gray's head. Both cocks went down at once and beat the air and ground with their wings, stirring up the dust from the hard earthen floor. The gray's mouth was open and it was spitting blood, its neck twisted viciously by the leverage maintained by the red rooster's strength and gaff.

"Handle that!" the referee bellowed. He was a squat, fat man wearing a white panama with a turquoise band and an orange tie-dyed T-shirt with the sleeves hacked off. He mopped at his round face incessantly with a red-and-white handkerchief.

The two handlers moved forward while the referee peered over their shoulders and made sure neither of them did any extra twisting of the metal spurs as they were pulled from the other rooster's flesh. There was little blood. The two handlers retreated to neutral corners and waited for orders to release their birds again.

The referee kicked dirt over the initial two lines with his bare feet. Using his walking stick, he drew another pair of lines in the dirt, closer together now.

More than a hundred people were inside the corrugated tin-covered building. The interior was as empty as a barn except for two sets of wooden bleachers that carried knife scars and beer stains. Most of the crowd was standing around the action, unable to fit in the bleachers. Against the walls, carrying cases and racks of cobbled-together cages held more roosters waiting to fight. The wild collection of voices was punctuated every so often by the challenge of a rooster's crow.

Money changed hands rapidly. Odds were given and taken. Beer and microwaved dishes were served in the corner, passed through open spaces cut through plywood sheets. It was almost four o'clock in the morning, but Crowe knew business would remain brisk until almost dawn. He owned a percentage of the pit.

The cocks were released again. Despite their wounds, their genetic programming sent them racing headlong at each other once more. The gray broke high again, kicking at the other rooster. But the red was waiting, and buried both spurs deep into the gray's abdomen. They went down in a tangle of feathers.

"The gray, man," a man in front of Crowe said, "he's had enough of the steel. Got no talent either. Better he should have his head lopped off and be done with it."

Crowe looked at the cocks as they were separated. Even after all the damage that had been inflicted on him, the gray still pecked at the red rooster as he was pulled away. Crowe leaned toward the other man. "I got fifty dollars against ten that the gray beats the red."

Grinning, the man looked over his shoulder. Then when he saw who he was talking to, the smile left his face and his eyes widened. "Meaning no disrespect, but I can't take your money."

The Golden Peacock cockpit was a gathering place for

Ocho Rios's outlaws and scammers. The night people and the dealers who liked seeing blood sports on a regular basis collected there to dream and scheme. For a time, police had raided the establishment. Cockfighting was legal, but occasionally they would turn up someone with counterfeit papers or someone with a warrant out for his or her arrest. However, Crowe had found a man who could grease the police department. They stayed away now. Whatever trouble happened at the pit, the on-site hardmen took care of.

"The gray," Crowe said, "he has heart. He's taken the steel twice and hasn't given up. He's hard to kill, too. You won't be taking my money."

The man nodded, but he wasn't as animated as before.

That suited Crowe fine. He liked people to be afraid of him, even when they worked for him or around him. Fear was a big equalizer.

He also knew Mestipen Seid would be filled with fear at this very moment. Seid had broken free of the death trap in Spanish Town and had yet to resurface. During the gunplay at the Great Salt Pond, Crowe had forgotten about the money and allowed it to get away from him. Too much had been going on around them, and he'd wanted to see whoever had dared challenge him dead—along with the women.

A message had needed to be sent. The next time he'd looked around, the money was gone—and so was Mestipen Seid. Now Crowe was waiting to hear from the team that had been sent to get Seid in Spanish Town.

The fighting roosters were released again. The gray was off balance this time, listing to one side with his broken wing dragging through the sand. The red came at him aggressively, then leaped into the air and started cutting with both feet. The gray became a blur of steel-shanked movement, battling ferociously between the red's outspread wings.

In seconds, the battling birds flopped to the sand again. One of the red's spurs had hooked through the gray's throat behind his bill. However, the gray had thrust both gaffs into the red's chest, striking the heart at least once. Frozen-eyed and his sharp bill open to struggle for one last gasping breath, the red shivered like a palsied man in winter and died.

The handlers came forward at once at the referee's signal. As it was pulled from the dead body of the other rooster, the gray pecked savagely at his opponent's head, ripping feathers free. The gaffs were cut off the roosters, and the corpse of the dead one was taken back to the pile of dead birds outside the building. In the morning, gasoline would be poured over the bodies and ignited so scavengers wouldn't be drawn. No one ate the dead birds because there was no way of knowing which ones had been doctored with strychnine to make them perform better during the fights.

The gray's handler slashed the gaffs from the bird, then held it high as the crowd alternately booed or cheered, depending on which way the money went. As the next fight was called, the handler held the gray's feet and turned the bird upside down. He put his foot on the gray's head and yanked. The head popped off at once and fresh blood spurted over the sand.

It wasn't that the rooster wouldn't have fought again after it had healed, but it would never again be near its peak physical performance. The owner didn't want to risk any more money on it, and whatever brood stock the gray was from was already known.

Crowe understood the mentality. Fights were won or lost, but they didn't stop. Only the strong survived. He took the money from the man in front of him.

"Mr. Crowe."

Crowe turned at the sound of the feminine voice. There were other women laced throughout the crowd, many of them the epitome of bloodthirstiness. A number of them also knew his name. He looked at the young woman standing before him. "I don't know you."

She appeared distraught, angry and scared. She was Hispanic, probably Cuban, from the lines of her jaw and the set of her dark eyes. Her hair was long and straight. She wore pants, sandals and a sleeveless shirt that hinted at her figure without being blatant. "My name is Natacha Liberto. I think maybe we could do some business together."

Crowe scowled at her. "I don't buy my women," he told her gruffly. Her face darkened with embarrassment for a heartbeat, and he knew he'd pegged her right. Her lips thinned, but she held back an angry retort. Whatever she wanted from him, she was willing to pay. He watched and listened.

"I know you are the man responsible for hijacking the ships and the kidnappings," Liberto told him.

"And how do you know this?" Crowe scratched under his chin and motioned for her to follow him outside. Most of the people inside the building knew that. He was there now recruiting for the run he would be making on the *Obsidian Princess* later that evening. In an hour or two, everything would be ready, and he could get some rest.

"I was told."

"By who?" Crowe halted outside the building. The cool of the night blew across them. The cockpit had established a beachhead against the jungle. The ocean bled into the tangled roots of the trees butting against the water, but there were three different docks hidden among them. Armed guards maintained a loose patrol around the perimeter.

"A man named Parboosingh." She looked up at him with earnest, angry eyes. Tears glittered within the depths, as well.

Crowe knew Parboosingh. The man was a young braggart and loved to be hard on the females that were kidnapped. He marked the man's name in his mind. If Parboosingh hadn't been one of the men who'd died in the battle at the Great Salt Pond, he would be dead by dawn. "That knowledge you think you have, girl, can be a very dangerous thing if you start waving it around."

"I know, but if I was going to tell someone, I think I probably would have by now."

"Yes. Then what do you want with me?"

"I think I can help you."

"How?"

"Have you heard of a man named Lyndon Palfrey?" Liberto asked.

Crowe nodded. He didn't know much about the man except that he owned his own island and appeared to have a lot of money. Palfrey was also reputed to make his living sponging off the black market and providing special services.

"You know about the construction he's had going on at his island?"

"Sure." Crowe had even sent some of his men to the job site to see if there was anything in it for his crew. Provided Palfrey invited the right people to his retreat and security was lax enough, Crowe had figured it for an easy score at some point.

"My uncle, a man named Gustavo Ruiz, was crew foreman."

Crowe watched as a weather-beaten Land Rover pulled through the narrow, rutted road leading to the cockpit. The yellow lights played over three armed men near the bottleneck of the clearing. Bouncing and erratic, the Land Rover came to a stop a few yards away and Domingo Krauss got out from behind the steering wheel. Four men armed with assault rifles jumped to the ground behind him.

"What's all this got to do with me?" Crowe asked the woman.

"A few weeks ago, my uncle disappeared."

"Men do that all the time," Crowe pointed out. "What makes this so special?"

"Because he was getting ready to blackmail Palfrey."

Crowe returned his attention to the woman, waving Krauss off. "How?"

"He never told us. He just talked about it a lot, getting his nerve up maybe, maybe just wishing. Then he disappeared."

"Palfrey?"

"We think so."

"Why?"

She looked at him as if he'd just sprouted another head. "To keep whatever secret he's guarding covered up, I'd think."

"You'd think?" Crowe said. "This bothers me, woman, because when people start thinking too much, they get themselves into all kinds of trouble."

"A friend and I broke into Palfrey's boat at Kingston a few hours ago," Liberto said.

"A man friend?"

She paused before answering, then nodded. "Yes. Tilo."

"Where is he now?"

"Palfrey got him."

"He caught you on his boat?"

"Yes."

"Not very good at breaking and entering, are you?" Crowe kept his voice flat without becoming condemning.

"It was my first time."

Crowe didn't believe it, but didn't choose to dispute it either. The woman intrigued him. He had a reputation as a man not to trifle with. She had to have known what kind of trouble she was stepping into, yet she'd come anyway. "What did you find?"

"The name of a boat," Liberto replied.

Crowe shrugged. "And what of it?"

"I don't know. Nothing was mentioned, but Palfrey had several papers concerning it."

"Maybe he was expecting a friend and wanted to make sure and meet the boat." Crowe turned that over in his mind, and even that glimmered with possibilities. He'd been counting on having that five million dollars Seid had ducked out with, and judging from the dour look on Krauss's face, that money hadn't shown up yet. He'd grown up in poverty, but that was no longer an acceptable position.

"No." The woman shook her head vehemently. "The ship is some kind of freighter, not a passenger ship. Whatever he and the Japanese are interested in has to be on board."

"Cargo?"

She nodded.

"What is it?"

"I don't know, and I couldn't guess." She gazed up at him with those hot, hard eyes. "We were discovered before I could find out."

"You said something about Japanese."

The woman started talking, relaying information she'd gleaned from her uncle regarding the monies that had gone into the reconstruction work on the island, how Gustavo Ruiz had reasoned that maybe the structure they'd built was actually all that had been intended. As she spoke, Crowe sensed the truth behind the words and it ignited a flash-powder store of greed within him. Things weren't desperate yet with the loss of the money Seid had taken, but their coffers were almost empty. He didn't have much in the way of a retirement plan, hadn't even planned on being this successful at his most recent craft.

"What do you want from me?" Crowe asked.

She gazed at him flatly. "Money. I want to get off this island. Maybe go to Miami. Enough money that I can set myself up in business when I get there." Her chin jutted out defiantly.

"You think what you have is worth that much?" Crowe asked.

"The Japanese," Liberto answered, "are very rich from what my uncle said. If they are involved with Palfrey, they will pay the money even if Palfrey can't. How much is up to you, how willing you are to squeeze them."

Crowe knew he'd already decided before she'd bottom-lined it for him. "Why do I have to pay you?" he asked in a harsh, threatening voice. "You're here."

"If I'd stayed there," Liberto told him, "I'd have been dead anyway. They can't let me live knowing what I know." Her voice broke slightly, giving away her fear, but she held on to her convictions. "If you try to get the information out of me, I might give you a false name. You won't know until you try to raid it, and by then—if it's the wrong ship—you won't have another chance to find out what they're protecting so much."

"Okay," Crowe said, reaching into his pocket for his watch. He rubbed his thumb around the worn form of Betty Page. "You've got a deal." Just as he was getting ready to ask the woman how much money she wanted, he noticed the shadows moving in the trees. They stood out against the darkness, their aggressive nature giving them away.

Crowe reached for the pistol snugged into his back at his belt. "Domingo," he called.

Krauss responded at once, reaching back into the Land Rover and coming out with a Tec-9 pistol.

For a moment Crowe thought he'd been set up by the woman, that maybe she was really some kind of cop. Then he noticed the black garb on the men spilling out of the woods. Swords glinted dully in the fists of some of them, splintering moonlight, and confirmed his initial identification. Japanese or not, they were definitely dressed in ninja clothing.

Even though he knew he probably wasn't going to hit anyone, Crowe fired at the advancing line, a string of five loud pops that set the rest of the cockpit into a snarl of action. He threw an arm around Natacha Liberto and pulled her toward the door of the building.

A man standing less than an arm's length away went down with an arrow through his throat. Bullets peppered the side of the sheet-metal building, passing through with ease and leaving gaping holes in their wake.

Still holding on to the young woman, Crowe yanked her along behind him as he raced for the relatively more secure area on the other side of the concession stand. A half-dozen men were already stretched out on the concrete floor. He whirled into position.

Krauss took shelter behind the wooden stands, which offered a little more in the way of protection. He covered the doorway with the Tec-9. "Fuck me, man," he bellowed.

"Those were Japanese." He held up a compact walkie-talkie in one fist. "Henri told me that before my chat with him ended so damn quick."

Crowe nodded and glanced at the girl. Perspiration filmed his face.

"I didn't know," Liberto said, shrinking.

"This thing you know, little girl," Crowe said, "it must be worth a lot for them to attack me here."

The screams of dying men and the restless cackle of the chickens filled the interior of the building, bouncing from the metal walls and ceiling. More bullets ripped through the tin sheets. Without warning, a grenade arced through an empty window and thudded against the ground. It rolled to a stop and started spewing white gas.

"We can't stay here," Krauss said. "They've got us surrounded."

"Get as many of the men as you can," Crowe ordered. "We'll form a group and head for the boats. If they haven't already found them, we might make it."

Krauss nodded and started to issue orders rapidly on the walkie-talkie. Not many of Crowe's team were equipped with them, but it could make a difference.

The big pirate shoved himself away from the wall and headed for the back. There wasn't a door there, but they might get through a window. If the Japanese had followed the woman, they couldn't have had time to know all of the setup. Krauss trailed after him, halting long enough to zip a neat figure eight of bullets that swatted a figure dressed in ninja black back through the door.

The building was rapidly filling with smoke, and Crowe could already feel a burning sensation clawing at his eyes. If they could make the boats, they had a chance. Even the men Krauss couldn't get hold of would be making their way to the boats. They were seamen, and that would be their first thought.

He stepped through the open window and pulled the woman after him. Spotting some of his men taking cover behind empty fifty-five-gallon cans, Crowe yelled at them and got them organized. The jungle started only a few yards away.

Gunfire lit up the night behind him. Crowe swung around and fired the pistol dry at the two ninjas who'd come around the building. Other men fired as well, so he didn't know if it was his rounds that took them down or someone else's. He yelled to his men, then led the charge into the brush.

LYNDON PALFREY STOOD on a knoll well protected by the thick jungle, and used night glasses to look down on the building. He was surprised at the number of men Hideo Shotozumi had been able to field at such short notice.

The Yakuza ninjas worked the battlefield expertly, cordoning off fields of fire and eliminating whoever was in their way. The return fire from the people who'd been inside the building was becoming more sporadic. He refocused the night glasses as the first wave of ninjas shoved their way inside the building.

"It will not be long now," Shotozumi said.

Palfrey put the glasses down and glanced at the man standing at his side. "No, I don't think so either." He didn't like the idea of wholesale slaughter, and didn't like the fact that he was part of it. Killing didn't bother him, but he liked the idea of doing it within a confined area and with time so that he could cover his tracks well. It bothered him that Shotozumi took this facet of their business so casually. But then, the Yakuza lieutenant didn't have to live on the islands once it was finished, either.

Natacha Liberto's trail to Ocho Rios had proved easy to follow. Crispus's contact had tracked her to her mother's house, but Liberto had already come and gone. She'd been emotional, her mother had said—emotional herself because the man questioning her hadn't taken long to show that he was willing to be more than physical. The woman had made a phone call and wrote directions on how to get to the cockpit. They'd left impressions on the next sheet of paper, which the man had recovered by rubbing a pencil across the surface. Then he left the mother with a slit throat. Palfrey wanted everything shut down against any possible police interest.

After he'd learned of the cockpit in Ocho Rios, Palfrey hadn't needed much more information. He knew of the place, and knew that it was a conduit for a number of criminal enterprises.

"Who owned this place?" Shotozumi asked.

"I don't know," Palfrey replied. He noted that the question was asked in past tense, but that was because the Yakuza attacking the building below were already starting to set fires that would consume it. "There are a lot of stories about this place and the people you can meet here. The local law is bought off or doesn't dare come around. For myself, I've never had business here."

"It would be wise," the Yakuza lieutenant stated, "to investigate this site within the next few hours. To see what stones we may have left unturned."

Palfrey nodded but wasn't happy about it. Further involvement would only heighten the risk of being exposed.

The fires converged on the building, turning it into a pyre. Corpses were strung across the grounds. The sounds of gunfire receded into the jungle behind the building.

Shotozumi talked briefly on the cellular phone he held, then put it away. "Come on," he told Palfrey. "Some of them have broken through the line behind the building and are loose in the jungle. Let's see if we can cut them off." He opened the door of the charcoal Pathfinder and slid behind the wheel.

Palfrey hesitated only a moment. Knowing he had no choice, and cursing himself for ending up in a position where he wasn't really in control of the events threatening to swallow him, he climbed into the 4WD. He didn't like the idea of driving through the jungle with armed men swarming around him. As Shotozumi let out the clutch and surged forward, the fat tires chewing through the soft earth, Palfrey slid his Browning .380 pistol from his pocket and held it on his thigh.

MACK BOLAN RAN through the jungle, moving toward the orange glow of the fires consuming the cockpit. He was a wraith among the shadows, moving silently and deadly. Togged out in the combat blacksuit, he was almost invisible. His combat harness supported his equipment and spare ammo. He carried the Beretta 93-R in shoulder leather and the Desert Eagle .44 on his hip. He cradled a 7.62 mm Vaime Mk2 sniper rifle to his chest.

Less than forty yards from the perimeter of the clearing surrounding the cockpit, a silhouette dodged out of sight behind a thick mahoe tree.

Instantly the soldier sidestepped and broke the path he'd been taking to the battlezone. He slipped the Vaime's sling over his shoulder and freed his hands. He secured the rifle more tightly to him and his movements with ties at his thigh and side that would slip as needed.

His face was tiger-striped in black combat cosmetics. He knew he'd be hard to spot even after he'd been noticed. Creeping through the trees and brush, Bolan brought himself close to the position where he'd seen the moving shadow.

He didn't think his quarry was one of the pirate group he was after. In the brief glimpse he'd gotten of the man, the Executioner had seen that the guy was dressed in black the same as he was. But there'd been a hood as well.

At first he'd wondered if he'd interrupted a strike by one of the law-enforcement teams who'd gotten a lead on the pirates as well. When the violence broke out at the cockpit without warning and little provocation, he knew that wasn't the answer.

He fisted the Beretta and pulled it from the leather. Moving quietly, tracking the other man, the Executioner came up on him from behind. Slightly more than an arm's length away in the darkness, Bolan reached out for him.

Some instinct triggered a response in the black-clad gunner the Executioner stalked. With a quick, twisting movement, the man turned and started to bring up his Uzi to fire.

Bolan uncoiled, covering the distance. He deflected the Uzi with his free hand, then slammed the Beretta's barrel against the side of his opponent's head. The impact sounded full and meaty. Out on his feet, the man sagged toward the ground.

The soldier caught him, knotting his fist in the material of the guy's shirt. Gunfire shattered the quiet of the night around him, wiping out all resonance of the local wildlife and insects. Bolan guided his prisoner to the brush as he scanned the surrounding jungle. He thought he'd detected movement in his peripheral vision.

When he raked the hood and mask away from the man's features, he saw at once that they were Japanese. No Japanese had been captured during any of the kidnappings. A series of brightly colored streaks imprinted on the flesh of the man's wrist caught Bolan's eye. He shoved the material up, then used his penflash.

A dragon of black, red, purple and green coiled up the inside of the man's arm. The tattoo was expensive and laboriously done, and must have required several visits to work in all the details and colors.

Bolan figured the man for Yakuza instantly. One of the Japanese Mafia's signatures was the tattoos, worn all over the body, but never creeping out anywhere that couldn't be covered by clothing.

For a moment, his mind flipped around the possibilities the Yakuza's presence presented, then he shelved the thinking. There were too many questions and not enough answers for the moment.

And the Yakuza member he'd taken down hadn't been alone.

Two more men dressed in black and wearing hoods fired at the soldier from concealment.

Bolan vaulted from his position ahead of the onslaught of bullets. Whatever business the Yakuza had there, he wasn't prepared to withdraw from the battlefield without gaining some Intel. If Santiago Crowe was working with the Japanese, whether for information or through some other arrangement, there was obviously bad blood between them now.

The soldier landed on one hand and pushed himself into a roll. As he gained his feet, he spun toward the left and fired from a loose profile position, his left hand sliding under his right smoothly to cup the pistol butt. He aimed at the Yakuza hardman's exposed head and gun arm. The Beretta bucked slightly in his fist, and the sound suppressor kept the noise from the subsonic rounds down to a thinned-out hiss.

The 9 mm parabellum manglers cycled through and hit their target. The gunner shuddered as his shoulder and side were peppered with bullets, as well as splinters from the tree he was using for cover. For a moment, his hooded face was exposed as he wavered off balance.

Bolan coolly put a round through the man's head, and was in motion before the corpse hit the ground. Autofire ripped into the brush where he'd been only a heartbeat earlier. He ran, angling the line of demarcation that separated the cockpit from the jungle. The sound of engines revving echoed around him, and he spotted the off-road vehicles shoving their way through the brush a little more than a hundred yards away.

Bullets shattered an outcropping in front of him and beat into the ground. He cut hard right and found momentary breathing space behind a stone shelf that thrust up from the earth. Reaching into his webbing, he took out a grenade and pulled the pin. He counted down, then heaved the bomb in the direction of the autofire.

The grenade detonated with a thunderous boom, tearing leaves and branches from the trees. A man screamed in pain.

Taking a kneeling position behind the stone shelf, the Executioner pointed the 93-R before him. Two figures stumbled blindly through the smoky haze left by the grenade. They fired in his direction but were wide of their target.

Bolan flamed them both with 3-round bursts. He ejected

the spent clip, rammed home a fresh one, and plunged back into the chase, running hard, trying to avoid any further encounters with the Yakuza. They were on the same agenda here, and the soldier knew he could use the Japanese firepower to harry the pirates.

He raced along the terrain, drawing the maps he'd looked at into his mind, fleshing out the details he spotted around him. The Golden Peacock bar-cockpit was almost two miles northeast of Ocho Rios proper, located near Little Bay between the resort city and Port Maria. It was probable that Santiago Crowe would have boats nearby. The number of cars and trucks in front of the cockpit had been low when considering how many people had been in the building.

Moonlight barely penetrated the dense vegetation. The incline of the ground changed rapidly and without warning. The earth turned springy underfoot, then gave way to marshlands in places.

Listening to the sounds of the pistol and rifle reports, Bolan knew he'd managed to close the distance. The 4WD units had halted slightly more than a hundred yards away, blocked by the fall of the land and the thick growth of trees. Armed men leaped from the vehicles and plunged into the brush, staying out of the flood of lights that projected into the jungle.

Bolan glanced down the incline and saw the surface of the water in places through the trees. An owl took soundless flight above him, gliding effortlessly through the branches. He shoved the Beretta into shoulder leather and climbed a tall elm that he thought would give him a vantage point. The Vaime sniper rifle was an excellent weapon, but due to the fact that it cycled subsonic rounds, its effective killing range was limited to little more than two hundred yards.

The soldier made the climb easily. He homed in on the splashes of muzzle-flash against the black backdrop of the night. Settling into a V against the main trunk, he saw that the pirates had effected a beachhead against the Yakuza.

He took the night glasses from their pouch and scanned

the area. Salty perspiration stung scratches along his cheek and neck from the climb. Mosquitoes from the stagnant water buzzed him, only slightly put off by the camou war paint.

Three cabin cruisers that showed years of usage were ground-anchored at the shoreline. Plywood ramps running from the ground to the railing allowed access. At least a dozen other craft, ranging from outboards to ski boats, flanked the cabin cruisers.

A line of pirates had taken cover aboard the ships and in the protection afforded by the broken ground and trees. The staggered line of fire had broken the approach of the Yakuza team and slowed it almost to a standstill. The exchange of gunfire was telling on both sides.

Then the unmistakable basso chattering of a .50-caliber machine gun joined the small war. At the other end of the line of cabin cruisers, a trio of pirates had brought up a tripod mounted Browning heavy machine gun and installed it on the rear deck of the boat. Belt-fed, it roared and spit flame and brass, driving the Yakuza back in places, becoming a pounding onslaught of death.

Bolan put the night glasses away after spotting Santiago Crowe running toward the boats. He was dragging someone after him, but the soldier hadn't been able to ascertain who it was with all the cover provided by the night and the jungle. He unslung the Vaime and pulled it to his shoulder. The sniper rifle was outfitted with a Simrad Optronics KN250 night sight. With the ten-by-fifty-six capabilities of the scope, he'd be able to put everything on an up-close and personal perspective.

He slid off the safety, then curled his finger around the trigger as he sighted on Crowe. The pirate leader was less than twenty yards from the nearest boat. No matter what else was going on between the pirate group and the Yakuza, his original agenda hadn't changed. Focused, the Executioner dropped his sights over Crowe and waited for his shot.

6

Mack Bolan captured Santiago Crowe's features in the scope and shifted slightly to bring his target securely into the crosshairs. The darkness and the canopy of patchy foliage over the man's route made the task difficult.

The pirate leader ducked forward without warning, vanishing from the scope's view.

Bolan kept both eyes open while he viewed his target, then changed emphasis to his left eye, tracking the big man again. He brought the rifle around, trying to bring him into view.

Naked steel gleamed in Crowe's right hand. He brought the machete down so suddenly that the black-clad Yakuza member who'd confronted him never had a chance to react. The massive blade split the Yakuza's head open like a melon. Crowe was still in motion as the corpse slewed to one side and disappeared in the brush.

At the same time, a female face skated through Bolan's crosshairs. The soldier relaxed the pressure on the trigger. It was one thing to try for a single target amid a field of them, but the presence of a possible innocent changed the odds.

Red tracer fire cut the air near the young woman's head.

Following it back, Bolan spotted the Yakuza gunner farther up the incline, leaning against a tree and using it for support, as well as cover. He put the Vaime's crosshairs over the shooter, then squeezed the trigger. The sniper rifle recoiled slightly, rolling across the soldier's cheek and staying on target if a second shot was necessary.

The 7.62 mm round caught the Yakuza in the center of the face and snapped his head back. By the time he hit the ground, the Executioner had sighted another black-clad target. He worked the bolt action, ejecting the spent brass and chambering the next round. With the sound suppressor, no one knew where the shot came from, even if they'd been able to discern it from the other sounds of gunfire. He took up the trigger slack and put another shooter down.

As he worked the bolt, Bolan realized the Yakuza members seemed more interested in acquiring the woman as a target than they did Santiago Crowe. She hadn't looked familiar at all, nor had she looked as if she belonged with the pirate band.

Crowe shoved his way through the final line of underbrush as he raced for the nearest boat. Sailors were already on board, waiting to shove off. The concentrated fire of the Yakuza slammed into the boat, sparking against the metal pieces of the railing and ripping splinters from the hull. The diesels churned to life with a throaty roar.

Bolan dropped a third Yakuza gunner and spared a glance toward Crowe and the young woman. She wasn't going along willingly, that much the soldier could see at a glance. She tripped and fell, yanking Crowe off balance.

Crowe turned and tried to muscle the woman from the ground. She resisted, throwing a handful of fingernails at his face. Crowe slapped her flailing arm out of his way and reached for her again, bellowing for help from some of the men.

Raking the Vaime back toward the pirates, Bolan centered Crowe in the crosshairs and took up trigger slack. Before he could squeeze the trigger, a fresh assault of autofire zipped through the trees only inches from Crowe. The pirate abandoned the woman and ran for the boat.

The death roar from the mounted .50-caliber machine gun smashed into the terrain and broke the invasion by the Yakuza. Bolan managed to pick off two more Japanese and one of the pirates before the woman pushed herself to her feet and began to run in the direction of the tree the soldier occupied.

"Get her!" Crowe roared above the sounds of the gunfire and the boat engines. He yelled at the machine-gun team.

The men operating the weapon were having trouble adjusting to the wave action taking place aboard the boat. Still, they ran a line of bullets in the woman's wake.

The Executioner put the crosshairs over the forehead of the man behind the machine gun. He stroked the trigger and worked the bolt action, getting ready for a second shot.

The bullet took the gunner high on the left side of the chest, maybe an inch or two away from his heart. The man spun from the impact, dipping the machine gun to blast an uncertain pattern across the shoreline and the water. The Executioner's second bullet took him in the throat. Bolan killed the guy feeding the ammo belt with his next two rounds, and the body tumbled in a lazy sprawl into the water.

Santiago Crowe swarmed the ladder to the upper deck, followed closely by a black man with blond hair. The starboard side of the boat was filled with muzzle-flashes from a dozen weapons.

Dropping the empty magazine from the rifle, Bolan slipped another into place and worked the bolt action, stripping the first round. He shifted his attention from the fleeing pirate vessel to the Yakuza members starting after the woman. Whoever she was, both sides intended to see her dead.

The Executioner worked a sweep pattern from left to right, peering under the scope to use the open sights. The brush and the movement of the men made it almost impossible to use the scope. His first bullet took a Yakuza gunner in the chest and stretched the man's body over a pile of brush. His second shot caught the next man in the shoulder and spun him off his feet. The Executioner put another round through his right eye before he could get up.

Aware that they were being fired upon from a different direction, the third and fourth pursuers took cover behind trees and the broken rock littering the shoreline. The woman continued on, making little whimpering noises Bolan could hear now that she was less than twenty yards away. He squeezed the trigger and put a round through the third gunner's exposed knee as the fourth man broke cover to chase after the woman.

Screaming in pain, the third Yakuza hardman went down, grabbing for his knee. The fourth man knew something had gone wrong, and tried to pull out of his trajectory.

Bolan drilled a round through the man's neck as he grabbed for a tree and tried to bring himself around. His body followed through on the redirection, but it was a corpse that finished the trip.

The woman managed a stumbling run through the undergrowth and brush beneath the Executioner's vantage point. He let her go, taking stock of the effort the Yakuza hardmen were making to follow. Pockets of the pirates and others from the cockpit had been left behind during the action and were still creating stiff resistance. In time, Bolan felt, the Japanese would level any opposition, but the cost would be great.

Evidently the people in charge of the operation didn't want to pay the price. Across the distance, Bolan heard the squawk of walkie-talkies. On top of the rise, the 4WDs started to back away. The shadows of the Yakuza melted into the trees, drawing back to the vehicles. They were harried by bullets from the survivors' weapons.

After recharging the Vaime with a full magazine and pocketing the partially used one, Bolan dropped lithely through the branches until he regained the ground. He slung the rifle and drew the Beretta, then followed in the direction the young woman had taken.

Not all of the Yakuza had pulled back with the vehicles. Some were flitting shadows racing through the night.

The woman ran erratically, pushing away tree branches that impeded her progress. She glanced over her shoulder often.

Bolan matched her pace easily, then started taking distance-eating strides. The chugging of the diesel engines in the background reached a higher decibel range than the gunshots. He overtook the woman quickly. She heard him coming and tried to push herself even faster.

Tracking the sound of brush breaking off to his left, the Executioner knew one of the woman's Yakuza pursuers had almost caught up to her. Bolan reached forward and grabbed her left arm. She attempted to wrench her arm away, but he didn't release her.

"I'm not going to hurt you," the soldier said softly into the woman's ear when he drew her close to him. He scanned the surrounding jungle, trying to focus on the noise being made by the other man. "I'm here to help."

Still, she continued to fight against him.

Bolan used both arms to restrain her movements. "They'll kill you if they catch you. If I wanted you dead, you already would be."

The woman began to calm down, shivering against Bolan, trying to draw away from the physical contact.

The Executioner backed into the brush, then turned as the Yakuza broke cover less than twenty yards away. He raised the Beretta as the black-clad gunner raised his assault rifle. The 3-round burst stitched the man from waist to shoulder, punching through his heart and lungs.

Bolan pulled the woman deeper into the brush as the dead man fell. At first, the woman resisted, then went along with him. Even with the pursuit, he knew they couldn't stay in the area long.

He covered another hundred yards, helping the woman to avoid most of the noise-making obstacles in the jungle that hovered in the shadows as they ran. Her movement became more fluid and compliant. A natural predator in the jungle environment, the Executioner let his combat senses scan the dark terrain around him. He detected the continued movement, felt it steadily on two fronts though there was no visual contact.

A tall elm tree jutted up in front of them, branches forked in every direction, bent in places from unrelenting winds blown by tropical storm systems. Knowing they were out of view of their pursuers, Bolan led the woman to the trunk.

"Up," he told her. "They're going to be covering the ground as quick as they can. With both of us moving, there's more chance of them finding us."

"Okay." The young woman didn't appear relieved with the prospect of the climb.

Bolan laced his hands together, taking her weight easily as she stepped into them. He pushed her up, then followed.

Fifteen feet up, he halted her movement. "Stay in close to the tree," he commanded. "You've got a shadow they might spot that doesn't fit in."

She nodded and wrapped both arms around the trunk, closing her eyes tight when she heard movement through the brush below.

Bolan shifted gingerly, stretching out along a thick branch with the 93-R before him. He pinpointed the locations of two gunners before he actually saw the men. They were good at moving through the undergrowth, instinctively seeking the passage of least resistance, remaining invisible. He dropped the Beretta into target acquisition, not wanting to fire. Getting the woman out of the tree quickly if he had to would slow him, and might mean the death of one or both of them.

But continuing hadn't been an option. The woman wasn't skilled to vanish in the brush.

The two gunners communicated silently, using abbreviated hand signals as they circled the area. One of them remained to cover the other, who walked down to the water's edge some forty yards distant.

The woman's leg against the backs of Bolan's calves was tight, tense.

The Executioner kept his gaze locked on the closer man, his finger resting firmly against the pistol's trigger. An owl burst from the treescape with a thunder of beating wings.

The Yakuza gunner sank back into hiding as the big predator glided past.

A heartbeat later, while the second man was on his way back, the first man lifted a slim-line walkie-talkie to his mouth. He talked too quickly to be heard, and there was no chance of overhearing the other end of the conversation because he wore an ear jack. After a brief exchange, he waved to the other man and they glided away, back in the direction they'd come.

Bolan remained frozen, watching the jungle around them.

"They're gone," the woman whispered in a trembling voice.

"Maybe," the Executioner replied in a whisper. He looked at her, knowing she offered a potential threat, too, if she thought he was the only thing keeping her from escaping. "Keep quiet and keep still. We'll know soon."

He didn't move, breathing in through his nose and releasing it through his mouth. As he watched, he shuffled events around in his mind, trying to make sense of them and where the Yakuza fit in.

"YOU THINK Palfrey followed you here?" Bolan asked.

"I don't know anyone else with Japanese friends," Natacha Liberto said with sarcasm. Since the arrival of dawn and the apparent absence of the Yakuza, and the acceptance that Bolan wasn't going to hurt her, the young woman had grown increasingly surly.

Sunrise had painted the jungle in a pink and purple-tinged incandescence. Shadows still clung in places, marking their territory with an inky black stain that would never be completely eradicated, even under a noonday sun.

Bolan had the lead, not worrying whether the woman would try to run. As far as she knew, he was the only one near that didn't mean her harm. She'd already told him about her uncle's presumed murder, Lyndon Palfrey's supposed guilt and the compliance of the Japanese in the cover-up.

They skirted the Golden Peacock bar and cockpit. Scavengers were still sifting through the debris despite the warning signs posted by the Ocho Rios authorities. A few of them were family, working the ashes and the tumbled-down metal struts for loved ones whose corpses hadn't turned up in the initial search by the local fire department.

The occasional sounds of voices and car engines drifted over the rise. Bolan had scanned the crowds diligently, but hadn't seen anyone matching the woman's description of Palfrey, or any Japanese in the group. He kept the Beretta in his hand and relied on his combat senses to warn him because the jungle was thick enough to cause problems if he relied on his visual skills alone.

"How did he know you would come here?" Bolan asked.

"I don't know." The cracked voice she answered in let him know that she had made some guesses, and none of them were good. In the daylight, she'd turned out to be even younger than he'd guessed. "Are you a policeman?"

Bolan halted beside a tree and glanced back at her. He scared her, too, and he knew it. "No."

"Then what were you doing there?" She folded her arms across her breasts and remained eight feet away, maintaining her distance.

"Looking for Santiago Crowe," Bolan replied honestly. Before she could think too deeply about that, he pressed her again. "What were you doing with Crowe?"

"I had some business with him."

Bolan nodded. "Sure. What?"

"It is no business of yours."

"Maybe. Looked to me like he was planning on killing you. Could be you misjudged him."

"My mistake," she said stubbornly. "I'll take care of it."

Bolan turned and went on, waiting to speak again until he heard her following him. She wasn't ready to cut loose from him yet, and that worked in his favor.

Fifteen minutes later, they reached the area where he'd left the car. He'd pulled it into the brush and left it under a lightning-blasted tree that had become stoop-shouldered from the damage.

The Yakuza had evidently found it all the same. All that remained of it was a burned-out husk. An old gray-bearded black man in a tattered jacket with crawling pink scars by his left eye was overseeing three boys young enough to have been his grandchildren as they removed parts from the car. There hadn't been much to salvage, but the wrecking crew worked at it diligently with crowbars and wrenches.

A battered green 1953 Ford pickup with wooden sideboards of uneven lengths lurched on its haunches like an arthritic dog, turning off the dirt road Bolan had followed to the Golden Peacock only a few hours earlier.

"Stay here," Bolan said in a quiet voice that the man and boys couldn't overhear.

"Where are you going?" Liberto demanded.

Bolan didn't answer. The woman started to follow him, but a glance froze her in place. He went east for a short distance and uncovered the backpack containing the cellular phone and notebook PC, and the duffel containing the ordnance that he'd cached there after parking the car. That the opposition would find the car during the gun battle the previous night had been a foregone conclusion.

He draped the backpack into place, feeling the weight of it settle across his shoulders. He was running on empty and knew it. Gripping the straps of the duffel, he lifted it from the ground and carried it at his side while he approached the car's broken and burned corpse.

The old man saw him first and met his gaze. He called out to the boys and waved them back into the jungle, taking a protective stance in front of them. One of the older boys, no more than twelve, moved uncertainly into position beside the old man, brandishing a short-bladed pocketknife.

Bolan holstered the Beretta and spread his open hands at his sides. "Do you speak English?"

The old man hesitated for a moment, then nodded. "Some."

"I want to buy your truck," Bolan said.

"Not for sale," the old man replied.

Reaching inside the combat rigging, the soldier took out a sheaf of American money. Converting anything over two hundred dollars a day in Jamaica was excessive for a tourist, because anything not spent over that amount couldn't be redeemed. "I'm offering two thousand. U.S." He counted out the bills and put the rest away.

"Maybe this old truck worth more, eh?"

"Not to me," Bolan told him. "It's worth two thousand dollars to me not to just take it."

The old man's nostrils flared. "Maybe it's worth something that I don't remember that I saw you."

"No," Bolan said. "If I pay you to forget, someone pays you more to remember. By the time you reach someone who's interested in me, I'll be gone. If I'm not, it won't matter that you said anything about it."

The old man nodded.

Bolan stepped closer to hand the man the money. At his side, the boy bristled, obviously torn between being afraid and feeling responsible for the old man's welfare.

The old man laid a reassuring hand on the boy's shoulder and spoke to him in a low voice. He took Bolan's money and made it disappear inside his clothing. "Keys are in it."

"Take a look around Ocho Rios," the soldier suggested. "You'll find the truck in the public parking areas around Turtle Beach. I'll leave the keys under the seat."

"Anybody going to be looking for this truck when you're done with it?" the old man asked.

"Not unless you say anything about it." Bolan opened the door. The creak it made was long and drawn out, and it listed heavily on the pins.

"What about me?" Natacha Liberto asked, standing in front of the truck.

"Your choice. But if you're coming with me, I want to know what you were seeing Crowe for, and why Palfrey's looking for you.'' Bolan turned the key in the ignition. The engine shivered to rattling life.

Remaining behind obviously wasn't an option the young woman relished. She glanced uneasily over her shoulder, peering into the shadows threaded through the jungle. ''Okay,'' she said, walking around to the passenger side.

Bolan put the duffel and backpack onto the seat between them. He flipped the restraining thong over the Desert Eagle's hammer and made sure the Beretta was loose in its holster. It was possible that the old man would send one of the boys to tell a scavenger working the cockpit about the truck, but he hoped to be lost in Ocho Rios before that could happen.

Liberto slammed the door when she got in, and sat pressed against the bare metal. Gray duct tape held the passenger window together.

Bolan put his foot down on the clutch and shoved the stick into first gear. Lurching slowly and steering hard, the pickup came around in a loose circle. He headed it back down the trail he'd used the previous night. ''Start talking,'' he said, ''and make it convincing. The first lie I hear, that's where you're getting out.''

A COUPLE OF MILES out of Ocho Rios, Bolan stopped long enough to change into jeans and a shirt he had bundled in the duffel. He stored his weapons, including the Beretta and Desert Eagle in the bag, and took out a 9 mm SIG-Sauer P226 in a calf holster to wear under the jeans.

It was a little after eight o'clock in the morning when he parked the pickup at the public area at the beach. A number of tourists were already up and moving into the deep blue water. Triangular sails of neon-bright colors cut the northern horizon where the sky met the sea. Farther east were the fishing boats and freighters with hard-working sailors aboard. In the distance, the Executioner could see two cruise liners, weighing anchor on their scheduled stops.

Natacha Liberto didn't say much as Bolan steered her

along by one arm. Clearly exhausted, the young woman pulled away from his grip at first, then leaned into it as they crossed the expanse of wet sand.

At one of the tourist kiosks loaded with film and souvenirs, Bolan found a bank of coin-operated rental lockers. He left Liberto in the café area and dropped coins into one of the lockers. He stored the duffel inside, hanging it from one of the hooks, then took the key that had dropped into the dispenser slot.

He was a little surprised to find Liberto waiting for him when he returned. She sat alone at a table, a cup of coffee in front of her.

Bolan sat across from her and picked up one of the menus from the slot between the condiments. He glanced over the items. "Did you find something you want?" he asked.

"No," she said pensively.

A waitress stopped at their table and held a pad at the ready. Her smile revealed a gold front tooth.

Bolan ordered the breakfast special, and, as the waitress turned to go, Liberto spoke up.

"Wait. Could I have a blueberry muffin and a glass of milk?"

The waitress nodded and went away.

Bolan relaxed in the booth and glanced out the nearby window. He could see the names on the liners; neither was the *Obsidian Princess*. The sun felt warm on his skin and it made him sleepy. But thoughts of Devon Catalano, Janet Gladsdale and Clarissa Thomasson stayed with him. He'd seen those victims, and there were others. Crowe was still his main target, but the presence of Lyndon Palfrey and the Yakuza had muddied the waters.

"So what now?" Liberto asked.

"In a few minutes," Bolan replied, "we eat."

She pushed her hair back out of her face. "I was talking about after that."

The soldier looked at her. "You're free to go."

"Go where?"

"Anywhere you want."

She looked at him with challenge in her eyes. "And you don't want anything else?"

Bolan looked her in the eye and knew what she was referring to. "No."

She gazed at him for a moment in silence, as if trying to understand. "I was going to make a deal with Santiago Crowe. Some money for what I knew. He knew he could have me with it."

"I don't work that way."

"You don't like girls?" Liberto raised arched brows.

"I like girls fine." Bolan knew the woman was searching now, trying to find a common denominator that would link them. It was possible she was trying to find something to work to her advantage, but he realized part of it was because she felt uncomfortable around him.

"Then why?"

"Another time, another place," Bolan suggested. The answer seemed to satisfy her. The waitress arrived with the food and served the plates. Conversation dwindled while they ate. Before he'd finished, the woman had added ham, eggs and toast to her order.

Bolan waited for her to finish eating before speaking again. Outside the window, a group of college-age students were stringing a volleyball net. He realized that they were older than the young woman sitting across from him, and that her experiences dealing with life had aged her far more than anything the volleyball players could have encountered.

Without warning, tears started to roll down Liberto's cheeks. "Palfrey killed my uncle," she said in a quiet, quavering voice. "He probably killed Tilo, too. Only I led Tilo there last night. I got him killed."

"You never told me what you were looking for," Bolan said. He figured the young man was dead, too. Palfrey was working with the Yakuza, and the Japanese gangsters weren't noted for leaving loose ends.

"We didn't know." Liberto wrapped her arms around

herself. "It has something to do with what he's building on his island. The only thing we found was the name of that ship."

"I'm going to look into that," Bolan said.

She gazed at him. "Promise me," she told him, "promise me, and you can have anything from me that you want. Tilo shouldn't have had to die."

The soldier promised, and he knew he'd make good on it. The Yakuza involvement had raised too many questions to ignore. He took out enough Jamaican dollars to cover the bill, added a twenty percent tip and left the money on the table.

As soon as he cleared the doorway, Bolan felt eyes lock on him and knew he'd picked up a shadow. "We're being followed," he said to the woman as he slid his hand under her elbow. She started to turn, but he restrained her. "Don't."

She stopped, but remained tense.

"In just a moment," Bolan said, "I want you to turn and point out some of those cruise ships in the harbor, like you're explaining something to me. Keep talking." He shifted the backpack containing the computer so it would be easy to transfer when he went for the pistol in the calf holster, if he had to. "Got it?"

"Yes."

They walked a little farther, skating around blankets and bronzed bodies. "Okay," Bolan said, "do it now. Take a step toward the sea."

The woman complied, leaving the soldier a line of fire. He turned with her, ready to shove her out of the way. Reggae music was thumping from some of the boom boxes teenagers had nearby, as well as from a bar near the shoreline.

As she started talking about the cruise lines, actually revealing an impressive store of knowledge, Bolan glanced around the beach. He spotted the tail immediately.

Mestipen Seid had marshaled a troop of island thugs as he redealt himself into the action. The Kingston PI turned as casually as possible and lifted a hand to his face as if adjusting his mirror sunglasses. He put his back to Bolan, squarely in the middle of four men who looked like they could bench press Toyotas. All of them were dressed in island clothing, shorts and open shirts. Necklaces and earrings glittered in the sunlight.

"Let's go," Bolan said, taking Liberto by the elbow again. He steered her away from the beach. Seid had been holding a cellular phone in one hand, so the men with him weren't the only resources open to him.

A flesh net had been formed around the area, and Bolan could feel it tightening.

7

"What are you going to do?" Natacha Liberto asked.

"I don't know," Bolan said. "I need to get you clear of this." He scouted the tourist attractions, the bars, souvenir places and bait shops.

"Do they know you spotted them?"

"No." Bolan quickly amended the answer. "I don't think so. Those five men aren't all there's going to be, either." His mind raced, sizing up the odds and the terrain. Seid probably wouldn't start anything in a public place, but he wouldn't wait long before making his move now that he knew there was a chance that he could be spotted, if he hadn't already been.

A fresh crowd of tourists were being greeted at the docks by a calypso band, flanked by an army of hagglers, craftsmen and taxi drivers all offering their services. Bolan directed their steps toward the knot of people, hoping they could gain some distance.

Seid was tracking the money, unable to let it go.

"If we can get away from here, there's a place we can go," Liberto said.

"Where?" Bolan asked, shouldering his way past a man hawking memorabilia that he swore was from Errol Flynn's yacht, the *Zacha*, during the time the movie star had spent on the island.

"A hotel," the woman said, "outside of town. The man who runs it rents the rooms for however long you like, promises no one will trouble you, then forgets you were ever there if someone comes asking."

Bolan didn't like the idea much. It put him off his game, and on the woman's turf, to a degree. But there weren't any other options at the moment, and he needed to contact Stony Man Farm. An earlier attempt showed quite a bit of material to download from e-mail, and he hadn't been sure the cellular phone's battery would be up to the task.

"Let's go." Bolan headed for the line of waiting taxis on the outer fringe of the crowd. Many of the tourists were heading for the shops and stores along the beachfront, but a number of them were taking taxis as well.

"Taxi, mister?" The voice was young and hopeful, and belonged to a boy who couldn't have been much over sixteen. However, he was parked in an advantageous position, the nose of his vehicle already pointing out into the flow of traffic.

"Yeah," Bolan replied, palming a couple bills and handing them to the boy.

The young driver was dressed in baggy olive-green pants cinched tight with a belt. A lavender tank top peeked out from a matching uniform shirt. He hustled around the cab and opened the rear door for Liberto.

The woman got in and slid over, gazing expectantly at Bolan.

The soldier glanced down the line of cars and saw Seid talking on the cellular phone. The Kingston PI and his four bodyguards were cutting through the line of cabs on an interception course with a long Oldsmobile that glided powerfully into position.

"Give me a minute," Bolan told the driver as he settled behind the steering wheel.

"Sure, man."

A magazine had been abandoned in the floorboard of the cab. Bolan picked it up, snaking the SIG-Sauer from the calf holster and concealing it beside his leg. He tucked the magazine under the bottom two fingers of his gun hand, concealing the pistol, his finger resting lightly on the trigger. He turned and walked toward Seid and the other men.

The Kingston private detective locked his eyes on Bolan, but talked quickly out of the side of his mouth. The four men around him moved uncertainly. Seid stood halfway in the open passenger side of the big car.

One of the men, a huge islander, walked forward. Brass knuckles gleamed across the broad expanse of his fist.

"Back off," Bolan warned. "The buy-in on this game is more than you want to ante." He showed the bigger man the snout of the SIG-Sauer tucked under the magazine.

"You think you can take on all of us, man?"

The Executioner stared at him. "Yeah. We can get this started and see who walks out of the smoke when it's over."

The big man backed off reluctantly, raising his hands and maintaining a distance that was more than Bolan could reach. "I got it, man. You can put that thing away."

Bolan ignored the suggestion. He kept his eyes on Seid, beating down the other man's glare, robbing the anger roiling inside him of any outlet.

Seid flinched from the direct eye contact and sidled inside the car. Before he could withdraw his edge from the frame, Bolan reached out and slammed the door shut. Finger bones cracked from the impact. The Executioner pressed in against the door, holding the hand in the impromptu vise.

The four men shifted, but the muzzle of the pistol never wavered from them. They held their ground.

Beads of sweat collected on Seid's face, and his skin paled. He worked hard not to scream out in pain.

"Last chance to walk away," Bolan said in a graveyard voice. He gazed at the men around him. "I'll know all of you next time." He turned his attention back to Seid. "The money's already gone. All I am to you from this point on is sudden death." Easing back, he moved away from the door.

"Fuck you, man!" Seid snarled, drawing his injured hand

inside the car. "You're going to get what's coming to you! People are hunting you!"

Bolan gave him a cold grin. "That's the way they tell it. I'm still here because I'm still looking for some people I have business with." He retreated, keeping his gaze on the car in case Seid or his men decided to get brave. "But I'll make time to give Don Catalano a call, let him know how hospitable you find Ocho Rios."

The soldier dropped into the backseat of the taxi. "Hit it," he told the driver.

The boy wasted no time in quitting the scene. He tapped the accelerator, and the engine's idling evened out at once. With professional ease and no trace of rancor, he cut off another cab and roared into the street.

"Give him directions," Bolan whispered, shoving the pistol back in the calf holster without letting the driver see it. "Close, but not the actual destination."

Natacha nodded and spoke rapidly.

The boy touched the bill of his cap, chattering away amiably about American baseball scores.

Bolan glanced behind them, but Seid and his people weren't making any attempt to follow. After a turn put them out of sight, he relaxed against the seat and started to organize his thoughts. The island was too small for him to remain there long, and the ocean around it was too big to start searching for Santiago Crowe without cutting it down. He hoped Aaron Kurtzman had something.

AFTER PAYING OFF the taxi driver, Bolan followed Natacha Liberto along a three-block walk to the motel she'd suggested. On the outskirts of Ocho Rios, civilization and technology had taken giant steps decades backward. The tourist dollars that had built the main city into a playground for vacationers that rivaled the ports in Kingston and Montego Bay had definitely ebbed in this part of the island.

Most of the businesses were tourist-related, offering handicrafts for sale from grass huts and semipermanent buildings made of woven split bark that had been white-washed and roofed in corrugated and overlapping sheets of tin. Signs were tacked to trees where a variety of pickups and aged vans sat, advertising guided tours and canoe trips along the rivers.

The motel was a single-story structure, stretching out some thirty or forty units in a U-shape branching back from the main office. The paint had peeled and left graying wood visible underneath. A vertical sign above the main door proclaimed the Amigos Inn. Birds had left muddy-gray streaks across its surface.

Bolan followed Liberto into the building. The sweltering heat that was forming outside was clumsily batted away inside the hotel lobby by the shade, a faulty air-cooling system hooked through one window and a trio of ceiling fans.

Two men sat in green-and-white metal lawn chairs behind a low counter across the short expanse of curling wood floor tiles. A lean black man wearing overalls without a shirt was working diligently at tying a fishing fly. The other man was ten years younger, in his late twenties, shaved bald and dressed in a vermilion shirt with the sleeves ripped off, and black swim trunks.

"Something I can do for you?" the lanky man asked, pushing himself to his feet with effort. He hooked the fly in the brim of a battered felt hat hanging on the wall over a *Baywatch* calendar that was three years and five months out-of-date.

"A room," Liberto answered.

The man looked Bolan over. The younger man remained unmoving in his chair, but his hand closed over something that was concealed by the loose swell of the shirt.

"Business?" the clerk asked.

"Yes. Extended."

The clerk nodded. "How long will you be wanting the room?"

"Two days," Bolan replied. He stepped forward and slipped a few bills from his shirt pocket.

"Pay in advance," the clerk said.

"Just tell me how much." When the clerk named the amount, Bolan paid, then asked for a receipt. The cost was on a par with the San Souci Lido in Ocho Rios proper.

The man grinned. "Man, got no receipt for this. You planning on writing this off on your account?"

"Sure," Bolan answered affably, stepping into the role of a corporate executive slumming in the red-light district. "You don't have a receipt, I'll just put it under PACR."

"PACR?" The clerk's brows knitted together in puzzlement.

"Yeah," Bolan said, signing the ledger the clerk offered with a phony name. "Pissed away—can't remember."

"Shit, man. You really get away with that?"

"Only sometimes." Bolan spotted the two pay phones to the right of the small desk, but neither offered enough privacy from the two men for his needs. And he didn't put it past them to tap the lines for a little additional blackmail to supplement the income from running a hot-sheet hotel. "Is there an electronics store nearby?"

"What you looking for?"

"Batteries for my camera. Few rolls of film."

"Lindy's," the younger man said. "'Bout two blocks down. Got a sign out front."

The clerk snagged a heavy brass key from the painted plywood board behind the desk and handed it to Bolan. The round plastic disk attached to it was chipped and worn. In white against the black surface, the number *61* was barely legible.

Liberto checked the number and took the lead. The room was at the end of the left leg of the U-shape of the layout. She took the key from Bolan and put it in the lock. The door opened with a creak and expelled a cloud of dust into the narrow, windowless hall.

Inside the room, there was only a sway-backed bed flanked by mismatched lamps with badly listing covers, and a small writing desk that was shored up with a dog-eared paperback porno novel. The bathroom was off to the left and looked little larger than a broom closet. The green carpet inside the room clashed with the burnt-orange carpet lining the hall.

Bolan took a quick recon of the room, half expecting to turn up audio or video equipment. Nothing was there, though. He closed the blinds over the room's sole window after checking the view. The only thing on the other side of the filmed glass was the jungle. Someone with a mower had shorn away a strip almost ten feet wide, but that had been days ago and the recent rains had inspired massive regrowth.

Liberto stood near the closed door, leaning against the wall.

"I'll be back in a little while," Bolan told her.

She gave him a small, troubled smile. "You're sure?"

"Yeah." Bolan walked through the door. "Keep it locked."

"I will."

Shifting the backpack with the notebook PC across his shoulders, the soldier headed for the back entrance he'd spotted. Staying around the woman was dangerous. If there'd been a safe place he could stash her, he'd have done it. But there wasn't, and abandoning her was out of the question until he found a place. He spotted Lindy's and made a dash for it, taking inventory of the cars parked around the motel.

A FAT MAN in a flowered shirt ran the electronics store. Besides a generous supply of tourist accessories, batteries, film, postcards, maps, books on local legends and flora and fauna, he also ran a line of black market goods.

When Bolan asked for a fresh battery for the cellular phone, the fat man said that he didn't usually carry merchandise like that. There were too many questions from law-enforcement people regarding the use of such items.

Bolan asked where he might purchase a battery like the one he needed, and the fat man had recalled that he did have one battery, though, a special-order item that the customer had never picked up. The cost was almost twice what the battery was worth, but the soldier paid with only a little haggling.

The fat man went into the small room behind the glass-encased counter and returned with the battery after a couple minutes. Bolan paid and left.

He crossed the street and walked in the narrow shadows allowed by the near-noonday sun. It took him less than a minute to make the young black man in the vermilion shirt from the motel. The tail tried to act nonchalant, thinking he wasn't noticed.

When the soldier went wide of the street and headed for a grassy knoll a hundred yards back from where a collection of fishermen worked the shoreline, the man leaned against a tree and watched.

Bolan stayed where the man could watch him. He sat on the knoll with his legs crossed and put the backpack beside him. While he opened the pack and removed the notebook PC, he also slipped the SIG-Sauer out and placed it under his thigh so he'd be ready.

He booted up the computer, then plugged the cellular phone into the PCMCIA slot and made the call to one of the Net servers he had numbers for. By calling from the open, he cut down on the chances of being tapped by someone with cellular phone capabilities. The knoll gave him an overview of the city, and almost a hundred yards in every direction. If someone came at him or showed too much interest in what he was doing, he felt he'd know.

A package was waiting for him in e-mail, complete with JPEG picture files and MPEG movie files. Bolan tagged them all, then signaled for a full dump of the information. The transfer took several minutes.

As he waited, he watched the men fishing while the children raced along the bank, showing little interest in the activity until a fish was hooked. Then they crowed in delight as the silvery catch fought the line and broke the water.

The soldier enjoyed the innocence of the children at play.

It was a constant wherever he went, even in war-torn lands, and in the worst circumstances that could be imagined. It made the hardships easier to bear for the people who lived there and for the soldiers who defended them. It was something to be protected from men like Santiago Crowe.

"File's done," the computer voice said through the small speaker.

Bolan broke the connection over the cellular phone, then detached it and made a call to another number. While he waited for the call to route through the various cutouts along the way, he worked back through the file management system and brought the new files on-line.

First up was one of the JPEG files. The monitor cycled through the data and reconstructed a picture on-screen. Bolan recognized the man at once as Santiago Crowe.

The pirate was in near-profile aboard a schooner in full sail, clinging to one of the ropes while the white sheets spread out behind him, caught in the wind. He was bare-chested, dressed in khaki painter's pants that had been hacked off at the knee. Only one strap was snapped over a broad, meaty shoulder, while the other dangled loosely. His bald pate glistened from droplets of the spray coming up over the side of the schooner. Crowe looked younger in the picture by five or ten years.

In the background, a man stood at the helm with his arm around a bikini-clad woman who was looking up at him and laughing. A life preserver hung on the rail not far from them. Blue letters spelled out *Avangelyn*.

Aaron Kurtzman picked up the phone on the first ring. "Yeah."

"Me," Bolan stated.

"I was wondering about you," the big cybernetics expert said. "You hadn't been in touch for a few hours, and I'd picked up some of the news about the shoot-out that went down in Ocho Rios early this morning. I was wondering if you were involved."

"Briefly. It wasn't exactly my party."

"Word I got was that you weren't alone in hunting Crowe," Kurtzman replied.

"Doesn't look that way."

"I went over the news reports myself. Even filched a couple police reports that went into databases less than an hour ago. They thought maybe members of the Yakuza were involved in a surprise raiding party."

"That particular rumor has gone gold." Bolan shifted, finding a more comfortable spot on the ground.

"What's the connection?" Kurtzman asked.

"I was hoping you'd be able to help me figure that one out."

"There's no ties to Crowe that I could find, and no real Yakuza action taking place on Jamaica that I could verify. They've got some connections with a core of Russian Mafia business on Aruba, mostly handling narcotics and rolling over money being pumped from there to Moscow for laundering. Barbara's been running that under her own personal microscope of late on orders from Wonderland."

Bolan considered that, but wasn't able to figure any way it linchpinned into what he was facing. Santiago Crowe's operation was strictly independently produced. "I've got another name for you."

"Shoot. I'll try to scope it out while we talk."

"Lyndon Palfrey. And there's a freighter called the *Jilly St. Agnes*. I'll need to know about that, too."

"What am I looking for?"

"I couldn't say. Start with Yakuza interests and go from there. I've got him made now as in bed with the Japanese Mafia in some way. I need to know where the *Jilly St. Agnes* fits in."

"Can do. You've got the file?"

"I'm looking at a shot of Crowe."

"That's the latest picture I could turn up on the guy that could be clearly labeled as Santiago Crowe," the Stony Man cybernetics genius said. "Guy's made the rounds throughout the Caribbean, but there's not much paper on him that I could track. A lot of those small places have only recently gone computer, and even if they bothered to put past reports and files on databases, it takes a lot of time. And maybe the investigating officers don't remember so well, or aren't even around anymore to ask.''

''You've got a story for this one?'' Bolan asked.

''The picture was taken by a tourist, a lady who'd made friends with the couple who owned the schooner. They were Jonathan and Kimberly Sebastian.''

''Were?''

''Yeah. Flip to your next picture.''

Bolan advanced the file, pulling up the next segment. It was another picture; this one looked like it had been yanked from the society pages of a newspaper or a magazine. The young couple featured in this picture was dressed for a black-tie affair, and looked like they enjoyed each other's company. Looking at them, the soldier already felt a chill from the part of the story he was certain he could guess.

''The Sebastian name ring any bells?'' Kurtzman asked.

''Some, but I can't tag it.''

''Jonathan Sebastian was vice-president of his father's software company. The elder Sebastian was no Bill Gates, but he made sure his company stayed in the black when the P&L statements came around. Kimberly Vannich inherited 2.3 million dollars from her grandfather's estate on her twenty-first birthday. Her father still runs the investment and manufacturing empire her great-great-grandfather started when he arrived in America. Together, they were worth a little over three million dollars. Living the good life.''

Bolan waited.

''Eight years ago, they both took a month off from their respective duties to business and family and vacationed in the Caribbean. They ended up crossing paths with Crowe, who hired on as their guide under an alias. Less than a week after that, they were dead. They'd been kidnapped, and the families had tried to pay the ransom, but things got botched. The reports I've seen hint at a falling-out among the people who held them captive rather than any misstep on part of the agency handling the buyback. The money didn't reach the kidnappers, and Jonathan and Kimberly Sebastian were killed. It was almost two months before their bodies washed up on the Grand Cayman shore. Their boat had been dynamited and put down, but the currents kept it moving along. The woman had been raped, and both of them had been tortured.''

"Crowe was working out the kidnapping scam," Bolan said.

"Or someone put the idea in his head and he smoothed out the wrinkles," Kurtzman agreed. "The reason I'm showing you this is so you'll be familiar with the details. Hal has leveraged some positioning in the State Department to get an interest in Crowe going again. Could be we can swing an umbrella your way if there's any fallout."

"I appreciate it," Bolan said. "Taking this guy out from a distance isn't going to happen. Too many people are tracking him."

"That's Hal's thinking. If you get in a tight spot, he might be able to wedge you free after the fact. Carl Vannich still has the ear of a handful of politicians on the Hill. When Crowe goes down, especially after he gets tied to these present kidnappings, everybody figures it'll be a blessing. This is the only thing I could find in the computers that names Crowe. I turned up a couple other leads to smaller crimes in different cities throughout the islands down there, but nothing that would encourage a federal task force of any kind. Guy's made sure there weren't too many witnesses around when he finished."

"What about Domingo Krauss?"

"Next up."

Bolan worked the built-in mouse and pulled up the third JPEG. He almost didn't recognize the man, except for the dark color of his skin, which conflicted with his strawberry-blond hair.

Krauss was dressed in a gray suit that had been tailored

to fit his lean build, and his hair was razored in a military cut.

"He looks different now," Bolan said. "Not as crisp and clean."

"The look he's got there doesn't match the jacket I pulled on him," Kurtzman said. "Says here his mom was an Olympic swimmer from West Germany who had a fling with an island guy, then abandoned the baby. Her name, whatever it was, didn't show up on the records anywhere that I've been able to find, but neither is there an explanation for the surname. Document I traced had his given name as Haile, but he changed it sometime in his teens. He was raised by his father and grandparents. Evidently Krauss couldn't stay on the right side of the law. He was popped a few times for burglary, and once for armed robbery, but the charges seemed to slide off him. The picture you see there was when Krauss hired on as bodyguard for a local reggae singer who made the big time four years ago and was looking to go international before he committed suicide."

"So the bodyguard phase ended."

"With a bang. Krauss was brought up on charges and nearly arrested. Gossip columns that I tracked the story through were broadly hinting that the singer had been helped to his suicide."

"By Krauss?"

"Right. Further speculation suggests that Krauss was doing the sweaty-sheet mambo with the singer's girlfriend. Everybody was surprised at the reading of the will when she was left with almost nothing. He'd changed it only a few days before he was found dead. My guess is that Krauss found Crowe and started running with the animals again."

Bolan figured it the same way. The suit in the picture was a veneer. A predator knew all about camouflage and used it to every possible advantage.

"I've forwarded some maps I thought you might need on the area surrounding Ocho Rios," Kurtzman went on. "They've been archived and established as separate files.

Point and click, and you can pull them up as you need them. Zoom magnification is built into all of them.''

''I don't think I'm going to be around here much longer. The game's moving away already. I need a fix on the other players.''

''Well, I've already scored a hit on the Lyndon Palfrey name.'' Kurtzman gave a description of a picture he'd found in a file.

''Sounds like the guy,'' Bolan said.

''What I've got on him so far, from a hit in London and one in Richmond, Virginia, suggests that Palfrey travels in the con-man circuits. NCIC came back with a conviction seventeen years ago in Richmond regarding fraudulent insurance claims, and Interpol tossed in a conviction over some fake antiques six years ago. Same scams, but he's gone international. Or at least to Europe.''

''That, coupled with the upscale fraud, suggests that Palfrey's been successful at it.''

''Oh yeah. I'm getting more stuff on it now. Guy's definitely connected with the bunco crowd, and for sure a high roller. Very, very few convictions, though, Striker, but a lot of people are looking at him. He has grease, and he knows where to put it.''

''How does he tie in with the Yakuza?'' Bolan asked.

''As far as I can see, he doesn't.'' A keyboard clacked at the other end of the connection, the keystrokes coming rapidly. ''I can check on his visa, provided he has only one in his name, and see if he's been in Japan lately. Maybe I'll turn something up. I'll let you know. But if he's scamming the Yakuza, Palfrey would have to be dumber than the information I'm looking at suggests. Or think he's really smart enough to pull it off.''

''I was told he owns an island somewhere near Jamaica,'' Bolan said.

''I'll look into it. Shouldn't be hard to turn up as long as it's in his real name.''

Bolan moved the file forward, tagging into an MPEG.

Onscreen, a crisp white liner cut through the deep blue of the sea while cotton-ball clouds skated through a sapphire sky. White breakers peeled back from the prow. Calypso music spilled from the notebook PC's small speaker, then letters overlaid the ship: Sunchaser Cruises. "I'm looking at a video."

"Right. This is the advertising circulating now on the *Obsidian Princess*. That's Sunchaser's flagship cruiser. She's going to be docking in Ocho Rios at seven tonight. Bump up to the next video feed."

Bolan tagged it and watched as the screen perspective collapsed, then refilled the monitor. The video focused on a black female singer dressed in a low-cut red satin dress, standing in front of a band. The MPEG file cycled through three different viewpoints, all centering on the singer and the dance floor.

"That's Hannah Raynes," Kurtzman said. "Not only does she sing in the lounge aboard the *Obsidian Princess*, but she's also the owner. Sunchaser Cruises was developed from a parent corporation you're probably more familiar with. Caliber Pro-Tech, an international security agency headed up by Foster Raynes."

"Related?"

"Just like the parent corporation," the cybernetics expert replied. "She's his daughter. If snatching her from the cruise ship for what she's worth isn't enough, Crowe and his people can tap into Foster Raynes's cash flow."

"He'll pay?"

"Every dime, and get his pound of flesh after if he can."

Bolan knew Raynes's name. The man had been to West Point and blooded in the Asian wars, Korea and Vietnam. He'd also served for a time with the CIA, then dropped out quietly in the 1980s during the Reagan administration. There'd been media interest, but Raynes hadn't said why he'd changed jobs. Since that time, he'd built up a mega-competitor in the growing security market, providing specialists to Third World governments and heavy metal rock stars. The man had a reputation for providing everything he promised, and being on the cutting edge of technology. Several of his clients were software developers in the intelligence and military fields.

"Is Raynes involved in Sunchaser operations?" Bolan asked.

"The elder Raynes, only as a silent partner. The daughter runs things there."

"Does either of them know the *Obsidian Princess* is a target for Crowe?"

"No. I've done what checking I could, but I couldn't be too heavy-handed. Hannah Raynes is sensitive about her father's involvement. The poop I get is that her father bought the failing cruise line under protest, but turned it over to Hannah to run. It took her almost two years to put Sunchaser in the black."

"Where'd the money come from?"

"Her father. Trust me, he can afford it. But once the cruise line got on its feet, she's been paying him back. She's very independent. She'd managed to cobble together enough loans to buy Sunchaser with a couple investors who were going to remain as silent partners. Her father waded in and beat the percentage rate the banks were offering, and promised to be as silent as the partners she walked away from."

Bolan moved through the file and pulled up the next still. Hannah Raynes sat at a patio table with a wall of plants and the liquid aqua sheen of a pool behind her. She was in a thinker's pose, one hand under her elbow, and the other under her chin, a confident smile splitting her full lips to reveal straight, even teeth. Obviously it was a posed publicity shot, but she came across acting naturally, at home and at ease.

"She did some television acting for a while," Kurtzman said. "Bit parts and walk-ons, trying to get her music career started. She made it into the club circuit and had a couple albums produced, but none of them pushed her career out of the clubs. She worked as entertainment on the cruise ships and decided she liked it enough to invest what money she had and could leverage into Sunchaser. For the last three years, it's been a growing success."

"What about security onboard?" Bolan skipped through the file, finding more JPEGs that revealed different shots of the cruiser.

"It's better than average," Kurtzman responded. "From what I've been able to find out, Hannah Raynes uses the latest security tech her father has, but she fills out the staff herself. Foster Raynes prefers guys with police or military backgrounds. Hannah goes more for the Hollywood security crews, private operators who've learned to keep their mouths shut about the indiscretions made by stars, and keep things on an even keel. Her people have handled stalkers, organized crime trying to blackmail into someone's career and paparazzi."

"But nothing like Santiago Crowe," Bolan said.

"No."

The soldier closed the file. Everything was there. He'd make time to go over it more in depth later, when he could use electricity instead of battery power. The fishermen were still working the water, talking animatedly to the children and bringing them into the sport as much as possible. In the distance, the man in the red shirt was still watching.

"I need passage on the *Obsidian Princess*," Bolan said.

"I thought you might." Kurtzman tapped more keys. "The liner usually docks at Ocho Rios to let off guests who're staying on the island, and take on new passengers. I've taken the liberty of booking you. Barb wangled a diplomatic courier to meet you with a pouch at seven. There's a place called Scudero's on the beachfront."

"I've seen it. Who's he going to be looking for?"

"Michael McKay."

The alias was an old one for Bolan. Not as seasoned as the Belasko or Blanski aliases, but slipping into the character was as easy as donning a fitted glove. McKay was a free-lance writer, specializing in travel articles and political intrigues. His presence on the cruise ship wouldn't be a surprise.

"The courier's going to have a set of bona fides for you," Kurtzman said. "But that's as far as we can stretch it at this point. Any other support and we get caught not going through channels in Jamaica, contact points to the Farm will be drawing heat."

"That's fine," Bolan said. "Get me that far, and I'll see what I can work out on my own."

"I work up anything more on Palfrey, the Yakuza or the *Jilly St. Agnes,* I'll dump it onto the Net for you."

"I've got someone I want to get clear of the area." Bolan quickly explained about Natacha Liberto.

"This guy should be able to handle that, too."

Bolan said thanks and broke the connection. He shut down the computer and put it in the backpack again. His war book held the next number he needed. After referencing it, he placed the call.

"Murphy's Copter Service," a young male voice said. "Leave a name and number, and I'll get back to you."

At the beep, Bolan gave the McKay name. "We did some business a while back down in Carriacou. I'm looking for the same kind of service out of Ocho Rios. I'll be calling back at eight." He punched the End button, then gathered his things.

The red-shirted shadow stayed with him all the way back to the motel, a grim reminder that paradise held her snakes.

"WE'VE GOT to call off the rendezvous," Lyndon Palfrey said. He didn't like the tight sound in his voice. For years he'd trained himself not to show the slightest quiver. Too many deals went sour if a mark picked up even the tiniest change.

"There is no way to do that," Hideo Shotozumi replied. "Earlier, perhaps, but not now. The die is cast."

They were in the parlor, surrounded by the Mediterranean-style furniture Palfrey had picked out piece by piece over the years until he was satisfied. Flowering plants and trees were thick, taking up the large space he'd designed in the room. Pots held dwarf trees, and hanging baskets sprouted bougainvillea, which spilled in rich texture over the sides to within inches of the varnished white ash floor.

It was Palfrey's favorite room in the house. The sections of floor-to-ceiling sliding glass doors were bulletproof, but when they were rolled back, it was almost as if the room had been built outside. Facing north, the rays of the dawn and the early morning never fully invaded the room. Nor did the noonday sun bring its full intensity. And the late afternoon and early evening provided an easy ambiance for relaxing at the day's finish.

He had the windows shut tight now, though. "What if Crowe attacks the *Jilly St. Agnes?*"

"A freighter? For what reason?"

Palfrey hated the way the Yakuza lieutenant sounded so calm when everything seemed on the verge of collapsing. "Your people never got the girl."

"No," Shotozumi agreed. "Even so, what could she tell Crowe? That you were interested in a freighter called the *Jilly St. Agnes?*"

"Maybe that would be enough."

"I don't think so."

Palfrey glanced at the Japanese. Shotozumi was totally at ease, sprawled out across the love seat. "Crowe is a desperate man now," Palfrey said.

"If they tied him to the kidnappings." Shotozumi waved at the forty-five-inch television recessed into one of the walls. "Your local news doesn't suggest anything like that."

"The attack at the cockpit could lead law-enforcement people in that direction," Palfrey said. "If they haven't already been leaning that way."

"Island law enforcement can't touch the freighter until it docks in Kingston. The cargo we're concerned with will be long gone by that time."

"If we can get to it," Palfrey said.

"We will." Shotozumi seemed unconcerned.

"Your people never found the man who took Natacha Liberto," Palfrey pointed out. He kept his voice as neutral as he could, but it felt good to pick at the Yakuza failings. "We don't even know who or what he represents."

"We will."

Palfrey turned and gazed at the landscaped sweep of beach that glided down to the swimming pool below. No one was at the house at present, and the pool furniture was abandoned under colorful umbrellas that showed bright against the bleached concrete and the ice-blue of the pool.

"I have men stationed along every road out of Ocho Rios," Shotozumi said.

Palfrey knew it was true, and it surprised him at how much manpower the Yakuza were willing to expend in the effort to get the toxic waste out of Kobe. Part of him regretted that he'd ever made a deal with them, but the other part was certain he could have asked for and gotten more money.

"If the man and this girl try to leave by road, we'll know. If they stay in Ocho Rios, we'll find them." Shotozumi's words held nothing but conviction.

The chill, however, wouldn't leave Palfrey. He'd watched as the black-clad warrior had taken on the Yakuza and made it past them with Natacha Liberto. From his position on the hill, Palfrey had caught only a glimpse of the man once, but there'd been no hesitation in the man's willingness to step into the fray. Any way Shotozumi chose to look at it, he didn't think the man could be dismissed so easily.

"We assumed he was there searching for Crowe," Palfrey said. "What if we were wrong?"

"It won't matter. When my men find him, then he's dead."

"I don't think he's a regular cop," Palfrey replied.

"He could be with the Mafia," Shotozumi suggested. "You have suggested that Catalano still has men on Jamaica who are searching for those responsible for what happened to his daughter.''

"For his money," Palfrey said automatically. His own research had indicated that the Boston don would be more interested in his money than in the welfare of his flesh and blood. He could tell by the lengthening shadows that dusk was upon them. The rendezvous with the *Jilly St. Agnes* was only a few hours away. "What are you going to do if this man finds your freighter first?"

"It will prove to be his undoing." Shotozumi reached into his shirt pocket and took out a package of cigarettes. He knocked one out against the first knuckle of his other hand. "I did not come this far to be defeated, my friend. The toxic debris aboard the *Jilly St. Agnes* won't be going back to Japan, no matter what. It was designed to be a one-way trip."

"What are you talking about?" Palfrey turned to look at the man.

Shotozumi waved the wreath of smoke from his head as he expelled his breath. "The *Jilly St. Agnes* is mined. I had a crew take care of that before the ship left the berth in Kobe. If there are any problems, we close in and set the explosives off by remote control."

"You'd release those chemicals into the ocean?"

Shotozumi's gaze was implacable. "Of course."

"Do you know what they could do to the ocean life?"

"That's not my concern."

Palfrey broke eye contact and looked back out at the rolling waves breaking against the beach.

"If Crowe and his people attack the freighter, it would come as no surprise that it was sunk," Shotozumi said. "As to the cargo aboard it, no one would be able to assign blame to where the toxic waste came from. Whether it's off-loaded and stored here, or whether it goes down with the freighter, my job will be done. And you will be paid."

Palfrey nodded. But silently, he prayed that the Yakuza assassins would find the big man and kill him, because he didn't think the man would stop with Crowe.

8

Dusk splayed out in thick royal-purple clouds that looked like scuds of foam against the smooth emerald surface of the Caribbean. Mack Bolan moved among the gathering shadows along the beach between the shops, sensing that he and Natacha Liberto were being stalked before he had visual proof of it.

"Something's wrong," the woman said.

"Yeah," Bolan responded. They moved among the tourist crowd gathered along Millards Bay. He wore denim shorts and joggers, and a short-sleeved shirt with the tails left out to cover the SIG-Sauer at his waistband and the two spare magazines in his shorts pockets.

"What?" Liberto had dark rings under her eyes from sleep that had been nowhere near restful.

When Bolan had returned to the motel room, she'd told him someone had killed her mother. She'd called friends back in Kingston and had found out. The soldier had held her while she cried, until finally exhaustion claimed her and he laid her on the room's bed. He'd managed a few hours of sleep himself in the chair, but it was barely enough to keep him going. He was moving on the professional soldier's edge, drawing on his last reserves. But he couldn't stop now, not with a possible confrontation with Crowe so close. "We're being followed. Keep moving."

She hesitated for just a moment, then kept walking. She skirted the tables and chairs of the outdoor café. Torches held on cane poles planted in the sand wavered in the light, fragrant breeze, combating the smell of the mosquito repellent.

Bolan trailed her, a half-step off her pace. Out in the distance, the *Obsidian Princess* was at anchor. Lights along all her decks formed small, rectangular windows, soft-yellow against the gathering night.

He made out three of their pursuers with difficulty, but knew from the pattern of their movements that they weren't alone. All of them were Japanese, dressed casual to get around indifferent scrutiny, all trained so their movements didn't draw attention.

"What are we going to do?" Liberto asked, raking her hair back out of her eyes.

"Walk. Scudero's isn't that much farther." The neon lights of the small club were already within sight. It wasn't quite seven. Bolan hoped the courier was early. Drawing attention to himself, then getting onto the cruise liner without notice would be difficult.

Neon tubing, twisted into script that spelled out the club's name, changed gradually from pale blue on the left to livid orange on the right. The entrance was double doors with multipaned glass that captured the soft lighting inside in a buttery glaze.

A man sat in the waiting area with a briefcase at his side. His tan was deep and burned in. He wore wire-frame glasses that gave him a scholarly appearance that was countered by the callused hands. He stood and approached Bolan. "Mr. McKay."

"Yeah." Bolan took the hand briefly.

"Henry Lafourt."

"Are you alone, Henry?" Bolan asked, scanning the interior of the club. Business was brisk. The stools along the bar were full, and he couldn't see any vacant tables. He shifted the backpack across his shoulders.

"No." Lafourt glanced through the doors. "Is there some trouble?"

"Could be. We're going to try to head it off."

"I see. I was told there was a possibility of Yakuza intervention."

"It's a fact."

"So I see. I've made arrangements." Lafourt took a package of cigarettes from his pocket and lit one with a battered but well-kept lighter embossed with marine insignia. He turned back to face the club crowd. "I believe a table's opening up for us now."

Bolan glanced through the glass partition and saw three men get up from a table, nodding at the embassy man. A busboy with a large plastic tray and two towels was already streaking for the table.

"Del," Lafourt said to the maître d' at the next door, "we'd like to be shown to our table."

"Of course, Mr. Lafourt." The tip the embassy man discreetly offered disappeared with the close of a hand.

By the time they reached the table, it was clean and new silverware had been laid out.

"They've got a really good menu," Lafourt suggested. "They specialize in Italian meals, but have added a number of Caribbean dishes." He crushed out the cigarette in the ashtray, then reached inside the fanny pack at his belt and took out a miniature radio. He plugged the receiver into his ear and cupped the transmitter along his thumb. The conversation he had was brief, too low for Bolan to overhear.

The soldier glanced around, checking the windows. The table Lafourt had chosen had obviously been selected to be near a spray of plants that blocked view of the table from outside. Unless a sniper was indiscriminate, no target would be offered.

The waitress arrived with water and asked for drink orders. Bolan and Lafourt ordered coffee, while Liberto asked for a screwdriver.

The woman had withdrawn into herself, and Bolan let her. He'd done everything he could to get her clear of the situation. The next moves she made would be her own.

"Those three men weren't the only ones I have for this

little operation,'' Lafourt said. ''Trust me when I say that you are secure here.''

''I do,'' Bolan said. ''However, remaining here isn't an option.''

''Yes. I was told that the matter you were working on had some exigency involved.''

''When does the *Obsidian Princess* leave?''

Lafourt pushed a cuff back from his watch. ''At nine. We have almost two hours to get you aboard.''

''I don't have two hours,'' Bolan said. He wanted to get aboard the ocean liner and move through her, to get a feel for the upcoming battleground, perhaps even be able to build a defense against the pirates.

''In that case, there is a back door.'' Lafourt gestured for the waitress and asked her to get Del for him.

The mâitre d' arrived in short order.

Lafourt scratched his nose delicately. ''My friend needs to leave, as unobtrusively as possible.''

''Of course, sir.'' Del looked at Bolan. ''If you will follow me, sir.'' He pulled his white gloves a little tighter.

Bolan touched his forehead in a small salute as he pushed himself to his feet. ''Take care of her.''

''Of course.'' Lafourt pushed over the briefcase.

The soldier took it and glanced at Liberto. ''It's your choice where you go and what you do from here. You don't have to go back to how things were.'' He took an envelope from his pocket containing ten thousand dollars U.S. ''This will buy you some time. I hope you use it.''

She looked up at him, the set of her jaw showing rebelliousness, but her eyes glazed with unshed tears. She took the envelope and said thanks.

Bolan trailed the maître d', leaving the dining-room floor quickly and entering the kitchen. No one tried to stop them.

Del used a key on the back door and disengaged the emergency alarm crash bar. ''Good luck, sir.'' Evidently he was familiar with subterfuges Lafourt ran.

Bolan nodded and let the night take him, wrapping himself in shadow. He headed south, away from the beach, intending to circle around and head back to the boarding-party area. Small boats were already ferrying liner passengers to and from the *Obsidian Princess*. Scoring one would be no problem.

The presence of the Yakuza was confusing, though. Earlier they had seemed intent on attacking Crowe's forces, and taking out the woman as well. But he got the impression they were stalking him also. He didn't know what threat he posed to them.

He paused at the mouth of an alley more than a block away, getting ready to turn east and make the loop back to the beach. A small Volkswagen cruised the street. Inside were two Japanese men who carefully studied the pedestrians.

Bolan knew they were aware that he'd left the restaurant. Natacha Liberto was safe with Lafourt, and they were content to leave her there.

The only warning he had of the attack was a whisper of steel being drawn along leather.

The Executioner came around instantly. The comforting weight of the SIG-Sauer was against his waistband, but firing it would only draw down more of his attackers. He pushed himself from the alley wall, opening up the space between himself and the man that lunged from the shadows.

The Yakuza hardman came at him, his face ricked back in a grimace of determination. The stiletto gripped in the man's hand looked like a glittering steel dart as it sought the Executioner's face.

Bolan stepped into the man, using his left hand to push away the knife. The slim, deadly blade slid past the soldier's face, less than an inch from his right eye, the skin across his cheek picking up the heat from the blade. Keeping the palm contact against the man's wrist, he forced his attacker's arm down and farther away. Crooking his right arm, the Executioner took another step forward and, before the man could evade him, slammed the inside of his elbow against his adversary's exposed throat.

The Yakuza's breath shut off suddenly with a wet croaking noise. The impact of the blow shattered the trachea, and the man's air passages filled with blood. As he fell, a tiny radio dropped from his pocket and lay on the asphalt floor of the alley.

Bolan left the corpse where it lay and made his way across the street before the Volkswagen returned. The numbers were speeding up on the play, and there were more players than he'd first guessed. He still didn't know what the Yakuza had at risk, but he felt that everything was coming to a head quickly. If the Japanese Mafia knew about the *Obsidian Princess,* things aboard the liner would be even more dicey.

THE RESERVATION in the McKay name was intact. After being shown to his room, Bolan made the rounds of the cruise liner.

The *Obsidian Princess* was huge. Besides the three main decks where passengers primarily stayed, there was also a garage complete with car lift, a gymnasium, pool and sauna, and chapel in the big ship's bowels. Topside held two more pools, a jogging track, and a miniature golf course. In addition, there were two bars, two full-service restaurants, a theater, library, launderette, barber shop and various other shops and areas providing goods and services. It was stocked as completely as any aircraft carrier Bolan had ever been on. Once it launched, it would be a complete world on the sea, having only to stop to replenish stock.

His room was on *A* deck at the bow of the ship. Reasoning led him to believe any attack from Crowe and his people would have to center around that end of the *Obsidian Princess* at some point.

Some of the ship's crew were dressed openly in light-blue security uniforms and wore badges. Normally, Bolan knew, those people would have been dressed to blend in with the rest of the guests. But with the paranoia cutting into the cruise circles, presence of armed security guards was part of the present PR package. The teams worked in pairs and kept in touch by radio.

Bolan's lack of luggage had triggered a remark from the ship's purser, but was quickly overlooked. He'd had to ditch the SIG-Sauer because metal detectors had been set up at the boarding ramp and security used wands to verify.

Thirty minutes after boarding, he stood on the sundeck and gazed out over the ship. The moonlight and other illumination coming from lights onboard lit up most of the decks so he could see easily. Despite the recent kidnappings, the cruise business hadn't been hurt much judging from the number of people still boarding and off-loading from the ship.

He used the night glasses to study the faces of the men coming aboard, hedging against the possibility that some of Crowe's people who could recognize him might board. The security people stayed on the move, acting sharp and efficient. The scare hadn't lasted long enough to generate any feelings that the threat would probably prove false. He leaned against a support pillar and remained out of casual view.

Eyes aching from the strain and lack of sleep, he found no one he knew or even thought he knew. There were Japanese passengers, but he didn't get the impression they were connected with the Yakuza. Most of them were with families or groups, and didn't give the appearance of doing any kind of recon.

At eight o'clock, he used the cellular phone to call Chase Murphy's number. The line rang once, then switched and started ringing again. In the distance, behind Scudero's, two police cars screamed to a halt, partially visible from Bolan's height and through the tangle of buildings. The cherries atop the vehicles whipped red and blue lines through the shadows.

"Hello," Murphy answered.

"You know the voice?" Bolan asked.

"With everything that came with it the last time," Murphy replied, "I don't think I'll ever forget."

The business before had involved a rogue Russian KGB agent who'd known about a secret stash of nerve gas off Carriacou, and intended to use it to reignite the cold war. Bolan had stopped the man, but Murphy had stopped a bullet along the way.

"I need a flyguy," Bolan said.

"The action's the same?"

"Down, dirty and mean," the soldier replied.

"With a chance of getting my ass shot off."

"Every chance. I'll understand if you decide to take a pass on this."

"You solo?"

"So far."

"Hell," Murphy replied, "I couldn't pass this up. If I leave you in the lurch like that, I wouldn't be able to live with myself. Plus, there's always Murphy's Flaw to consider. I'm a sucker for women with a sad story, and a champion of lost causes. What do you need me to do?"

"How soon can you get here?" Bolan watched the lights flashing around the area where he'd left the dead Yakuza gunner.

"Man, I'm already on the island," Murphy answered. "As soon as I got your message, I set the machine to forward my calls and made the jump on down here. The rotors haven't exactly cooled off yet, but me and the bird are ready to rock and roll. Just tell me when and where."

Bolan smiled. "I'll have to wait on that. I'm aboard a cruise liner called the *Obsidian Princess.*"

"Out in the harbor now?"

"Yeah."

"Damn, I'm looking at you."

"I left some of my gear on the island," Bolan said. "For starters, I'll need you to pick it up. I'm empty-handed here."

"Tell me where, and I'll get it."

Bolan gave the details, then explained that the key to the

locker had been left with the front desk of the Hibiscus Lodge Hotel under the McKay name, where McKay was registered by a clean credit card.

"I take it this is gear I don't want to be found with," Murphy said when he finished.

"Right."

"No prob. I got a hidey-hole in the chopper that'll accommodate anything you can squeeze into a locker. I didn't come down here unprepared, either. What's the plan?"

"You've got a cell phone?"

"That's what I'm talking to you on now."

"I'll need the number."

Murphy gave it.

Bolan committed the number to memory. "I'm going out on the liner. I'll need you ready to jump when I call. Probably be an in-and-out. Pick me up and run."

"From whom?"

"The local authorities, among others. You've heard about the kidnappings going on in the area?"

"Oh, yeah. Coverage on the Mafia guy's daughter and the daughter of the politician has captured a lot of attention in the local dives of Key West. But I'd been paying attention before then. You dealt yourself into that?"

"Yeah."

"Never anything small for you, is it?"

"It gets more complicated," Bolan said. "There's also a contingent of Yakuza working around the edges of this thing. I don't think they're connected with the kidnappings. They've got an agenda of their own, but I haven't figured out the angles yet."

Murphy was silent for a moment. "People around me have been talking about a dead Japanese guy that just turned up in an alley not far from here. I take it you'd met."

"Briefly."

"Who are you after?" the pilot asked.

"The kidnapping ring," Bolan replied.

"So the Yakuza is a bonus."

"Something like that."

"Terrific," Murphy said. "It's us against the pirates of the Caribbean, with ninjas thrown in. Sounds like a nightmare straight out of Walt Disney hell."

"I'll be in touch," Bolan said.

"Do that. Don't worry about your gear. I'm on my way to get it now."

Bolan broke the connection, folded the phone and put it away. He went back to watching the boarding passengers, but he didn't hold out much hope for spotting someone. Crowe had taken time to set up the raid on the ship, and the man's animal cunning made him a dangerous adversary.

The soldier also suspected that the raid would come in the early hours of the morning. With effort taken to select the victims, Crowe's people would already know where their berths were. During the lean hours before dawn, when most of the ship would be asleep, an attack would be devastating and the confusion would be a weapon in Crowe's arsenal.

He waited, playing out the scenarios as best he could, keeping himself mentally and physically ready. However it went down aboard the *Obsidian Princess,* with Murphy only a phone call away, he could begin pursuit within minutes by air.

And the *Jilly St. Agnes* threw an unknown into the pot. It was a card on the play that was totally wild.

HANNAH RAYNES WORKED the lounge's small stage like the professional she was. Dressed in a blue satin dress that hugged seductive curves and kissed the tops of her high heels, with provocative slits from hemline to hipbone, she captured the attention of every male in the room.

Her voice was throaty and deep, a challenge rather than something that could be relegated to background din. Her repertoire was extensive. She began with torch songs that Bolan remembered from his father's records, seasoned it with Aretha Franklin and Eartha Kitt, then topped it off with a couple selections Bonnie Raitt had made famous.

The band followed her voice with the grace and elegance of a shadow following a dancer. As the last song ended, the baby spotlight irised shut, leaving the lounge sheathed in darkness. A few seconds later, canned music spilled from the sound system and returning subdued lighting rendered the surroundings nocturnal.

Bolan sat at one corner of the bar and nursed an Evian water with a twist of lime. Two bartenders worked the serving area, one male and one female. Both were dressed in blacksuits and set the tone for the lounge. The soldier wore a suit he'd purchased from an onboard clothier who'd sent out to fill the order. For off-the-rack, the clothing fit well.

The *Obsidian Princess* had been under way for almost two hours, bringing the time to a little after eleven p.m. They were reaching the end of the safe waters Bolan had predicted for the journey.

After checking back into his room, Bolan had downloaded the files Kurtzman had sent concerning Lyndon Palfrey and the Yakuza. There wasn't much.

The reports Kurtzman had turned up on Palfrey suggested more than they confirmed. The man was definitely a con man by trade, and had been around some impressive scores even though nothing the law-enforcement agencies involved could turn up involved him enough to prosecute. However, there had been a run of bad luck for the past ten months. Kurtzman had dug deeply enough into the man's background to discover that Palfrey had been selling off part of his stock portfolios to live on. And Fire Dolphin Island did belong to Palfrey. The money financing the building of what was reputed to be a paramilitary training complex on the island was somewhat mysterious.

Kurtzman had also gotten information from Lafourt concerning the dead Yakuza Bolan had left in Ocho Rios. After getting copies of the tattoos on the dead man, the Stony Man cybernetics expert had linked the corpse to the Moon Shadow clan of the Yakuza. The Moon Shadow clan specialized in the corporate world of Japan, hostile takeovers, extortion, prostitution and gambling. All of them were tools aimed at ownership of businesses and profits, which were used to turn money from illegal activities into legal tender.

The Moon Shadow clan operated chiefly in Tokyo. But of late, they'd been branching into recovery efforts in Kobe after the earthquake. With the new building of businesses, and the reconstruction of the industrial area, Bolan knew the city would be ripe for criminal interests with fluid cash to invest to come in and take over almost whatever they wanted. None of that, however, explained the Yakuza's presence in Jamaica or its dealings with Lyndon Palfrey.

Hannah Raynes approached Bolan directly, moving into the space beside him long enough to order a nonalcoholic and noncaloric drink from one of the bartenders. She turned to face him, then sipped her drink. Over her shoulder, out on the small dance floor, couples were moving under the swirling multicolored dance lights.

"McKay," the woman said in that whiskey-deep voice.

Bolan returned the frank gaze, knowing it wouldn't do any good to play the opening numbers in a coy fashion. "Do you always make it a point to get to know your passengers so quickly?"

"No. As a good businesswoman, I make sure I get to know my share of them. Repeat bookings are nice to have."

"I'd assume so."

"You, however," she said, "have never been on one of the Sunchaser cruises."

"No," Bolan admitted.

She gave him a slight smile without amusement. The soldier figured it was more for the other people watching them than for his benefit. "I'm told you're a travel writer."

Bolan nodded, going along with her agenda. Excusing himself from the conversation wasn't a good idea, and might not have been even possible. He noted three hulking security men in street clothes flanking the cruise line owner.

"I had that checked out. It didn't take long to turn up a

half-dozen articles by you in the past four months. You're a busy person."

"I try," Bolan responded. Kurtzman kept the McKay byline active in the freelance circles, hiring ghosts as they were needed, usually retired military men who had no problem keeping State secrets.

"But I have to ask myself what you're doing here," Raynes mused. "Are you here to review the cruise, or is it something else?"

"The cruise," Bolan answered.

"Then I'd have thought you'd arrive a little better equipped." She looked into his eyes.

Bolan tapped the backpack against the bottom of the bar with a toe. "I have everything I need."

"Except a suit for tonight," Raynes said. "And clothing for the rest of the trip. I had you run through the computer and found out about the clothing purchase, and all bags have to go through security at this point. You had none. You were registered at the Hibiscus, but not until today. And there was no mention of your arrival at one of the airports."

"I came in on private charter," Bolan replied.

"Damn, honey," the woman said in a voice that dripped sarcasm, "they must pay reporters really well these days. Most of the people I knew in the biz would have tried to scab a berth on a cruise liner from their editor, or from me in return for PR. You don't even bother to tell me you're here."

"I was going to get around to it," Bolan said. "Once I knew for sure whether I was going to say anything good about the cruise."

The man sitting behind Hannah moved off his stool. The singer wasted no time in taking the seat. She regarded Bolan coolly, and he could feel some of the edge off now. "Well, are you going to?" she asked. "Say something good?"

"The music," Bolan told her honestly, "is worth the trip in itself."

The smile this time held genuine warmth. "If I was less

secure in my ability,'' she said, ''I might think you were trying to bullshit me, Mr. McKay.''

''No.''

''I know. But I also know you aren't telling me the whole truth. I noticed you sitting in the crowd while I was doing the first set. You know who my father is?''

It was a loaded question. Denying knowledge would indicate he was covering up. Admitting that he knew her father could be read more than one way. However, as a reporter, he felt he would know. There was no hesitation. ''Yes.''

''Personally?''

''No.''

She looked into his eyes and sipped her drink. ''Should I believe you?''

''That's up to you,'' Bolan replied.

''In this day and age, I find it hard to trust anybody.''

Bolan nodded.

''You remind me of a lot of men I've seen around my father. You've got that clean-cut American military look. The agencies down here, CIA and DEA, kind of let their guys go cowboy. You look for that smug, superior attitude, though, you can still nail most of them before they open their mouth and start lying to you.''

Bolan didn't say anything.

''I just want to know if my father sent you down here, Mr. McKay.'' Her gaze returned his full measure.

''No.''

''I thought he might have,'' she said. ''On account of the kidnappings. You know about those?''

''Yes.''

''Before you got here?''

''Yes.''

''So are you here for the cruise, or the kidnappings?''

''What do you think?''

''I think that no matter how you answer that question, a lie is going to fall right out of your face.''

Bolan sipped his drink.

"If my father sent you here to watch over me, I've got my own people who can do that. I brook no interference in my personal affairs."

"I'll bet he knows that, too."

"You bet. But something else."

Bolan watched her expectantly as she finished her drink then rose from the stool.

"If you're not connected with my father," she said, "then I don't believe you're here to do a story on this cruise. You'd have arrived with luggage, and you'd have set up an itinerary with me, then tried to sponge a better class accommodation from me. It makes me wonder what you're really here for."

"I'm not connected with your father," Bolan said. "I didn't arrive with luggage because I'm not planning on staying long, and I hadn't planned on a formal gathering here in the lounge. I didn't set up an itinerary because I want to do the story my way. I'm not trying to sponge because the accommodations are fine. But the way you're acting makes me wonder about your hidden agenda."

Her nostrils flared slightly in anger as she regarded him. "These kidnappings aren't spur-of-the-moment things, McKay. Whoever is behind them has a front-runner, someone pointing the way. However this works out, I don't figure you've got clean hands. I don't want any of my passengers hurt." She turned from him.

"You might want to look out for yourself, too."

The woman whirled. "Is that a threat?"

"No, just a friendly reminder. Whoever else is on this ship, you'll be a top target. Stick close to your security people."

"I can take care of myself."

"I had that figured."

She walked away without another word. Heads turned as she passed. The three security men dropped into sync with her, forming a defensive triangle before she made the door.

Looking into the dark mirror behind the bar, Bolan watched her go. She was a hell of a lady, and her nose for trouble was dead-on. He killed another ten minutes while finishing his drink, then quit the lounge and headed outside.

He hesitated at the railing, looking out at the sea. The full moon left shimmering waves of silver over the dark water. An approach by any kind of craft wouldn't go unnoticed.

Movement started to his right, a jerky ebb that didn't fit in with the casual strolls several other passengers were taking. A couple dozen small white tables sat out on the deck, surrounded by chaise longues. Most of them were full, occupied by people taking quiet time for themselves or conversing with others.

Beyond them, the ebb of jerky motion became a wave of panic that spread outward in increasing ripples. The deck became strangled with the press of bodies.

"The pirates!" bellowed a florid-faced man in Bermuda shorts and an open Hawaiian shirt. "The pirates are here!"

The sharp crackle of autofire rattled across the deck. Several people screamed in fear and frustration as they ran for shelter.

Bolan stayed to the inside of the railing, rolling with the buffeting he took, trying hard not to knock anyone down to be trampled, and made his way aft. The chaise longues had been reduced to twisted wrecks of aluminum and shredded nylon bands. He took the first companionway going up. The crowd was thinner there, and it gave him the high ground.

At the end of the deck, near the florist shop that had closed hours ago, he halted and peered down into the stern of the *Obsidian Princess*. Four boats lay aft of the ship, and two had already secured lines to the railing. Armed men scurried up the hawsers carrying bundles of rope ladders over their shoulders, while other men in the boats provided covering fire. A half-dozen passengers had already fallen to the pirates' attack, their bodies littering the deck.

Three uniformed security guards pushed the.. way through the crowd under Bolan's position and started returning fire. A rapid basso drumbeat boomed from a platform high in the mast of a motor sailer where a heavy machine gun had been mounted. The lambent green tracer fire ripped across the liner's deck, taking out another half-dozen passengers and ripping huge gouges in the flooring and the walls of the bar below before cutting down the security guards.

Bolan had to dive for cover as the sustained blast gained elevation. The heavy .50-caliber bullets smashed into and through the railing, tearing out whole sections. As soon as it let up, the Executioner pulled himself up and dropped over the side.

He landed on bent knees but crashed to the deck anyway due to the blood slick that had poured from the corpses of the security men. Searchlights whipped across him, picking him up. The pattern got tighter as the men working the lights tried to bring them on line. Bullets skipped across the deck and thudded against the wall behind Bolan as he took the weapons from the dead men. He found only two pistols, both Glock 17s. The third one had skittered away or remained trapped under one of the bodies. Each of them had been carrying three extra clips. He took them all, shoving them into the pockets of his jacket.

Then he turned to meet the pirates as the first men surged over the railing.

9

"The radio's out, man," Domingo Krauss said. "They won't be doing no calling from that ship."

"Good." Santiago Crowe stood in the prow of the stolen motor sailer and glanced up at the crow's nest that had been rigged in the main mast. The .50-caliber machine gun kept up a deafening chatter, and falling brass tumbled and spun as it fell toward the water and the motor sailer's deck.

Krauss was dressed in black, as was most of Crowe's crew. The bulletproof vest under his shirt made him look bulky. The strawberry-blond hair made him easily identifiable. He went forward, talking over the radio handset he held, coordinating the activities of the boarding crews.

Crowe wore a vest that looked small on him, and didn't wear a shirt. His bare arms glistened in the moonlight, the sheen of oil he'd applied making his skin look even darker, almost like a shadow come to life. The machete was sheathed over his left shoulder, and he held an Ingram MAC-10 in his right fist.

He watched as the rope ladder was secured to the railing above. One of the men waved, urging the others below to begin the ascent. Without warning, his head came apart and his corpse dropped over the side, spiraling toward the water and disappearing with a splash.

"Domingo!" Crowe roared.

"Yes," Krauss responded.

"Get the gunners to clear those decks!" Crowe waved his

pistol toward the men who'd frozen after seeing the dead man tumble into the sea.

"They *were* cleared, man," Krauss yelled back. "One guy. He's up there holding off the boarding crew."

"One man?" Crowe said.

"No shit." Krauss looked as if he couldn't believe it himself. "That man shoots, somebody dies."

Crowe remembered the sniper from the jungle the night before. He'd gotten only a glimpse of the man as he dropped from the tree and covered Natacha Liberto's flight. "A security guard?" he asked.

"Man in a suit," Krauss replied. "Can't tell."

"Japanese?"

"No."

Crowe roared again, ordering his men up the flexing rope ladder onto the *Obsidian Princess*. They went reluctantly. "Get the others we have on board to come around and flank him."

"Already done, man. He's dead, and he don't even know it yet."

The machine gunner in the crow's nest let out a sustained burst. The green tracer fire whipped across the liner and chewed into the fantail.

Shoving some of the men aside, Crowe grabbed the rope ladder and climbed it. The pitch and yaw of the motor sailer made the climb difficult. The liner was heavy enough that it sat securely on the uneven ocean surface.

The man ahead of him reached for the railing and tried to pull himself aboard. The movement became erratic, then the man drifted toward Crowe, struggling to hold on to the webbed squares of the ladder. His lower face was a mask of blood, and his jaw was together only on one side. Light went out of his eyes, and the struggle to hold on died with it. Motor nerve control gone, the man pitched from the ladder and fell, thudding against the hull of the ship on the way down.

For one frozen moment, Crowe felt fear take him and he

hated it, but in another breath it was gone, leaving only the need to destroy whoever was standing in his way. Gunfire sounded all around him as he surged to the top of the ladder.

Crowe shoved the MAC-10 forward over the railing and pulled the trigger, holding it down. The machine pistol jumped in his fist and blasted a swath of bullet holes across the liner's trim. The grim flickering of the tracer fire from the .50-caliber machine gun drew his attention to the lone gunner on the other side of the swimming pools and miniature golf course.

The man was a shadow with two guns. Both sparked in deadly rhythm, cutting down a three-man attempt to overrun his position. Two of the men went down across the slick surface of the deck, and the other pitched into the closer pool. Crowe had no doubt that they were all dead.

After reloading his weapon, Crowe raised up over the railing and charged forward, yelling to rally his men around him. The split deck left the man three feet higher than the pirates, and created a wall on the other side of the first swimming pool that could be used for cover. Crowe fired the MAC-10 as he ran, seeing the shadow drift back although the guns continued blazing in his hands.

Crowe felt a bullet slam into the vest at his abdomen. For a moment, it took his breath away, then he was sliding, feet forward, into the shelter offered by the split deck. He dropped the empty magazine and shoved another into place. Glancing back the way he'd come, he saw there were four men in his wake. Two of them wouldn't be moving again.

Crowe raised his walkie-talkie. "Are you sure their communications are out?"

"Damn sure," Krauss reported. "Collie already drop a grenade in there. But even with the radios down, man, there be a lot of cellular phones onboard. They get satellite access, they can still make the call."

Crowe knew that, but he was also counting on none of the callers knowing who to call, or even where to tell the people they got in touch with to start looking for the *Obsid-*

ian Princess. Still, it left them only minutes to accomplish the kidnappings.

"Can we get those people around to the port side of the liner?" Crowe asked.

"You thinking of getting them off over the side?" Krauss asked.

"While we hold this man down," Crowe said. "Yes."

The sharp crack of machine pistols and rifles, as well as the deep basso of the .50-caliber gun, growled across the liner's deck. In the background were other noises, people screaming.

"I'll send the boat around," Krauss said, "and tell the others where to take their hostages."

"Get it done." Crowe motioned to one of the men near him. "Boy, don't be hiding your sorry ass here. I'm going to cut you right out of your money if you don't earn it."

The young man nodded and shifted to get up.

"And give me that grenade you're wearing." Crowe took the proffered explosive, turned it in his hand and pulled the pin. He released the lever and counted down, then stood up above the ridge. Spotting the man in almost the same position as before, he brought his arm around in a whipping motion. As he released the grenade, something whacked him in the chest.

Knowing he'd been hit, he dropped below the ridge and gazed down at himself. The bullet had shattered the skull hanging around his neck. Yellowed bone shards clung to the chain hanging broken against the bulletproof vest.

A heartbeat later, the grenade went off.

Crowe stood, holding the MAC-10 in both hands, and tried to peer through the smoking wreckage that had been left by the grenade. With the way the area had been torn up where the gunner had been, he didn't see how anything could have survived.

At least, not anything human.

The realization that the thought had crossed his mind made a chill run down his back. He turned his attention to the mast of the motor sailer moving around to the port side of the ocean liner. The boat was smoothly cutting through the water, easily overtaking the *Obsidian Princess*.

"Santiago," Krauss called over the walkie-talkie.

"I am here." Crowe glared back at the smoke cycling over the debris left by the grenade. Nothing moved there.

"The explosives have been set. In minutes the hull will be ruptured and the ship will begin to sink. Better be for getting your ass away from here."

"What about the people we came to get?" Crowe ripped the broken chain and dropped it to the deck at his feet. The bone shards thumped away in different directions.

"We got most of them, man. Best we could do."

"Okay. Signal the men and let's get out of here." With only one backward glance, Crowe took off for the port side of the liner, drawing his machete and waving his men into action.

A struggling knot of men erupted from a doorway further amidships. Crowe recognized Hannah Raynes at the forefront of the men working with him, flanked on one side by Domingo Krauss. Her guards, in uniform and in plainclothes, were making a valiant effort to get her back, but were unable to use their weapons with the woman in the middle of things. Krauss wasn't so encumbered. His .45 banged rapidly, knocking men down from almost point-blank range.

Coming up from the side of the men, Crowe swiped the machete across the men struggling against Krauss and his group. The keen-edged blade sliced through one man's arm as he raised a pistol and pointed it into Krauss's face. The amputated limb flopped wetly to the deck as the man went to his knees, stunned and staring at the bloody stump pumping his life away.

Crowe shoved the MAC-10 into the side of another man's face as the guy tried to wheel around to face the new threat. Crowe stroked the trigger. A 3-round burst shattered the man's face and knocked him into two more guards, taking them all down.

The liner security people didn't last for a moment against the other wave of violence Crowe carried in his wake. Bullets hammered the fight out of them, then chased the handful of survivors back into cover amidships.

Krauss grabbed Hannah Raynes roughly, slapping away the woman's attempts to fight clear of him. A backhand split her cheek and left her dazed for a moment. Before she could recover, Krauss shoved her over the side and she dropped toward the dark choppy brine stirred up between the *Obsidian Princess* and the motor sailer. He followed her before she had time to hit the water.

Crowe took a last look at the cruise liner and nodded in satisfaction. There were still some pockets of resistance, but they were token and futile. He'd gotten most of what he'd come for, and it would be enough to pay for them all to go into hiding for a while until it was safe again.

The big .50-caliber machine gun continued to rake the liner's deck, keeping any would-be defenders and avengers in check, and adding new layers of destruction to the carnage.

Sheathing the machete over his shoulder and slinging the MAC-10, Crowe stepped over the side of the ship and shoved himself outward in a dive, arching for the water. No one could stand against them; he knew that with a certainty. Then the cold water closed over him, taking away the sounds of the continuing battle.

EARS STILL RINGING from the explosion, Mack Bolan shoved the debris from his body and fought his way to a standing position. He'd seen the grenade even as Crowe had thrown it and recognized it for what it was, then had jumped as far away as he could. Flat against the deck when the explosive blew, he was mostly protected, but the grenade had ripped the canopy above his position loose and it had tumbled down on him.

Flames still clung to some of the wooden finish that had been reduced to shards. He brushed a patch of fire from one of his coat sleeves, and tasted the acrid bite of the smoke against the back of his throat.

Gazing out over the impromptu combat zone, he spotted three bodies floating in the charcoal wash of the nearer swimming pool. More bodies lay sprawled across the miniature golf course. He couldn't tell who had attacked the ship and who had defended it.

The .50-caliber machine gun whipped back around in his direction. The tracer fire spit green blips at him, and the heavy rounds slammed through the skeletal remains of the canopy over his head.

The Executioner snugged into the wall at his side and shoved his right hand forward. He'd managed to hang on to both pistols, but a trio of long, bloody scratches decorated the back of his left hand and wrist as he used it to prop up his other arm. The Glock wasn't a distance weapon, but it was all he had. He figured almost seventy yards separated him from the crow's nest where the gunner was perched.

He took up trigger slack, working to absorb the pitch and yaw of the motor sailer and time the shot he needed to make. He concentrated on the target, then pulled the trigger.

The first shot didn't seem to hit its mark. Without hesitation, he was already firing again. The fourth bullet evidently caught the machine gunner, because the man staggered off balance, then plunged from the makeshift crow's nest.

The second man was taking the dead man's place even as the motor sailer slid around the port side. A heartbeat later, the machine gun was rattling again.

Bolan fell back from his position and sprinted for the twisted metal pig's tail of the companionway leading to the next deck. The Glock he'd used last had blown back empty. He slipped the other pistol into his belt long enough to put in his last full clip.

Only two dead men were on the sundeck, their bodies torn by the heavy machine-gun bullets, twisted wildly in improbable positions.

The soldier rushed across the space to the railing. Passengers and security people were at the port-side railing below, milling around the fallen corpses that sprawled across the deck, covered with scarlet threads of blood. Flashlights in the hands of a few of them played across the water, then became targets for the pirate gunners. When the heavy machine gun opened up and drove them down for protection, the flashlights were extinguished.

Bolan watched the four boats breaking away from the port side of the ocean liner. They were rapidly drawing farther out of range, running with no lights. Crowe and his people had gotten what they'd come for.

As the crowd below started to get to its feet again, a vibration suddenly coursed through the *Obsidian Princess*. Immediately afterward, warning sirens wailed and emergency lights flared to life, further illuminating the pockets of death that had been left on the ship.

Crowe hadn't been content to merely quit the scene.

Bolan charged down the companionway on the port side of the sundeck. Two of the security guards pointed their guns and flashlights toward him.

"Put your weapons down now, sir!" one of them yelled. He kept his barrel pointed at Bolan's face.

Moving easily, the soldier laid both pistols on the deck. "Easy. I'm on your side. I'm a passenger."

"We'll make sure of that."

Bolan stood with his hands locked behind his head. The sirens were almost deafening, and the warning lights took away all the festivity of the low-wattage bulbs that had been on display until that time.

"Let him go, Smitty," a voice behind Bolan said. "That guy held off those assholes at the fantail. Kept them from flat-out overrunning the ship."

The young security guard nodded nervously and slowly put away his side arm. "Yes, sir. Just wanted to make sure. Hell, half of those guys with the pirates were part of the passenger list or crew."

"I know, kid. We'll get it all sorted out." The guy that lumbered into view was a bear of a man. Big and broad-framed, and built like a wrestler, he ran a bloody hand through his white-gray hair and left crimson streaks without knowing it. He was dressed in a lightweight white suit and turquoise shirt that were bloody and dirt-caked. He carried a partially crushed fedora in his left hand. A snub-nosed .38 was shoved in the front of his belt.

"Mr. Jarrett!" The yell came from a white-uniformed ship's officer caked with grime and soaked to midchest.

"Yeah, kid," the big man said, stepping forward.

"Those bastards set charges against the hull before they left. The blast cut through both hulls. We're taking on water."

"Shit. Can you get a patch over it?"

"No way. Unless they get a salvage team out here damn quick, this ship is going down."

"Where's the ship's captain?" Jarrett demanded.

"Dead. I was standing right beside him when he got his head blown off."

"What about Hannah?"

"They took her," one of the security guards said.

Jarrett nodded. "Start off-loading passengers into the life-boats. Fenwick, you go with him. Make sure those people took all their guys with them." He turned to Bolan as the ship's officer and the security man ran back amidships. "Son, you might want to pick up those pistols and help out some."

Bolan retrieved the Glocks.

"Hunter, you and Kennedy find me somebody who knows where the hell we are so we can radio this in to coast rescue and get some help out here. You got a cell phone?"

"Yeah," the taller of the two men said.

"Call it in now if you can get through, and keep them on the line until you find out."

"Keep the channel open," Bolan suggested. "The rescue

teams should be able to triangulate an approximate location using the ship's cell phone tree and the one on shore.''

Jarrett nodded. "Get it done." When the man had left, he looked at Bolan. "You some kind of federal cop, son?"

"No," Bolan replied.

Jarrett clapped his fedora on his head and hauled a bent cigar out of his pocket. "You aren't exactly cherry to this kind of shit, are you?" He lit it with a lighter, then noticed the blood on his hand and tried to wipe it off against his pants.

"No."

"There's going to be a lot of confusion for the next few minutes." Jarrett got into motion, taking a small walkie-talkie from the back of his belt. He listened intently, eyes constantly roving.

Bolan nodded but didn't say anything.

From the orders he gave, Jarrett was evidently chief of security aboard the ship. He didn't get emotional as he worked through the rescue procedures, raising his voice only when he needed to get someone's instant attention. "Bastard didn't take no chances this time," Jarrett said to Bolan. "Already had the ship mined. With all the confusion going on in the area, and the communications tied up with the rescue operations, they'll be gone real damn quick. Doesn't give a damn about how many people he kills in the process."

Bolan knew that. He and Jarrett swept back along the fantail, checking through the bodies spread across the deck.

One of the pirates, already mortally wounded, tried to lift an arm and shoot Jarrett, but the security chief calmly drew his .38 and put a bullet through the man's head. No emotion showed.

The ocean liner's crew acted quickly, deriving organization from the confused and frightened masses spilling up onto the deck. There were wounded among them as well, but they helped each other. Families were separated. Children cried and screamed for their parents, while frantic mothers and fathers shoved their way through the crowd trying to find their sons and daughters.

Cables whistled through the boom housings as fully loaded lifeboats dropped into the sea. Once in the water, the lifeboat crews started the small outboard engines and powered away from the sinking ocean liner.

The *Obsidian Princess* had started to sink slowly but surely, and as the ruptured hulls lost buoyancy, it sank more quickly. Bolan knew that if the first of the emergency rescue teams didn't arrive with pumping and balloon equipment in the next few minutes, the ship would be lost entirely.

While he was helping, Bolan had recovered the notebook PC in the backpack. He carried it slung across his shoulders as he helped pass out life vests to the children. Whenever he could, he tried calling the Stony Man Farm number. So far, the lines had all been busy.

The wind whipped the ocean spray over the side, stirred up even more by the motors on the lifeboats. Everyone on the deck was drenched in short order. As the water hit the generator and engine rooms, the ship lost its primary power and went to the battery reserves. Many of the lights went out entirely, while others dimmed to a gloomy incandescence. The pull on the battery reserves wasn't going to last long. The flashlights in use confused things further, but there was no way not to use them.

After helping a young boy find his mother, Bolan hit the redial button on the cellular phone. There was a click, then the number went through and started to ring at the other end.

"Striker," Kurtzman answered at the other end, "CNN just broke in with the news about the ocean liner a couple minutes ago. Where are you?"

The connection sounded fuzzy and broke up every few seconds. Knowing it could go out at any moment, Bolan cut to the chase. "I'm on the ship. Everything here seems to be going okay. I need to get a message to my backup and get him out here."

"Give me the number and hold on."

Bolan did, grabbing the railing as the floundering ship suddenly dropped farther into the sea and tilted a few degrees starboard. Frightened voices accelerated and rose in volume, momentarily blotting out the sounds of the winches, hoists and engines battling below.

"I've got him," Kurtzman said. "He's already in the air, winging your way."

"Has he got a fix?"

"No," the cybernetics expert said, "but I'm going to home him in. I've got him and you on the satellite recon I've had set up in the area."

"Good. What about the rescue efforts from Ocho Rios?"

"They're on their way. CNN relayed that at first they were having trouble locating the ocean liner even though they knew what course she was supposed to be taking. She isn't where she's supposed to be now."

"Crowe's people must have taken over steering before the raid went down," Bolan said. "Or altered the navigational computers in some way." Either was possible. Crowe hadn't left much to chance.

Another lifeboat whined down the length of the cables at the side of the vessel. It banged against the side on the way down, testament to the fact that the liner was rolling over on its side as it went down.

"They'll be there in minutes," Kurtzman said. "Your guy should be there before then."

Bolan scanned the skies, then spotted the winking triangle of lights coming from the southeast. "Have the locals organized any kind of pursuit?"

A harsh blast of static burst across the connection. "I repeat, that's a negative, Striker," Kurtzman said. "I've tapped into their communications enough to know that the only thing they're working on is the rescue of those passengers."

The winking lights flew closer and started to lose altitude. "Can you get a fix on the four motor sailers that just left this ship?"

"I can try, but there's a lot of traffic in that area. It's not going to be easy. Have you got a heading?"

Bolan gave it.

"If I find something, I'll get back to you."

"Good enough. I'm going for the freighter. I'm probably not going to be able to call you back through regular channels over the cell phone with the traffic on the lines."

"I'll keep the line open for you," Kurtzman said. "Just punch your phone on hold. I'll force the computer host on your PC from here when you get ready."

"Done. I'll talk to you soon." Bolan punched the hold button and watched the tiny light flare to life. He could make out the lines of the helicopter circling above the ship now.

Spotting Jarrett, he made his way over to the big man. A number of other people had noticed the helicopter, as well. The liner lurched again, dropping another few feet into the sea. Most of the passengers had off-loaded from the ship, but space aboard the lifeboats was almost nonexistent.

"I saw you talking on the phone," Jarrett said. He pointed his cigar at the dark sky. "That yours?"

"Yeah," Bolan replied. "I talked to a guy who's keeping an eye over this area—"

"Keeping an eye on the whole Caribbean, huh?" Jarrett said. His gaze narrowed. "Vacation, eh?"

"Busman's holiday." Bolan glanced up, seeing the chopper drop closer. "I was told the coast rescue ships will be here in the next few minutes. They couldn't find the ship because it wasn't on course."

"Kind of figured that, son. You going to be leaving us now?"

Bolan nodded.

Jarrett fitted his cigar into the side of his mouth. "What you did back there on the fantail, holding that position with just those pistols, I've never seen that done before. You going after the people who did this?"

"Yeah."

"Well, then, good hunting." Jarrett offered his hand.

Bolan took it and held it for just a moment, then made his way toward the companionway running up to the top deck. Once he reached a clear area, he used the flashlight one of the security personnel had equipped him with to signal Murphy.

The ship shifted again, and deck furniture scattered in the open spaces came racing across the deck to smash up against the wall under the funnel.

The helicopter banked and drifted sideways back toward Bolan's position, dropping to within thirty feet above him. A rolling coil spilled out the passenger side of the Bell Model 222B. When the roll hit the end of its length, it was still five feet from Bolan's outstretched grip. Murphy jockeyed the chopper around and cut more altitude, bringing it within reach.

Bolan grabbed the wooden rungs and started up, buffeted by the winds hurled down by the spinning rotor blades. He was aware of the people gathering behind him, thinking maybe the helicopter was another means of escape. Murphy powered the engine and drifted away from the *Obsidian Princess* before anyone else could grab the ladder, hovering over the ocean.

In seconds, the soldier climbed into the cabin and started to pull the rope ladder back inside.

"Which way?" Murphy shouted over the noise.

Bolan pointed northeast. When he finished storing the ladder, he closed the door and slipped into the headgear, not bothering with the belts. He needed to be free to move. The cabin was empty behind him, the other seats taken out to make room for him and his gear and the things Murphy had brought.

The aircraft gained altitude and shot off in the direction the four motor sailers had taken.

"Long time no see," Murphy said over the radio headset. He had an M-14 canted forward beside his door, and wore a .40-caliber Delta Elite in shoulder leather. Both looked like they were work tools, not just for show.

"I was told you were already in the air," Bolan said.

Murphy nodded and made an adjustment to the yoke. The helicopter responded fluidly, more bird than machine. "Before I left Key West, I put in the spare fuel tanks I sometimes use." He grinned. "With you, I learned to expect the unexpected. Figured reserve fuel would only be an opening bid. When your buddy came through with your location, I got the jump on the rescue troops. But we didn't beat them by much." He pointed south.

Bolan looked. A mass of red-and-white lights were descending on the stricken ocean liner. He recognized some of the emergency choppers, stalwart sea horses capable of handling the ferrying of the passengers. Dotting the horizon behind them were the running lights of several vessels that easily made better sailing time than the big cruise ship.

"Good enough." Bolan retreated to the rear of the helicopter and quickly stripped. He donned the combat blacksuit and webbing, then strapped on the Desert Eagle .44 and Beretta 93-R.

"I packed a wet suit back there that should fit you," Murphy said over the headset. "That water's going to be cold if you have to go into it."

Bolan spotted it in Murphy's gear. There was also an accumulation of weapons, including an Ithaca Model 37 Stakeout shotgun cut down for easy concealment and a CAR-15. The pilot had packed for trouble. The soldier tied his hightop joggers and went forward, dropping into the co-pilot's seat.

"Got a flask of hot coffee here." Murphy passed it across, then added a foam cup with a matching lid.

Bolan took it, then removed the notebook PC out of the backpack. He jacked it into the power outlet on the chopper's instrument panel, then used attachable suction cups to seal it to the comfort station between the seats. He wired the cellular phone into it, then brought it on-line.

Clicking off the hold button on the cellular phone, he said, "Okay, Bear."

The PC's screen cleared, showing the desktop setup for Windows 95. The cursor pulsed expectantly.

"I'm taking over through the host program," Kurtzman said. "You want to talk to me verbally, you'll have to use the phone interrupt."

"Affirmative," Bolan said.

"I found your four boats, I think," the Stony Man cybernetics expert said. "They're dead in the water. I'm taking over at your end—now."

The PC screen cleared abruptly, then shifted into a slate of gray-green. A neon-blue compass formed in the upper-left corner, followed by a yellow blip that pulsed brighter rhythmically, never quite dying away. Four red triangles waited ahead and to the right.

A line of script ran in a narrow band across the bottom of the screen. *Your keyboard's active. ???s?*

Murphy peered at the screen. "High-tech. Zowie. Can you get me a heading on that?"

Bolan tapped the keys. *Heading?*

Present course—018.3 degrees.

"Terrific," Murphy said, then made the course correction. Bolan made another entry. *ETA?*

Present speed—7 mins.

???s Jilly St. Agnes?

There was a slight pause. *Freighter. Out of Malaysia. Trade ship, working import/export biz. Company-owned, some black-market activity, but nothing big according to CIA.*

Palfrey's interest?

None showing.

Ties to Japan?

Made a stop in Kobe a few weeks back. Other border biz in that region.

History?

Been there before. Import/export.

Bolan considered that, drawing a blank as to why Palfrey would be interested in the freighter. It was a drug area, but if the shipping line wasn't already involved, there was little chance of it going into business so suddenly. The Yakuza and the Chinese Triads would police small competitors and eliminate them.

Ties to Yakuza?

None that I could find. Still looking.

What about a location?

Looking. You'll know when I do.

Bolan checked his watch. It was almost midnight.

"There," Murphy said, pointing ahead of them.

Taking his night glasses from a pocket, Bolan trained them on the spot the pilot had indicated. Through the light-amplifying lenses, he was barely able to make out the shape of the four motor sailers anchored only yards from one another.

Murphy dropped his altitude and closed on the boats.

Bolan adjusted the binoculars, scanning the decks. No one was visible. A heartbeat later, all four boats blew up, sending a huge gout of orange-yellow flames clawing skyward. The harsh, fiery light peeled back the night, and lit up the sea in all directions. Flaming debris from the boats looked like confetti from hell as they arced across the air before dropping into the ocean and disappearing.

"Damn," Murphy said. "These guys are serious about covering their tracks."

"Take us down closer," Bolan requested. When the pilot complied, he searched through the dark waters. He didn't think he'd find any of the pirates who'd survived the series of explosions, but there was a possibility they'd left some of the hostages from the ocean liner.

A handful of minutes passed, but nothing turned up. Huge sections of the twisted wreckage left of the motor sailers had already dropped through the sea, on their way to the bottom.

Glancing back at the PC screen, Bolan found a new message already waiting for him. A long green rectangle was north and east of their present position.

Found the Jilly St. Agnes. *Confirm destruction of the 4 boats?*

Bolan hit the keyboard. *Confirm. Visual ID. No survivors. No victims. Got coordinate lock?*

Coordinate lock done and done. Inform local law?

In time. Let them work rescue first. Heading for Jilly St. Agnes?

Heading 93.6 degrees. Max speed of 160 mph your craft, ETA at 12 mins.

"Let's go," Bolan said.

Murphy nodded and let the helicopter catch the wind like a hawk winging into a kill path.

10

Chase Murphy managed to intercept the *Jilly St. Agnes* in just under eleven minutes. The Bell helicopter performed like a thoroughbred, racing across the dark surface of the ocean.

Bolan used the night glasses to scope out the freighter. She was cutting through the water easily, flying the Malaysian flag proudly on her bowsprit. Men roved her decks easily, in greater numbers than he thought would normally be the case. None of them appeared to be armed.

"They're expecting trouble," the soldier said.

"How do you want to work this?" Murphy asked.

"Approach them and see about radio contact," Bolan replied.

Murphy nodded and jockeyed the helicopter closer, reaching over his head to cut in on the maritime radio.

Bolan glanced back at the PC's screen. Besides the green rectangle of the freighter and the yellow blip of the helicopter, there was now a trio of black specks closing on the freighter from the southwest.

Tagged your boat crews. Hit Enter if you want pics.

Bolan tapped the Enter key, then waited a few seconds while the pictures loaded. The screen cleared in sections, adding detail and definition.

All three boats were big power cruisers. A lime-green rectangle formed around the head of one of the men standing at the pilot's area. The screen blinked, then began opening up another picture. The screen split down the middle and images began forming on both sides. The one on the left finished first, revealing itself as an infra-red shot of a face that resembled Santiago Crowe. On the right side, the computer enhanced the IR-shot and added flesh tones, confirming that it was Crowe.

"Got the communications guy," Murphy called out. "They weren't overly excited to hear from me, it seems."

Bolan switched the toggle on his headset to the secondary channel.

"—is this?" a rough voice demanded in heavily accented English.

"A friend," Bolan said. "Let me speak to your ship's captain."

"Why?"

"Because there's a good possibility you people are about to be attacked," Bolan said.

"Who by?" the com officer asked.

"A convoy of armed men are already headed your way."

"Who are you?"

"Give me some time," Bolan said, "and maybe I can explain."

Murphy continued to drop altitude. The crew was easily seen on the deck, scurrying to take up positions at the railings. Weapons were clearly visible now, and had obviously been tucked back for instant use. A deck-mounted searchlight suddenly flared to life and swept across the black velvet sky. While it had disappeared into the star-studded heavens before, when it touched the helicopter, it lit up the aircraft like a stage-show production. The harsh white light frosted the Plexiglas nose, reducing visibility.

"Are you a policeman or Coast Guard representative?" another voice demanded.

"No," Bolan replied. "Are you the captain?"

"Get the hell away from my ship," the new voice said.

The accent was British, but there was an island cadence in there, as well.

Bolan tapped the keyboard. *Ship's captain?*

Gelmann.

"Captain Gelmann," Bolan said, "your ship may be in danger. There are people on their way here now that are planning to take over your freighter if they can."

"Who are these people?"

Murphy held the helicopter at a matched pace nearly a hundred yards above the freighter's deck. The searchlight stayed on them.

"Pirates," Bolan said, "led by a man named Santiago Crowe."

"That name means nothing to me."

"If you let me board, I can show you some files."

"You were told to clear off," Gelmann said. "That was your only warning." The connection went dead.

A second later, automatic weapons fire opened up. Bullets cracked the Plexiglas windows, shattering into crystal veins in the searchlight. Other rounds holed the helicopter's fuselage and ricocheted off.

Murphy heeled the helicopter around and gained altitude like a kite caught in a strong wind. In seconds they were out of range.

"Damn," the young pilot said, levelling off. "Either they didn't believe you, or they're hiding something."

"They're already expecting trouble," Bolan said. "They're protecting something."

In the distance, the searchlight winked off and a cloak of shadows dropped over the freighter as she continued on her way.

"So what are you going to do?" Murphy asked.

Bolan glanced at the PC. The black specks were quickly overtaking the *Jilly St. Agnes.* He tapped the keyboard. *Crowe's ETA?*

15-17 mins.

"I'm going to take a closer look," Bolan said. "I need you to take a flyby and drop me. I saw scuba gear back there. Is that tank charged?"

"Yeah, but what chance do you think you have of getting on board?"

"Guess I'm going to find out. I'll tell you when." Bolan tapped the keyboard again. *Monitor com bands rescue to Ocho Rios, Kingston?*

Already there, guy.

Word from Jilly St. Agnes?

None. They're running quiet.

"We could drop a line to the Coast Guard," Murphy suggested.

"They've got their hands full," Bolan said. "If the call was placed by the freighter, maybe they'd get someone on it. But the *Jilly St. Agnes* evidently doesn't want any outside interests around." He turned his attention to the keyboard. *Can do sat-com connect through helo to headset, give me com to you and flyguy?*

Satellite's in place with clear channel. Can-do. Farmer Brown has spec ops unit on yellow in Gitmo. Your call.

Gitmo was Guantanamo, the U.S. naval base on Cuba. The special ops unit would undoubtedly be SEALs. *Hold off. Int'l incident. Bump the pot, see what's up.*

Affirmative. Sat-com on-line 5 mins.

Bolan pushed up from the seat. "We're going live com in five minutes," he told Murphy.

The pilot nodded. "I trust we're not going to be throwing our names around over the air."

"No."

"So what do I call you?"

"Striker."

"Fits." Murphy smiled. "I'll be Rebel. You get ready for that flyby, let me know."

Bolan went back into the cargo hold and quickly dressed in the wet suit. He put the combat rigging in an underwater pack with a neutral buoyancy setup, then added the joggers and the Vaime Mk2 sniper rifle. "I'm taking the Ithaca, too," he told Murphy.

"Help yourself. And don't worry about serial numbers. That stuff can't be traced."

Bolan slipped the shotgun into the bag, then added ammo for all the weapons. He pulled on the mask and slipped into the air tank rig. "Go," he told the pilot.

Murphy whipped his craft around with the reflexes of an attacking wasp. He dropped altitude and skimmed across the top of the ocean surface, on a direct intercept course with the freighter. "At this speed, that water's going to be like jumping onto rock if you hit wrong."

"I've done it before," Bolan said. "You just worry about keeping in one piece. I'm going off-line now. I'll be back as soon as I can." He slid open the side door.

"Good luck."

Tracer fire leaped from the *Jilly St. Agnes* and flashed toward the helicopter. At two hundred and fifty yards, the gunners were putting their shots closer. At two hundred yards, some of them hit the chopper. At one hundred and eighty yards, the onslaught started to drum like a slow rain. The approach path put them headed toward the freighter, slightly to port of it.

Grabbing the equipment bag, the Executioner threw it out the door, then tumbled after it immediately. He was aware of the helicopter rising behind him, the engine thundering and protesting against the strain. He held a pair of fins in one hand as he turned in the air and came down feetfirst.

The equipment bag shattered the top of the ocean, breaking the surface tension and along with it the threat of smashing into it and causing injury. Bolan dropped through the ruptured area and the black sea closed over him.

"THE HELICOPTER would be faster," Lyndon Palfrey pointed out as he took over the helm of the yacht. Crispus and the regular crew cast off quickly as the Yakuza filed onto the craft. In the background, the main house was mostly dark, minimally lighted.

"A helicopter would also be more easily noticed," Hideo Shotozumi replied.

Palfrey started the twin diesels, and they obediently roared to throbbing life. Part of him was stunned that he was actually contemplating going to sea in an attempt to rendezvous with the *Jilly St. Agnes.* It was ludicrous. His best bet was to simply walk away from it, cut his losses.

Except that Shotozumi couldn't do that. Failure in the Yakuza wasn't accepted. The toxic waste couldn't be allowed to track back to the corporations in Kobe.

The Japanese stood at the railing of the helm and shouted orders down to his men. Black equipment cases were quickly lashed into place, while others were sorted through and inventory taken out. In seconds, the Japanese Mafia members bristled with weapons.

Palfrey powered out of the bay, watching the white spumes slip to the sides as the yacht knifed through the waves. He glanced behind the boat, easily spotting the running lights of the four vessels Shotozumi had arranged to have on hand if things aboard the freighter went ballistic. "Crispus," he yelled above the noise of the engines.

"Sir." The man was on the lower deck, dressed in black with a watch cap.

"Get the boat's ID covered now."

"Yes, sir." In seconds, he had teams covering the yacht's name and number with magnetic and adhesive black strips.

She was the *Jade Pearl,* and she was the same model as a number of other yachts in and around Jamaica. Palfrey had made sure of that at the time he'd purchased it. When he wanted to seize the spotlight, he was capable of that, but many times it was in his best interests to fade away.

Shotozumi joined him at the wheel, a walkie-talkie in his fist. "I have your course heading."

"Tell me," Palfrey said. He tried to keep any sign of discomfort from his voice. Aside from getting caught, the thought of the toxic waste washing up on his island almost made him ill.

Shotozumi gave him the heading and Palfrey quickly made the adjustments.

"Don't worry, my friend," the Yakuza lieutenant said. His smile was easy, natural, as though they were out for a pleasure tour and not heading into the jaws of possible death. "Once we get close enough, a simple press of a switch and the freighter will be no more. We'll return to your island, have a few drinks, and perhaps plan our next bit of business."

"How close?" Palfrey asked.

"No more than a half-mile, as long as we have visual contact," Shotozumi answered.

"Where's the ship?" Palfrey asked.

Shotozumi snapped his fingers at one of the two men who'd come up the ladder and stood silently behind him. The man passed him a nautical map. The Yakuza lieutenant unfurled it and spread it across the instruments at Palfrey's side.

A red *X* had been drawn east of Jamaica, north of their present position.

"The *Jilly St. Agnes*," Shotozumi said, "is headed in our direction. Finding her will prove to be no problem. We're already locked on to her through a satellite receiver."

"Then why don't you blow the damn thing up from here?" Palfrey demanded.

"We can't." Shotozumi rolled up the map again and passed it back to his subordinate. "Tracking her is no real feat given our technology, but setting off the detonation switches is impossible. They're intentionally designed to be short-range only, as well as very discretionary. It would have been catastrophic to put in a receiver that would have gone off if someone aboard ship had simply changed radio frequencies. The band the present signal is on is very short. But it will suit our purposes. Trust me."

Palfrey didn't want to, but he didn't see that he had a choice. He handled the yacht mechanically, then bellowed at Crispus to get a team and get the fabric top erected.

"How long before we reach that point?" Shotozumi asked.

"An hour," Palfrey answered. "More or less."

"Make it less."

Rather than argue, Palfrey only nodded. "Is the freighter under attack?"

"There has been an unidentified helicopter in the area," Shotozumi said, "and brief radio contact about Santiago Crowe coming for them."

Palfrey had seen the reports just now breaking on the news from the various media that had collected off the coast of Ocho Rios. Rescue teams had arrived at the *Obsidian Princess* and were now engaged in trying to keep her from going completely under. The local law agencies were stretched thin trying to make sure the medical people were able to arrive and depart without being cut off by the arrival of the media. Even if they knew where Santiago Crowe had gone, it would have been hours before they could organize any kind of pursuit. "Crowe hasn't arrived there?"

"No," Shotozumi replied.

"Then who's in the copter?" Palfrey asked.

"We don't know," the Yakuza lieutenant answered. "Yet."

Palfrey focused on his handling of the yacht while Crispus and his people erected the canvas top. Shotozumi might not be saying it, but Palfrey got the impression that they both knew who was in the helicopter.

DEEP IN THE COLD and dark of the sea, Bolan used a wrist compass with luminescent hands to seek out his target. The air tank he wore was a military-styled rebreather setup that didn't leave the telltale rush of bubbles in its wake. By the time he reached an interception course with the freighter, he could hear the preliminary bursts of gunfire splitting the hum of the ship's big engines.

He surfaced, going through the shadow of the water until the cool silver kiss of the moonlight thinned it out to where he could pick up a few details. Murphy was to the north, out of the line of fire, hovering low over the water. The three pirate vessels under Crowe's command were moving into the attack position, closing on the *Jilly St. Agnes* from three sides. Muzzle-flashes sparked on all four ships.

Bolan estimated the distance between himself and the freighter to be a little more than a hundred yards, and it was closing fast. All hands aboard the *Jilly St. Agnes* were moving to repel the attackers. None of them seemed concerned about the port side of the ship where the Executioner lay in wait.

He treaded water and spit out the mouthpiece. Reaching to his harness, he removed a collapsible grappling hook and knotted nylon cord. The railing around the freighter was almost thirty feet above the ocean's surface. The throw was going to be hard, but not impossible.

As the *Jilly St. Agnes* closed, her bow started pushing waves ahead of her. Bolan got caught up in them, bobbing in spite of the weight. Fifteen feet out, the soldier popped the hooks open on the grapnel, then spun it around his head in growing arcs. As the freighter came alongside him, he made the throw.

The effort pushed him below the waterline for a moment, but the grappling hook sailed true, arcing low over the railing on the freighter's top deck. The big ship passed, but the hook didn't catch on anything at first and only skipped along the deck. The noise was lost in the crash of gunfire.

Then it caught, pulling the line taut. Bolan held on with both hands, plowing through the water after the freighter dragged him under. The cold blackness enveloped him again, and it felt as though gravity had tripled. At first he fought to simply hang on, then struggled to hand-over-hand his way up the nylon cord. His back and shoulder muscles burned with the strain. Without the air tank, his lungs screamed for oxygen.

His hand broke the surface and he took a fresh grip, managing to clear his head and one shoulder with the next pull. Halfway out of the water, he dumped the air tank and rigged a climbing loop in the nylon that would support his weight. His equipment pack was across his shoulders. He pulled himself up out of the water and slipped his foot into the loop, using it to step himself up the cord more quickly.

The small-arms and rifle fire was joined by a basso thumping. Large sprays of light and thunder blazed and crackled across the *Jilly St. Agnes*'s upper deck and superstructure. Two explosions created brief waterspouts on the port side of the ship. Evidently Crowe had managed to secure grenade launchers and wasn't shy about using them.

At the top of the cord, Bolan caught the deck's edge in one hand and pulled himself aboard. He knelt in the shadows of a lifeboat, stripped off the wet suit and fins, and pulled his gear into place. He donned the joggers and bulletproof vest from his equipment pack as explosions strafed the freighter's upper deck. Clipping on the waterproof ear-throat headset, he heard only gray static over the frequency.

A grenade sizzled onto the deck near one of the amidships hatches and blew up. The detonation cleared three of the freighter's sailors and stretched out their flaming corpses. The phosphorus round kept burning, throwing a wave of heat over Bolan.

The soldier slung the Vaime sniper rifle, barrel pointing down, then slipped the Ithaca shotgun's sling over his shoulder. Released, it would hang within easy reach. He held the pistol stock firmly as he rolled in the lifeboat to take a better look at the battlefield.

There was no doubt that Crowe would take the freighter.

The three ships circling the *Jilly St. Agnes* were quicker and armed to the teeth. At least ten gunners were lobbing grenades across the freighter's deck with increasing accuracy. And all three of the powerboats had machine guns bolted atop the steel-framed tuna towers. The .50-caliber chatter was devastating as it raked the bigger ship.

Bolan estimated Crowe's crew at fifty or sixty men. The powerboats were big ocean cruisers, easily capable of handling twice that number. Somewhere in their bellies, the soldier knew, the hostages from the *Obsidian Princess* had to be locked up. Sinking the ships, even if possible, wasn't an option until he could guarantee the safety of those people.

A man in captain's braid ran out onto the deck and started to yell orders at the freighter's crew. Twisting red and yellow flames from the phosphorus grenades had taken root aboard the *Jilly St. Agnes* like some spreading virus. Men were pulled back from returning their attackers' fire to hose down the decks with fire extinguishers. Gray clouds steamed around them.

One of the pirate vessels came alongside the freighter and matched speeds. The ship's captain bellowed and pointed out the new threat to his men. A half-dozen responded to his orders, but were summarily cut down by heavy machine-gun fire.

The Executioner knew it was only a matter of time before Crowe seized his prize. Before that happened, he needed to know his chosen battleground. If Brognola had managed to get a SEAL team on standby alert in Guantanamo, they'd need an idea of what they were getting into.

Abruptly the headset came to life with a burst of white noise.

"Striker," Kurtzman called over the frequency.

"Go," Bolan responded. He launched himself from the lifeboat and streaked for the nearest hatch leading into the bowels of the ship.

"Rebel," Kurtzman said.

"I'm here," Murphy replied.

"Your sat-com link is go, gentlemen," the cybernetics expert declared. "What do you need?"

Bolan almost made the hatch without being spotted in the confusion of the attack. A small number of the freighter's crew had risen up to challenge the pirate ship's attempt to get on board. They'd managed to throw back a section of cargo netting once, but the combined firepower of at least two of the heavy .50-caliber machine guns drove them back. Crowe's men were starting to climb on deck, breaking the resistance.

One of the fleeing freighter sailors spotted Bolan as the soldier reached the hatch. The man lifted his rifle, shouting a warning to the others.

Bolan raised the Ithaca and squeezed the trigger. The shotgun boomed, spitting a pattern of deadly double-aught buck that caught the sailor and knocked him from his feet. The scattergun blast was lost in the other sounds of the battle.

Leaping over the side of the hatch, Bolan landed on the metal companionway and quickly dropped into a defensive position.

Two sailors were on their way up, clutching assault rifles to their chests. Both were caught by surprise but struggled to bring their weapons to bear.

Bolan lashed out with a boot. The kick caught the lead man under the chin with a meaty crunch. Reeling off balance, the sailor fell over the side, losing the flashlight he had in one hand. The man tumbled into the darkness of the hold and disappeared from view, but the flashlight pinwheeled and dropped, expiring with a shatter of illumination when it struck bottom.

Operating on instinct when the other sailor's beam raked across his eyes, the Executioner stepped into his second opponent's space and slammed the Ithaca's barrel against the lifting rifle. The weapon issued a short burst that stuttered sparks from the metal cross guards framing the ceiling, then fell from the man's hands.

Whirling black comets spotting his vision from the flashlight, the soldier reached out and grabbed the second man by the shirtfront. He rested the shotgun barrel against the bridge of his nose. "Any wrong moves," he promised in a graveyard voice, "and I clear your sinuses permanently. Understand?"

"Yeah," the man said.

"Hands behind your head."

The man complied instantly, showing familiarity with the process.

"Turn around." Bolan guided the man down the companionway, nestling the Ithaca in the small of his prisoner's back. "How many people down here?"

"Two. Maybe three. I'm not sure."

The light in the hold was dim, with only a few scattered bulbs to illuminate corridors and security areas. The battle overhead went on, but none of it trickled into the hold. Bolan guessed that Crowe was probably consolidating his control over the freighter. The soldier wasn't worried about getting out of the hold when he was ready. In the confusion, it wouldn't take much to break free of the ring Crowe had set up. Crowe would be interested in getting what he'd come for and leaving as soon as possible.

With his prisoner leading the way, Bolan worked his way between the aisles in short order. He contacted Kurtzman and Murphy over the headset, letting them know where he was.

"The team's ready and standing by in Guantanamo," the Stony Man cybernetics expert said. "Give me a green light and they're on their way, courtesy of Farmer Brown, with all the backing of the Man himself."

Bolan didn't question why the President would be interested in the pirate ring or the freighter. With the hits against American citizens, including the senator's daughter as well as the daughter of Foster Raynes, the soldier didn't expect the chief executive to stay out completely. With the terrorist acts against the U.S. starting to multiply, including domestic ones, a hard line had to be drawn.

"Where's the cargo you're holding for Lyndon Palfrey?" Bolan asked his prisoner.

"I don't know who you're talking about," the man replied. His English was serviceable, but little more than that.

Bolan repeated the name more clearly, but drew the same response. The cargo was stored in an orderly fashion, though not necessarily neatly. Most of it was trading goods, gathered from the half-dozen or more ports the *Jilly St. Agnes* had stopped at on its way from Kobe, Japan, and Malaysia proper.

The dry goods and machinery were kept toward the middle of the hold, spread out to the sides and stacked three and four crates high, more than twice the height of a man. A forklift was bolted to the center of the deck, attached to twin rings mounted in the floor. The perishables were kept toward the front of the hold, with easiest access to the main hatches. They were usually the first off at any port. A freezer and cooler area were toward the back.

"What about the Japanese cargo?" Bolan asked. "You made a stop in Kobe before coming here."

The man obviously didn't want to answer the question, but didn't know how not to. The soft illumination from the security lights showed the indecision on the guy's face as he nervously licked his lips. "I don't know what it is."

Bolan was grimly aware that Crowe's men might be rushing into the hold at any moment. "Where is it?"

The man started to shrug, then obviously thought better of it. "This way." He turned down an aisle and started to walk forward.

Bolan followed. Dealing with Crowe was going to be tricky, since the man had the hostages from the *Obsidian*

Princess with him. If the SEAL team had to be called in, the Executioner wanted the hostages out of the way.

The sailor stopped beside an immense stockpile of crates. "These are the ones we picked up in Japan."

Reaching into his gear, Bolan took out a penflash and played the beam over the wooden crates. They were marked with a variety of addresses, not many of them from Japan. Most were from Hong Kong, but none of the labels indicated businesses Bolan was familiar with. None of them gave any real clues to what was inside, though some indicated they contained farm implements.

Drawing his Randall survival knife from the chest sheath on his harness, Bolan rammed the broad blade under the top of one of the crates. He kept the sailor covered while he worked. The nails came out of the wood with long shrieks and gleamed in the light of his penflash as he scoped the contents.

Inside, shrouded in foam popcorn packing, was a fifty-five-gallon drum. Painted all in black, with a series of white and yellow numbers and letters stenciled on it, the drum was tightly sealed with a thick retainer collar. The soldier checked some of the names on the barrel against the ones on the bill of lading attached to the crate and found matches.

"You don't know what's inside?" Bolan asked.

"No," the prisoner replied. "Captain Gelmann doesn't let us know everything. This, he was even more quiet about."

"You picked all of these crates up in Kobe?"

The man nodded. "I'm pretty sure."

Bolan shifted the penflash and read more of the names. Topside, he could hear the rate of gunfire gear down. The blasts were coming more placed now, ringing with a finality. Most of the crates indicated Hong Kong as point of origin, while the rest came from across Southeast Asia. Only a few were listed as Japanese, and none of them as coming from Kobe.

A pack of men suddenly hit the top of the companionway. Flashlight beams stabbed in every direction, searching.

Bolan flicked off the penflash after memorizing some of the names. His prisoner chose that moment to attempt an escape, and the soldier let him go.

The sound of running footsteps attracted the advancing group of gunners. Two of them moved quickly down the companionway and trained their guns in the direction of the fleeing man while others up above pinned the sailor in their light. Sustained bursts caught the man in midstride and nailed him against one of the crates containing the fifty-five-gallon drums.

Bolan let the darkness take him, staying away from the weak pools of illumination provided by the security lights.

Crowe's men advanced cautiously, compelled by the shouted orders of a man who'd obviously had some military training in the past. He made them secure the area while he went forward to examine the dead man. Gunfire rattled at the other end of the hold, followed immediately by a man's death scream.

The hardman who'd taken charge waved a couple men in that direction. Another one yelled back that it had only been another sailor.

In the flashlight beam, the sailor against the crate looked like a broken and twisted doll. He'd been shot through one of his eyes, and the back of his head was spread over the crate behind him.

One of the men holding a flashlight stepped forward and stuck the barrel of his weapon into it. It parted easily. "Oil?" he asked, looking back over his shoulder.

"Try and see," the man in charge ordered.

Bolan had made his way up the side of the hold, climbing crates, the small noise he'd made covered by the natural sound of the ship passing through the water and the noise made by Crowe's men securing their prisoners. He paused near a closed emergency hatch that was designed only for crew and not cargo. So far, no one had bothered it. He watched the events below, shielded in the shadows.

The man took another step forward, then stuck his fingers into the coal-black goop. Immediately, he started screaming that his flesh was burning. He threw down his gun and frantically tried to wipe the thick liquid from his hand. He succeeded in smearing it over his clothes and making the problem even worse.

Crowe appeared in seconds, looming like an ebony giant over his men as he parted their ranks with brute force. The burning man continued to yell, throwing himself against the crates and other people, out of his mind with pain. Crowe lashed out with the machete, bringing the flat of the blade crashing against the man's skull.

The impact of the blow was wet and meaty. The pirate dropped to the deck unconscious, but his body still jerked involuntarily in response to the pain he had to have still been feeling.

"Domingo," Crowe roared, "bring me the captain."

The man's blond hair made him easily recognizable to Bolan, even from where the soldier clung to his perch. The Ithaca couldn't have made the shot to take down Crowe, and there was no way to reach the rifle. The Desert Eagle would have accomplished the job, but there was still the matter of the hostages. At least with Crowe in charge until a better time came, there would be a semblance of control.

Krauss shoved Gelmann ahead of him. The captain's hands had been tied behind his back, and he bled profusely from a ragged cut over his left eyebrow. The pirates fanned out around Crowe and Gelmann as Krauss drove the ship's captain to his knees.

Crowe reached out with the keen-edged machete, laying the blade just under the captain's chin. He leaned forward, making himself even more threatening. "You tell me, man, what's in these here barrels. You do, I maybe let you live a little longer."

Gelmann tensed, steeling himself for a final show of bravery. But it was hard with Krauss holding his head back by the hair and the blade at his throat. Crowe moved the machete slightly, enough to break the skin. A few drops of blood crawled down Gelmann's neck, black in the glow of the flashlights trained on him.

"Toxic waste," Gelmann said in a strained voice. "All of it's toxic waste."

"The Japanese," Krauss said in disbelief, "they're worried about a cargo of chemical poisons?"

"Yeah," Gelmann croaked. "They couldn't get rid of it anywhere else, so they paid us to transport it."

Bolan scanned the number of crates, thinking about the way the man had been burned by the contents of the first barrel. The guy was still unconscious on the ground, twitching in pain. A fiery red flush had spread up the length of his arm.

If the *Jilly St. Agnes* went down with her deadly cargo, the damage done in the area would be incredible. It would take years to repair the ecosystems, if possible at all. And the toxins wouldn't stay in the water. Bolan knew they'd eventually find their way to the coastlines, in fish or birds or other sea life, and possibly in whole molecules that would infect the land itself, finding their way in through underground streams.

"We've been on a fool's errand, man," Krauss stated. "There's nothing here to take."

"Maybe not." Crowe let the machete drop from Gelmann's neck. "But maybe we got something else to sell, man. These chemicals." He took in all the crates with a wave of the big blade. "How much you think the Caribbean governments and the others are going to be willing to pay to keep this vile shit out of the water?"

A cruel smile formed on Krauss's lips. "You thinking maybe we should ask?"

"No." Crowe shook his head. "I'm thinking maybe we

should tell them. Us having this, it'll give us more time to figure out how we're going to disappear when the time comes.''

Bolan moved farther up the emergency companionway. As he neared the top, a brief ghosting of his penflash ignited a matte-black surface that didn't fit with the thin film of rust that coated the hull to one side of the stairs. He reached out a hand, feeling the metallic rectangle's surface. He knew what it was at once, identifying the greased-wax feel of the C-4 plastic explosive and finding the angular lines of the remote detonator.

Hooking an arm around a metal rung of the stairs, the soldier slipped his hands around the demolitions package and freed it from the wall. The adhesive was strong, but there weren't any wires to set it off once it was loose. He turned it over in his hands, working by feel, and tugged the trip wires loose so it wouldn't detonate.

Krauss and Crowe kept talking in the background, giving orders to their men to bring the hostages from the *Obsidian Princess* down into the cooler area, under guard.

Bolan stored the C-4 inside a chest pouch and shoved the remote control into his pocket. He watched as the prisoners from the cruise ship were brought into the hold, guided by flashlights and armed pirates. They passed by the crates containing the toxic waste, having to step over corpses, on their way to the cooler section. They were herded without conversation.

Hannah Raynes objected to the treatment, but a pirate stepped forward and hit her in the mouth. The singer fell backward, but immediately tried to get to her feet and attack the man who'd struck her. Two fellow prisoners grabbed and retrained her. She cursed them as they pulled her into the cooler.

Bolan watched as one of the men ran a wrench through the handle, barring the door. They were living on borrowed time, and the soldier was grimly aware of that. He reached and freed the latch on the emergency hatch, then went up.

Someone below had to have seen the moonlight flash through the open hatch. A fierce voice roared out a challenge as the Executioner gained the top step, followed almost immediately by the thunder of gunfire.

Bolan hauled himself up on deck. The bag he'd left containing the wet suit and the fins was across the ship. He sprinted hard, aware of the pirates spread out around him, depending on his speed and the darkness to mask him. Bullets chopped the deck and masts in his wake.

A man whirled around a mast before him, the assault rifle already chattering in his hands. At least two of the bullets caught the soldier in the side, bruising his ribs beneath the bulletproof vest.

The Executioner lifted the shotgun in his fist without breaking stride. Another round caught him in the stomach, knocking the wind from him. Bolan's finger slipped around the trigger and squeezed it. The tight pattern of double-aught buck caught the man in the upper chest and face, knocking him away like a rag doll, spinning him against the lifeboat behind him.

Then Bolan was past him, hooking the bag with his free hand. He took three great strides that brought him to the railing and threw himself over. He released the bag on the way down, then let go of the Ithaca and, hands stretched out and feet together, arced his body for a swan dive that would take him deep and allow him enough speed through the water that he could be yards away before he had to surface.

Bullets churned the water around him as he struck. Then he twisted and stroked, pulling himself along at an angle that would take him away from and behind the ship. For a moment, he felt the pull of the massive screws driving the freighter, then he was past them.

He waited until his lungs were burning before heading for

the surface. When he did, the freighter was a hundred yards away and gaining distance.

Reaching inside the collar of the blacksuit, he pulled the waterproof headset into position and hit the transmit button. "Stony Base, this is Striker."

"Go, Striker," Kurtzman responded. "You have Stony Base."

"Rebel."

"On-line, dude," Murphy responded.

"As soon as the freighter's away, I need a pickup."

"I'll be there, Striker."

Bolan's mind worked steadily as he treaded water, looking for the equipment bag. He compartmentalized the information he had about the *Jilly St. Agnes*. "Stony Base, we're going to need that Gitmo special ops unit."

"One phone call," Kurtzman promised, "and it's away."

"We're going to need some specialty items," Bolan said. "What?"

"Salvage gear," Bolan said, spotting the equipment bag and heading toward it. "For starters. We've got a situation here that we hadn't counted on."

11

Bolan sat in the co-pilot's seat beside Murphy, working out the logistics of his plan in his war book. The roar of the rotor overhead had become a brain-numbing sonic backdrop. Some of the details he'd gotten from Kurtzman over the PC; the rest were from his brief recon aboard the freighter. It was risky at best, but it was the only chance they had to free the hostages and keep the toxic waste from getting into the ocean.

"I got a read on your remote detonator," the Stony Man cybernetics expert said.

"Yeah?" Bolan responded.

"Japanese manufacture," Kurtzman replied. "Like you thought."

Bolan looked back at his notes. "Means that Gelmann probably didn't mine his own ship to explode."

"That's the way I read it, too. More good news is that I can jam a signal to those detonators, assuming they're all on the same wavelength."

Bolan guessed they were. The remote detonators also had timers built in, and he figured the explosions were set to stagger, to get a more powerful effect that would rip the freighter to pieces. He looked at the paper in his lap. He had torn blank sheets from his war book, then used black ordnance tape across the backs to hold them together. The drawing he had produced of the *Jilly St. Agnes* wasn't to scale, but it was technically good enough for what he would need to brief the SEAL team from Guantanamo. "What about an outside signal source?"

"With the transmitter setup, whoever triggered the explosives would have to be within a half-mile, line-of-sight."

"Or already on the ship," Bolan said. Self-sacrifice was an old concept with the Yakuza, one that was enforced.

"If that was the case," Kurtzman said, playing devil's advocate, "why haven't the charges been set off before now?"

Bolan had known the explosive device he'd found hadn't been the only one. Logic dictated that there were others. "Maybe because the mole onboard the freighter, if there was one, was killed by Crowe's people. Or maybe he's waiting on a rescue."

"That's a slim possibility."

"Yeah." Bolan rubbed his chin, finding coarse stubble there from the past couple of days of not shaving. "Either way, we have to figure on a backup team. You're still locked on to the *Jilly St. Agnes*?"

"Tighter than a tick," the cybernetics expert replied. His voice went away for a short time, murmuring in the background.

Bolan knew that the operation in the Caribbean wasn't the only one Kurtzman was covering. Phoenix Force and Able Team weren't lying idle, and Kurtzman coordinated Intel for all of them.

"Striker," Kurtzman said, returning to the conversation, "you should have a visual on Indigo Phantom."

Bolan craned his head to the north, northwest, searching for the arrival of the SEAL unit. Forty-three minutes had passed since the special operations team had been put on green. The helicopters came in low and lightless, flying totally on instrumentation from information channeled through the satellite link with Stony Man Farm.

"You got them?" Murphy asked.

"Yeah," Bolan replied.

"Three?" the pilot asked.

"Three," the soldier confirmed. He watched the ruby running lights of the Sikorsky CH-53E Super Stallions grow steadily nearer. He tapped the transmit button on the headset. "I've got three, Stony Base. Confirm. How about a com patch?"

"Com patch working, Striker."

Bolan listened to the buzz of static in his ear, then it faded into the background, leaving the connection crystal-clear.

"Striker, you have Indigo Phantom on-line," Kurtzman said.

"Glad to have you with us, Indigo Phantom," Bolan said.

"Indigo Phantom's proud to be here, sir." The male voice was strong, confident. "And we're ready to rock and roll."

"Stony Base," Bolan said, glancing at the PC, "I need those breakdowns."

"You've got them, Striker," Kurtzman replied. The notebook's monitor flared, then fragmented into a rough blueprint of the freighter. "Confirm link on Phantom's computers. You are go."

Bolan leaned in to the PC. "Phantom, you know the situation we're facing."

"Hostage intervention," Phantom Leader said. "Also, your target craft has been mined and carries a deadly cargo."

"Right," Bolan said. "The cargo's toxic waste." After reviewing the facts and the names, Kurtzman had made his best guess that the toxins had come from Kobe's industrial waste during the cleanup after the earthquake. By dumping the waste on Palfrey's island, which Bolan had surmised had been the plan after considering the ties to the Yakuza and the blueprints Kurtzman had liberated from architectural files in Kingston, the companies getting rid of the waste would be saving millions of dollars in reclamation and elimination efforts. The Yakuza and Palfrey had taken a cut of the savings. "Our problem is twofold. We have to take the freighter without harming the hostages or the ship's integrity, and we have to do it before the explosives can be set off. If that ship sinks, even the barrels that aren't ripped in the explosions are going to rupture when they reach a depth that's too much for them." Bolan pushed F1, which had been redesignated by Kurtzman.

The PC's screen cleared, shifting to a close-up view of the top deck.

"I'll orient you to how the top view fits with the cargo hold," the Executioner said. "We're going to need three teams. One to exfiltrate the hostages, one to secure the ship in the event that it's inadvertently holed, and one to hold the deck and the pirates while the other two teams operate." He hit F2, showing the drawing he and Kurtzman had put together. "This is how we're going to do it."

LYNDON PALFREY USED his own field glasses to recon the dark slate sea ahead of the yacht. Hideo Shotozumi stood beside him, talking rapidly over the cellular phone connecting him to Tokyo. The satellite coordinates they'd been given had showed they were close to the *Jilly St. Agnes*. The yacht rocked quietly on the ocean's surface.

"I have them," the Yakuza lieutenant said, loud enough to be heard over the waves slapping against the craft.

Palfrey refocused his glasses in the direction Shotozumi was looking. He raked the lenses slowly across the horizon until he found the awkward lines of the freighter against the smooth curvature of the sea. She was cutting through the water on minimal running lights.

"Blow them up," Palfrey said, "and let's get the hell out of here." During the voyage over, he'd come to terms with the toxins being released into the sea. His bottom line was that it was better if some of the local flora and fauna suffered than if he did.

"You don't quite seem so reticent as before," Shotozumi observed. He snapped his fingers and one of the men standing behind him passed up an electronic transmitter.

"Boiled it down to me against them," Palfrey said. "They lost."

"And the spill of toxins into your sea?" Shotozumi asked.

"If it gets that bad," Palfrey said, "I'll be able to take an extended vacation in Venice with the money you're paying. Maybe even think about buying a new place. I could use a change."

"Come to Tokyo first," Shotozumi said. "There's a piece of business we have going on in Hong Kong where I think your talents would serve both our interests."

"We'll talk," Palfrey said. A soft mist was falling over the sea, given more body by the gathering anemic-gray clouds starting to skate low over the ocean's surface.

Shotozumi made adjustments to the device he held, then uncovered and pressed a button with an audible click.

Palfrey waited for the explosion, pulling his shoulders tight in anticipation.

Instead, nothing happened.

The Yakuza lieutenant pressed the button again, harder this time. There was still no response. Angrily he tossed the remote control device over the side of the yacht.

"Do you think they found the bombs?" Palfrey asked. "Or Gelmann did?"

"I don't know," Shotozumi said. "But there is a manual timer aboard the freighter that can be set."

Palfrey shook his head. "You can't be suggesting that we do that."

The Yakuza lieutenant gazed at him without emotion. "There's no other choice. People will be hunting Crowe and his group soon. If they aren't already. Put us in motion."

SANTIAGO CROWE ENTERED the wheelhouse of the *Jilly St. Agnes,* his thumb rubbing against the surface of the Betty Page watch. He gazed through the misted panels of Plexiglas to the south, watching as roving groups of his men covered the deck, throwing the dead into the sea.

"Storm's coming," the helmsman said. He was a weathered fisherman from the Kingston area who'd spent more hours on the sea than on dry land. "Going to blow up a big one too, man."

Crowe put away the watch. He felt the older man was right, but the storm would do them a favor by further shielding their activities from anyone who was looking for the freighter. They'd veered from the planned course a half-hour earlier, heading for one of the smaller islands to the east of Jamaica where the ship could be hidden.

Krauss entered a few minutes later. "Getting cold out there, man. Going to be wishing I'd brought a coat."

"Another few hours," Crowe said, "you'll be some place warm and toasty, getting ready to count your money."

"I've been thinking about how we should work this deal," Krauss said, taking up a position on the other side of the helmsman. "I think we ought to find some lagoon and sink this boat. Not so deep the damn barrels are crushed by the pressure, but deep enough so this ship isn't found so easy, man. You know?"

"Yeah," Crowe said. "I've been figuring on that too." It sounded like a good idea, better than any he'd come up with. Hiding the freighter wasn't going to be easy, and offloading all the toxic waste sounded too complicated. It was better never to take the deadly poisons away from the ocean. That would nullify the threat they had to use as leverage.

"That way, we blackmail whoever'll pay to keep the toxins out of the waters, then we can blow up the ship, release everything in those barrels, let them know there was an accident and where it is. During the confusion of people zooming here trying to fix the problem like they did after that *Valdez* thing, we get the hell out of these islands for a time."

Crowe turned over the plan in his mind, liking the sound of it, and the simplicity. "That's how I had it figured." He squinted into the roiling haze of the fog settling across the sea in front of them. "Where you got them boats, man?"

"Our boats?" Krauss asked. "They're following us. Just like we agreed."

"You're sure?"

"Yeah, man. Wouldn't be no mistake about a thing like that."

"Then who," Crowe asked, "the fuck is that?" He pointed at the yellow lights barely visible in the gloom ahead of them.

"Don't know, but I'm going to be for finding out. Damn quick."

"Get those whore-hounds on deck," Crowe roared, fisting the machete. "Tell them they got to earn the money I'm going to steal for them."

Krauss left in a hurry, starting to shout as soon as he cleared the door.

"Keep this course," Crowe told the helmsman. "Those bastards want trouble, they're going to bite off more than they can chew." He pushed through the door and walked toward the prow while men rushed around him, taking up defensive positions. A backward glance told him that the three boats they'd used to overtake and attack the freighter were lingering astern.

That left only his enemies ahead of him. If it had been the police, they'd have had some kind of aircraft in the area. Since the initial contact the *Jilly St. Agnes* had with the small helicopter, there'd been nothing else. That left Palfrey and the Japanese. Somehow they'd discovered he'd taken the freighter.

Crowe found a corpse taking up room in the prow. He reached down and grabbed the shirt, then heaved the dead man into the sea. With the machete in one hand and his machine pistol in the other, he awaited the arrival of his enemies. No one was strong enough to stop him.

"THE YAKUZA JUST made the party," Kurtzman said over the com link.

Mack Bolan stood in the open cargo hold of the Bell helicopter. The winds whipped around him. The aircraft were more than a mile away and holding at twelve thousand feet above sea level, well above the fog. He knew Crowe and his people couldn't see the choppers cutting through the night.

"You're sure, Stony Base?" the Executioner asked.

"I've got five boats on-screen now," Kurtzman replied. "And the system I've got jamming that detonation frequency in the area showed a hit less than twenty seconds ago. There. I'm reading a couple more. They're definitely trying to set off the munitions."

Across from Bolan, one of the CH-53E Super Stallions settled into a matching speed and altitude that left only ten yards between the rotors of the two machines. The cargo door at the back of the other machine dropped open, and the doorway filled with black uniformed SEALs. Like Bolan, they had a white band around their right biceps, there for identification purposes.

"They're closing in, Striker," Kurtzman added a moment later.

"We're on it, Stony Base," Bolan transmitted.

"Phantom Leader, are you ready?" he asked.

"Say go, buddy."

"Go." Dressed in combat blacksuit and webbing, carrying his two pistols and the M-16/M-203 combo, the Executioner leaned out the cargo door and let the wind take him away.

"Good luck," Murphy called over the headset. "You need me, call. I'll be there quicker than two shakes of a lamb's tail."

"I'll hold you to that," Bolan said. Without goggles, his eyes teared against the force of the wind. But he made himself watch as a dark shadow pulled free from the rear of the Sea Stallion across from him. Murphy had parachutes aboard the helicopter, but none of them were the black silk rectangular style the SEALs had brought with them. They would be invisible on the approach.

The soldier assumed a skydiving position to track across the sky and slow his fall. He watched as the SEAL commander came closer, a spare parachute gripped tightly in one hand.

Seconds later, the SEAL fisted Bolan's combat rigging and handed over the parachute and a pair of goggles. "Need help getting it on?" the captain asked as they plummeted toward the sea, yelling to be heard.

"This part I know," Bolan replied.

The SEAL was in his late twenties and still had a boyish grin that didn't fit with the death's black he wore. "Captain Drew Carson," he shouted through his cupped hands. "It's nice to be working with you, Colonel Pollock." He gave the warrior a thumbs-up, then stuck his feet straight down and fell like a rock, clearing Bolan's area.

Colonel Rance Pollock was the military ID the Executioner worked under while involved in a Stony Man-backed operation.

As he pulled on the parachute, Bolan glanced up at the staggered line of SEALs spilling from the backs of the military helicopters. Some of the men had equipment lashed to them, trailing by a cable umbilical below their feet. The Executioner donned the protective goggles to shield his eyes. The aircraft would trail behind at the same distance until they were called in for fire support and evacuation.

At eight thousand feet, Bolan gave the order to crack the silk. He pulled the rip cord and watched the giant sheet of honeycombed black silk stretch to fill the sky. Above and around him, the team of SEALs did the same. Kurtzman guided them through the satellite transmission.

For a moment, Bolan was above the layer of scudding fog, then he was a part of it. He focused on Kurtzman's calm voice as the cybernetics expert guided the raiding party toward the target, counting down the ETA to less than a minute.

Within three hundred yards of the *Jilly St. Agnes,* Bolan was able to make out the lines of the freighter. He tugged on the shroud lines, making adjustments to his approach. He overtook the ship in seconds, spotting the three boats behind the freighter jockeying for position against the five powerboats that were forming a semicircle around the big ship's prow. Gunfire flashed on all of the craft as the crews engaged each other.

"We're going to be coming down hot," Bolan said over the com link. "Indigo Phantom Wing, can you confirm audio?"

"Roger, Striker. Indigo Phantom Wing One reads you five by five."

"Affirmative. Rebel?"

"Chilling," Murphy responded.

"Team One," Bolan called out. "You're on."

"Yes, sir."

Glancing over his shoulder, the Executioner watched as a third of the SEAL team pulled at their shroud lines. In response, the chutes lost altitude and gained speed, swooping in on the freighter like a horde of giant bats. Bolan gathered his shroud lines and went with them.

The sensation of floating changed to one of speed. The ocean surface below Bolan looked like a sheet of flat, black glass. Team One came up on the *Jilly St. Agnes* from behind, with no warning to the freighter's crew or the boats that surrounded her.

Bolan didn't try to avoid the masts. The parachute caught in the netting of the aft mast and brought him up short, dangling some fifteen feet above the freighter's deck. One of Crowe's men spotted him and started to raise his weapon, yelling out a warning that went unheard in the din of battle.

The Executioner drew the .44 Desert Eagle smoothly and centered the sights over the man's chest. He squeezed out two rounds, knocking the pirate down and back, shucking the life from the husk of flesh. Still holding the heavy pistol, aware of the other parachutes dropping all around him, hanging in the masts and sail rigging like withered mushrooms, he worked the quick-disconnects of the chute harness.

He held on to the shroud lines and extended the full length of his arm, taking away another two feet from the drop. At the end of the cord, taking up the freighter's motion now, he started to twist.

Below him, a trio of gunners ran to intercept the landing SEALs.

Bolan released the cord and dropped into a controlled parachute roll that brought him up on his feet. Taking a modified Weaver's stance as bullets cut the air over his head, he worked from left to right, running through the hand cannon's magazine.

The three pirates spun away as the bullets smacked into them. None of them moved after they hit the deck.

Leathering the Desert Eagle, the Executioner slid the M-16/M-203 off his shoulder and wrapped the strap around his left arm as he kept moving forward. Automatically his mind marked out areas of the battlezone, recognizing threat and opportunity.

The pirates were torn, trapped between two enemies and finding themselves in a deadly no-man's-land. Some of them kept fighting desperately against the attacking ninjas trying to force their way onto the ship.

The Executioner worked in short bursts. A triburst of 5.56 mm tumblers caught a pirate in the face and stretched him out. Then the soldier shifted to a new threat as a black-clad Yakuza grabbed a rigging line and hauled himself over the side. A rope ladder clung to the railing behind him.

The Yakuza gunner lifted his Uzi and raked a blast at Bolan, only scoring once against the bulletproof vest.

The Executioner reached forward and squeezed the trigger on the M-203 grenade launcher. The 40 mm phosphorus warhead exploded against the Yakuza's chest, turning him into a flaming specter and shoving him back over the side in pieces.

Moving quickly, Bolan recharged the M-203 with an HE round. Peering over the side of the freighter, he spotted the powerboat below. He lined up his shot and took it, sending the 40 mm hell flower into the steering section of the boat.

Bodies jerked away from the concussion. When the smoke cleared, all that was left of the steering section was splintered carnage. Two of the Yakuza hardmen had managed to cling to the rope ladder even through the force of the explosion. Plucking the Randall survival knife from his combat harness, Bolan severed the rope, then watched long enough to see the men fall.

He fed another round into the grenade launcher, then burned down two more pirates. Crowe's people were beginning to break and run, not holding against the Yakuza as they swept over the freighter from the prow.

Tapping his headset transmit button, he said, "Team Two."

"On our way, sir," Carson radioed back.

Bolan scanned the battlefield spread across the ship's deck. The SEALs had dug in, finding positions that would allow them to hold the center of the main top deck and provide covering fire. "Snipers?"

A chorus of three "ayes" came back to him, accompanied by the numbers one, three and four. "Where's two?" Bolan asked. He took cover behind crates of cargo that had been lashed into place on the deck. Bullets gouged the soft wood as they searched for his flesh.

"Two got hit," one of the men answered.

Pulling the M-16 to his shoulder, Bolan looked through the sights at one of the men pinning him down. They were taking cover at the side of the wheelhouse and behind a firefighting station, above his position. He aimed slightly over a muzzle-flash, then stroked the trigger once.

The 5.56 mm sizzler caught the man in the face and jerked him back.

Bolan put two more rounds in his target before the man dropped dead. He shifted slightly and picked up another man falling into position beside the other two. Before the gunner could get completely into cover, the Executioner put a round between his eyes. His ribs hurt from the earlier impacts, but he kept pushing himself. The numbers on the play were falling fast and deadly, and the rescue effort had started out behind in the count anyway.

Glancing into the rigging and masts above, he saw the freighter had been shrouded with the discarded parachutes. Not all of the SEALs had managed the landing. Some had been cut down while approaching. So far there'd been no confirmed casualties.

"Team Three?" Bolan said.

"Ready."

Shifting to the other side of the crates, Bolan reloaded the assault rifle and the Desert Eagle, then releathered the pistol. He yanked a pair of flash-bang grenades from his harness, then tossed them toward the prow and the small knot of Yakuza that were working on gaining an offensive edge.

The grenades landed on the deck in front of them and they tried to pull back. Before they could get organized, the explosives detonated in a blinding flash of light and loud booms.

Bolan knew the hostages trapped in the cooler below were probably in the dark and able to hear the battle going on above them. The panic filling them was going to be a problem for the rescuers, too.

"Team Two's ready," Carson transmitted.

"Go," Bolan said. "Team One has your back." He whirled around the crates and opened fire, hosing any area where the Yakuza or pirates might be hiding. The rest of Team One's firepower joined him. The ruby dots of the sniper's laser sights touched gunners and put them down, while the autofire briefly drove back the opposition on both ends of the ship.

Team Two burst from cover, carrying the preset packages of shaped charges the squad's demolition men had designed to take out the top deck. In seconds they were laid out in a rough oval between the main mast and the stern mast. The SEALs' sudden vulnerability inspired a new wave of return fire from the pirates and Yakuza.

Three of the Navy specialists went down. One was able to get back up and stumble to cover. A second was helped by two of his comrades. The third man was less than ten feet from Bolan.

The Executioner broke cover as a line of bullets from a machine pistol tracked the downed SEAL. He ran to the man's side, grabbed his arm and yanked him back to the cover of the crates.

Bolan propped the man against the crates and quickly checked him over. A pair of rounds had torn through the man's neck. His breath was a black-speckled froth from the hole in his windpipe, but he was breathing. The man's eyes were already glassy, and his grip on Bolan's arm was weak.

"Take it easy," the soldier told him. "We're going to get you out of here."

"Yes, sir," he replied in a choked voice.

Bolan hit the transmit button on the headset. "I need a medic over here. Now. Got a man down with a neck wound. Through and through, and tracheal rupture. I don't want him to drown in his own blood."

"On my way," a man said.

Bolan fed a new magazine into the assault rifle as another SEAL carrying a medikit dodged a hail of bullets and slid across the deck to the wounded man.

"I got him, Colonel," the medic said, rummaging through his kit.

"Keep him alive," Bolan said, then glanced at the

wounded man. "And you don't have my permission to die. I didn't call you out on this to get yourself killed."

A slight smile twitched the man's lips. "No, sir."

Bolan keyed the transmit button. "Team Two."

"Sir!"

"Confirm your readiness."

"Clean and green," the gruff answer came back.

"Do it," the Executioner said, turning to shelter the wounded man and the medic.

"Fire in the hole!" the demolition leader yelled over the com channel.

An instant later, the upper deck erupted in smoke, fire and thunder. A hole opened in the deck, fiery embers clinging to the edges in places.

"Go!" Bolan ordered. For a moment the gunfire coming from the pirates and Yakuza hit a lull. With the sound of the explosions, it could have been conceived that the ship had been destroyed, or come near to it.

The Executioner was in motion at once. He moved his head, taking in the changing fields of fire. Twice, he touched off 3-round bursts that took down targets. He kept scanning the area for Crowe but didn't see the man. Evidently the big pirate had assumed a low profile after being attacked on two fronts.

Rappelling lines spilled from men stationed in the main and stern masts, creating a new webbing. The SEALs jumped through the hole, holding on to the ropes. A portion of them were assigned to the extraction of hostages, while the others readied the salvage gear for quick use.

Glancing into the rigging, Bolan watched a team unfold a ten-foot by ten-foot bulletproof cloth in the lines near the main mast. It was going to be a staging area for the extraction, providing cover for the hostages.

"Colonel, this is Team Two Leader," Carson said.

"Go." Bolan took up a position behind the main mast.

Wood had been ripped from the smooth bore by bullets in a number of places.

The gunfire from the cargo hold sounded thunderous as it rose out of the hole.

"We have the hostages. We're bringing them through on your go."

"Hold up, Team Two Leader," Bolan said.

"Be advised our position here is tenuous at best, Colonel," Carson replied. "These people are going schizo from all the fireworks, and they're not exactly sure about us. Also, there's a lot of the opposition down here with us."

"Understood." Bolan glanced around, watching the Yakuza ships jockeying for position. He estimated their number to be greater than the SEALs. "Indigo Phantom Wing Leader."

"Roger, Colonel. You have Indigo Phantom Wing Leader."

"Bring on the heat," Bolan ordered. "You and Wing Two. Both sides of the freighter. Strip those other ships out of the water, build us some space and some time."

"That's affirmative, Colonel. Indigo Phantom Wing Leader and Two are on the move."

"Team One Leader," Bolan said, "you've got the sitcon."

"Roger, Colonel. We'll hold the fort until you get back."

A sudden explosion at the side of the ship shivered through the freighter. Bolan was staggered, and barely avoided a wave of gunfire that burned tracers within inches of his face. He whirled with the M-16 to his shoulder and returned fire, cutting down one man with a blistering figure eight and taking out another with a burst that crunched through his face.

"Colonel, this is Team Three Leader. We have a hull breach at the waterline."

"From inside or outside?" Bolan asked, changing magazines in the M-16.

"Outside. Dammit, we're taking on water and they're sending people through."

"Starboard or port?"

"Starboard."

"Patch it," Bolan said. "I'm coming down." He stepped forward and grabbed one of the ropes leading through the hole the demolition team had blown through the deck.

"Indigo Phantom Wing, did you copy?"

"Affirmative, Colonel. I got your starboard side."

The helicopters came with a sudden wave of thunder created by the spinning rotors. Little more than fifty yards above the ocean's surface, the CH-53Es looked like giant insects coming in for a landing.

Only they didn't land. With unerring accuracy, the combat choppers unleashed everything at their disposal, targeting the eight boats surrounding the *Jilly St. Agnes*. Twenty millimeter cannons, chain guns and rocket pods lit up the night in an incendiary display of total destruction.

Two of the powerboats were decimated before Bolan gripped the rope and slid into the hold.

12

Chaos reigned inside the belly of the freighter. The cargo had slipped loose from its moorings during the battle, and crates spilled across the floor. The impromptu maze became hazardous for everyone. Flashlight beams lanced across the open spaces and burned shadows away from the walls, floor and ceiling wherever they touched. Muzzle-flashes jumped and jerked like sparks thrown up by a greenwood fire.

The slide down the rope came close to burning Bolan's hands. The dark almost made NVGs necessary. The hole in the starboard side was made even more visible by the fragments of the powerboats burning just on the other side. The water came through the ruptured hulls in silver streams.

Indigo Phantom Wing leader had made a good run.

Touching bottom, Bolan released the rope and grabbed the assault rifle. The black-clad Yakuza were hard targets against the backdrop of shadows filling the cargo hold, but he managed to put three of them down before return fire drove him to cover.

Bolan stayed low as he made his way through the tangle of cargo. Crates lay broken and shattered around him. Pieces of equipment, skeins of cloth, canned foods and preserves were only part of the debris left from the explosions. Some of it was starting to float and move, eddying in the growing pool of water. When Bolan stepped into it, he was surprised to find that it had already risen to a depth that reached his midcalf.

Tagging the headset transmit button, Bolan said, "Team Three Leader, this is Pollock."

"Go, Colonel."

"How soon before you're ready to attempt resecuring the integrity of this vessel?" Bolan made his way to the cooler area. The corpse of a pirate lay facedown in the water, one arm flopping loosely in the scarlet-threaded water.

"A minute more. Maybe two. The resistance down here is hell. Pirates trapped with us are putting up more of a fight than they would have if the Yakuza hadn't forced them to retreat down here."

"Understood. Let me know when you're functional." Eyes more adjusted to the lack of light now, the Executioner scanned the hellzone from his vantage point atop the forklift strapped in the center of the room.

Team Two had already begun extraction of the hostages. Limned against the lighter patch of the hole blown in the upper deck, one of the hostages was being hauled up the block-and-tackle arrangement, worked by ropes dangling into the hold. The hostage went up fast and easy, disappearing from Bolan's sight.

"Team Two Leader, get me a count on the hostages," Bolan said.

"I make it nine," Carson replied.

"Confirms what I had earlier," Bolan replied. Even with the radios, the gunshots trapped inside the hold were so loud that he had to shout to be heard.

"Got a feisty lady here who tells me that number is dead-on."

Bolan figured he knew who the lady was. "Count them off as you get them out. Team One Leader, I want confirmation on each and every hostage taken out."

"Acknowledged, sir. Total stands at two now. Healthy and waiting to get the hell out of here."

Bolan sighted on a pirate who was firing at the extraction crew near the cooler from a prone position on the catwalk scaffolding near the emergency ladder he'd used earlier to escape. He stroked the trigger, riding out the minimal recoil in case he needed a follow-up round.

The bullet took the man through the head. Without motor control, the body rolled from the scaffolding.

"Colonel, this is Team Three Leader."

"Go, Three Leader," Bolan responded. A flurry of action drew his attention to the cooler area. Gunshots rang out a frantic staccato.

"Damn!" Carson swore. "Team Two is jammed!"

Bolan dropped from the forklift and ran toward the cooler. The water was swirling around his knees now, making progress harder.

"Team Three is set up now, Colonel. We'll need the air supply standing by. If we don't get some flotation working on this vessel, we're going to lose her."

"Affirmative," Bolan answered. He scanned the Yakuza gunners ringing Carson and two other SEALs. One of the Navy special ops was in the water, flailing off balance and trying to find cover. "Indigo Phantom Wing Three, do you copy?"

"Wing Three copies, Colonel. We're inbound now."

The Executioner raised the M-16, staying in the slight cover of a toppled aisle of boxes and bundles of cloth. He sighted on one of the gunners firing on the downed SEAL and squeezed the trigger twice in rapid succession.

The 5.56 mm tumbler caught the man below his left eye and punched his brain through the back of his head. The Executioner lowered the sights on a second man before they knew there was a wolf amidst them. Two more men dropped before they could react to the new threat. Bolan secured one more hit on the back of a target's head as they turned and fled.

Carson was holding a defensive position against the back wall by the cooler, in a crouch and partially behind an overturned crate that had been viciously scarred by bullets. Hannah Raynes crouched beside him, fighting against the arm the SEAL commander had thrown around her protectively.

"He's hit, damn it!" she screamed at Bolan. Her hands were hooked in the back of Carson's gear, and it was obvious she was trying to help him stand.

Bolan moved forward through the water swirling around them. The freighter was starting to list, heavier now in the stern than in the prow. The water was above the soldier's knees. He shoved floating boxes out of the way, and one corpse, as he neared Carson.

"How bad is it?" Bolan asked.

"Take her and get the hell out of here," Carson said through gritted teeth. "I can make my own way." Blood slicked the black uniform. The entry wound appeared to be under his left arm, less than an inch from the protective weave of the bulletproof armor. With that trajectory, the bullet had to be lodged deep in the SEAL's chest, possibly in a lung.

"The hell he can," Raynes yelled. "He's barely standing on his own now." The woman looked ragged and worn from the hours of captivity, but her spirit was as abrasive as ever.

"Stand down, soldier," Bolan told the man. "Your bit's done. We're getting you out of here." He slung the M-16, then picked up Carson in a fireman's carry. "Anyone else here?"

Raynes fell into step beside him, shoving aside floating debris. Flashlights raked the darkness ahead of them. "No. They got us all out."

"She stayed," Carson said weakly. "Wouldn't go until we got all the others."

"They were my passengers," Raynes said. "I'm responsible for them."

Bolan kept moving, avoiding as much of the bigger cargo as he could. The footing was slippery now that water covered the deck. He tried not to think about the toxic waste that might have poured from bullet-riddled containers. There was still a chance the SEAL team could salvage the ship before it went down.

The hostage count at topside held at eight.

"Indigo Phantom Wing One and Two, lock into retrieval position and begin evacuating the civilians. Three, we need that pressure line down here now."

All the Wings responded.

As Bolan helped Carson tie onto the line, Raynes screamed a warning. He whirled at once and found himself face-to-face with Santiago Crowe.

The pirate chief leaped at him like a giant black panther. The machete was back over his shoulder ready to cleave. Blood spattered his clothing.

Bolan didn't have a chance to stand his ground. Crowe grabbed a fistful of the Executioner's combat harness, using his bigger size and greater weight to drive his prey to ground. In a heartbeat, Bolan's face was under water. Crowe was on top of him, holding him under. There was no way to bring the M-16 into play, and the Desert Eagle was pinned in its holster under him.

"Been looking for you, man," Crowe snarled. "Seeing all these people here, I knew you had to be on the ship someplace. Had me a feeling." The machete arced down in a sudden blur, coming straight at Bolan's face.

Reaching up, Bolan blocked Crowe's swing, ramming his forearm against the inside of the pirate's arm hard enough to deflect the blow. Lungs aching for air, he rolled enough to shove the bigger man from him.

Crowe got to his feet at the same time as Bolan and immediately swung the machete again, giving the Executioner no time to draw either of the weapons.

Bolan ducked to one side and kept his hands up in a ready defense, circling in the now waist-deep water. In the background, he saw the yellow plastic of the inflatable flotation bags going up around the cargo hold as SEAL Team Three got them in position.

Giving no quarter, Crowe came at him again immediately, slashing at Bolan's midsection.

The soldier jumped back and the blade slashed through the front of the bulletproof vest. Protection against bullets, the vest wouldn't last long against the machete.

Crowe bulled at him again, growling in rage. His size and strength gave him the edge to push Bolan back against one of the crates containing the toxic waste. The wood was rough against the back of the soldier's neck. He caught the pirate's wrists with difficulty and strained to push him back.

Carson was already being hauled away, slumped like he'd dropped into unconsciousness. Hannah Raynes had been attacked by Domingo Krauss, blond hair bloody in the combination of moonlight and flashlight beams. The rest of the SEAL teams were busy securing the salvage equipment or protecting the men who were.

"Little man," Crowe shouted, "I'm going to crush you, then I'm going to gut you and strangle you with your own intestines."

Bolan lifted a knee and planted it in the bigger man's groin, feeling the shiver run all through Crowe. Still, the deadly grip didn't break. He kicked again and felt the hand loosen. Moving quickly, the soldier bent his knees and dropped, pulling Crowe off balance. He twisted an arm across the pirate's, tearing free of the grip. Before Crowe could recover, Bolan drew the Randall survival knife from its sheath on his chest. The gleaming, sharp blade whisked free in a heartbeat.

"Kill the bastard, man," Krauss urged from behind Crowe. "Kill him and let's get the fuck out of here now." He held Raynes easily against him despite her struggles against the forearm under her chin.

Crowe straightened, lifting the machete. He smiled at the knife in the Executioner's hand. "Man, that's only slightly better than taking me on with a butter knife. I'm going to chop off your head, make a new necklace with it after the fishes eat your face off.'' He snapped the blade out in an overhand swing, intending to bury it in Bolan's skull.

The Executioner moved, dropping his right leg and his knife hand back and away. His left hand swept across his body, catching Crowe's elbow and shoving it aside. The machete whistled past Bolan, the point nicking his shoulder.

Still in motion, completing the move he'd set himself up for, the Executioner gripped the haft of the Randall knife tightly and whipped it forward, stepping into the blow with his full weight. The point of the survival blade penetrated Crowe's bulletproof vest like tissue paper, then plunged to the hilt just under the big man's sternum. The force and angle carried it into and through Crowe's heart.

A look of surprise dawned on the pirate's face as he stared into Bolan's eyes. He tried to speak, but blood trickled from his soundless lips, threading down his chin. He quivered once and died, starting to collapse.

''You kill him, man?'' Krauss demanded.

Bolan shoved Crowe's corpse from him, dropped the Randall survival knife and drew the Desert Eagle. The pirate's falling body blocked Krauss's view of him for a heartbeat. It was enough.

Krauss stood with a pistol to Hannah Raynes's temple, turned at a ninety-degree angle to Bolan. His eyes narrowed as he saw Bolan still standing, then he shoved his gun out and started to fire.

None of the three rounds Krauss got off touched the Executioner. Then the Desert Eagle was up and he fired from the point.

The 240-grain boattail took off the top of Krauss's head and sent the corpse spinning away from Raynes.

''Go,'' Bolan told her, guiding her to the rope with his free hand.

The woman stepped into the waiting loop just as a long hose dropped through the hole that had been blown in the deck. Members of Team Three splashed through the rising water and grabbed it, taking it to the various feeds they'd set up to the air bags that would keep the freighter afloat. In seconds they began to swell.

"Colonel, this is Team Three Leader. We are go on keeping her up. Once we get her stabilized, we'll work on patching that hole."

"Affirmative, Three Leader. If there's anything else, let me know." Bolan stepped into the loop with Raynes, still holding the Desert Eagle as he gripped the rope with his free hand.

"Just let us know how the captain makes out. He's a good man."

"Will do." The rope started up with a jerk, then gained speed. Bolan stared up through the hole, watching as the three massive helicopters came into view.

The Super Stallions were in a triple-decker stack above the *Jilly St. Agnes.* Wings One and Two were on either side of the staging area made in the rigging around the main mast. Both had rope ladders stretched out taut to the sides, leaving enough room for Wing Three above them to drop the pressure line pumping the flotation bags full. Hostages, each escorted by a pair of SEALs, were climbing both of the rope ladders to safety.

The deck was clear except for scattered pockets of resistance from the Yakuza and pirates. SEAL teams were systematically digging them out and taking them into custody.

Rising above the deck, Bolan saw the remaining broken fragments of the powerboats scattered around the freighter. Flames still burned on some of them. Then one of the powerboats came to life, spitting white spumes behind it as it turned and raced toward the open sea.

"Damn," Wing Two said over the com link. "We missed one."

Bolan could tell from the damaged bridge-work on the powerboat and from the corpses lying on its deck that it hadn't been missed entirely. He swung out and dropped six feet to the deck, watching the powerboat. The freighter had stopped dead in the ocean, still taking on water, and the three Super Stallions were committed to holding their positions. They were sitting ducks if anyone in the powerboat wanted to take a shot at them.

LYNDON PALFREY HEARD the movement behind him and turned, not knowing what to expect. The aerial bombardment had been worse than anything he'd ever been through. He kept the powerboat steady, though, and left the engines wide open, moving away from the freighter as fast as he could go.

Hideo Shotozumi stood there uncertainly. His clothing was ripped and torn, and blood stained his face and shirt. If it was all his, Palfrey didn't know how the man was still alive.

"Turn the boat around," Shotozumi commanded in a croak.

"What?" Palfrey knew he couldn't possibly have heard the man right.

Shotozumi lifted his hand, showing Palfrey the pistol he was holding. "Turn the boat around. Now!"

"The hell I will." Palfrey waved back at the freighter. The three helicopters were all linked to the *Jilly St. Agnes.* For how long, he didn't know, but he hoped it was long enough for him to get clear of the area.

Without a word, the Yakuza lieutenant shot him through both legs.

Stunned and hurting, his legs no longer able to hold him up, Palfrey fell. "You crazy son of a bitch!" Palfrey screamed. "What the hell do you think you're doing?"

Shotozumi grabbed Palfrey's shirt collar and yanked him back from the controls with surprising strength. He limped to the wheel and brought the powerboat around in a tight turn. "My duty," he said. "In failure, I am a dead man anyway."

In disbelief, Palfrey watched as Shotozumi aimed the powerboat at the freighter, vectoring in on the hole the Yakuza had blown in the ship's side in an attempt to bring it down and provide them egress. They were at least eight hundred yards out. There was still time to escape. He reached for the small pistol he kept in an ankle holster, managed to get his fingers around the butt of it and was starting to draw it when Shotozumi turned and looked at him with eyes that showed the pain within.

Palfrey tried to bring up the pistol, but knew he was too late. Shotozumi raised his own weapon and fired.

Never feeling the impact that shattered his head, Palfrey's world turned black.

BOLAN SAW the powerboat turn around then head straight for the freighter, coming at the weak spot that had already been created in the ship's side. At that speed, with the bulk it had behind it, there was every chance that the powerboat would rip through the hull of the *Jilly St. Agnes* and send her down in minutes before the salvage equipment could finish being set up.

"Oh, shit," someone said over the com link.

There was no time for any of the Super Stallions to break away and engage the powerboat. Hostages were still on the secured rope ladders, and the pressure line couldn't be jostled much without possibly getting tangled in the rotors of the helos below it.

SEAL gunners lined the starboard side and fired at the powerboat. It was seven hundred yards out and closing like a hungry shark.

Bolan tapped the transmit button. "Rebel."

"Already heard," Murphy responded. "I'm on my way."

Checking the horizon, Bolan saw the Bell chopper on an approach pattern. "Meet me on the prow."

"Roger."

Scanning the line of SEALs, the soldier spotted a man

taking a LAW from his equipment pack. "I'll take that," Bolan said.

The SEAL flipped the collapsible light antitank weapon to Bolan. "Figured I might get a shot, maybe put that boat down before it reached us."

Bolan didn't answer. Firing down on the powerboat, even if the man was able to hit it, would only wreck the top deck. If it was close enough, whatever was left of the powerboat stood a good chance of plowing on into the side of the freighter and possibly succeeding in bringing the ship down with it anyway.

By the time Bolan reached the prow of the freighter, the powerboat was at four hundred yards, the LAW's optimum range. Murphy dropped the helicopter over Bolan. The soldier reached up and caught the nearest landing skid. "Go," he called over the headset.

The powerboat was at three hundred yards, rising up out of the water from the hydroplaning action. Tracer rounds from the SEALs' guns were scoring it now, but it showed no hesitation in the approach.

"How do you want to handle this?" Murphy asked. His voice over the com link sound distant and hollow in the deluge of noise that filled the air. The chopper leaped away from the freighter's deck and spun toward the powerboat.

"Go in low and head-on," Bolan replied, stretching himself into position along the skid. It took all his strength to hang on as the wind, centrifugal force and gravity pulled and pushed at him. He closed his left arm around the forward strut and wrapped his ankles around the skid. "I need a shot at the waterline."

"You got it," Murphy said. The helicopter jinked, dropping some altitude as it lined up on a collision course with the approaching powerboat. They were a hundred yards out from the *Jilly St. Agnes,* little more than the same distance from the powerboat.

The blurred ocean surface was less than five feet under

the helicopter's skids when Bolan opened the LAW. The sections snapped into place and he flipped up the crosshairs. He knew the 94 mm warhead wouldn't destroy its target, but if it hit at the waterline, the resulting hole should create enough drag to stop the powerboat's approach, or at least slow it so when it hit, it wouldn't be as damaging.

The Executioner slipped his finger over the firing stud and tried to bring the shot on-line. "Steady," he told Murphy.

"You're getting the best I've got to give," the pilot replied grimly. "And we're for damn sure running out of time."

Resting the rocket launcher's tube over his shoulder, Bolan rolled slightly onto his side. The powerboat was headed straight for them, spitting up twin plumes of froth on either side of the prow.

If the powerboat succeeded in ramming the freighter, the resulting confusion might bring down the helicopters as well, drawing them all into a web of destruction, connected by the various umbilicals they'd set up. Whoever was piloting the powerboat, Bolan knew it was a last-ditch effort to get rid of the incriminating toxic-waste canisters.

He held the LAW steady as the distance separating the helicopter and the boat dropped to less than sixty yards. The combined speeds put them only a heartbeat away from each other.

"Now!" Bolan said. "Pull up and to the right!"

Murphy swerved his craft with expertise. Even at that, the miss was only going to be by a handful of yards once they gained the proper altitude.

The Executioner pressed the firing stud when the shot he wanted came into view. The warhead jumped from the rocket launcher's mouth, trailing smoke and flame in its wake. At that range, the powerboat's hull looked incredibly huge.

The explosion threw out a wave of heat and debris that washed over Bolan with enough force to rip loose his hold on the helicopter's skid. He flailed with one hand as Murphy continued the climb, shooting through the orange-and-yellow flames that licked up from the stricken vessel.

The disposable LAW dropped from his hand as he reached to secure another hold. He glanced down.

The warhead had struck the powerboat at the waterline, where Bolan had intended. The resulting hole had stopped the boat's forward progress little more than eighty yards from the *Jilly St. Agnes* before the explosions on board had ripped it to shreds. Debris rained across the ocean surface.

"Damn, Colonel, that was some good shooting," Indigo Phantom Wing Leader called out over the com link.

"We'll make time to pat each other on the back later," Bolan said. "Get those people out of there."

"We're on it, buddy."

With effort, Bolan pulled himself onto the skid, then made the stretch to reach the co-pilot's door as Murphy reached across and opened it. He dropped tiredly into the seat. A quick conversation with Team Three Leader assured him that the flotation bags were going to hold up the freighter until transport ships could arrive from Guantanamo.

By the time dawn touched the sky, Bolan knew the sea would reclaim much of the damage showing now. It would cover its scars, hiding them from view and go on as it always had. He knew those who'd survived Santiago Crowe's cruelties would do the same. It was nature's way, allowing survivors to go on in spite of the wounds and terrors they'd faced.

But the soldier felt that nature had never intended for the kind of predators to be loosed on the world that came in the form of Cannibal Man. As long as he could stand and he could fight, the Executioner intended to hold against those predators, and he would draw the line of demarcation between civilized and savage in their blood.

Iran ups the ante in Bosnia with new weapons of terror....

TRIPLE STRIKE

A kidnapped U.S. advisor and a downed recon plane pilot are held in a stronghold in Muslim Bosnia, where Iranian forces have joined with their Bosnian brothers to eradicate the unbelievers.

The President and Stony Man must use their individual powers of influence to bring the agents of doom to justice—if there's still time....

Available in November 1998 at your favorite retail outlet.

In the badlands, there is only survival....

JAMES AXLER

DEATH LANDS®

Crucible of Time

A connection to his past awaits Ryan Cawdor as the group takes a mat-trans jump to the remnants of California. Brother Joshua Wolfe is the leader of the Children of the Rock—a cult that has left a trail of barbarism and hate across the ravaged California countryside. Far from welcoming the group with open arms, the cult forces them into a deadly battle-ritual— which is only their first taste of combat....

Journey back to the future
with these classic

titles!

A preview from hell...

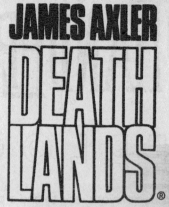

JAMES AXLER
DEATH LANDS®
Dark Emblem

After a relatively easy mat-trans jump, Ryan and his companions find themselves in the company of Dr. Silas Jamaisvous, a seemingly pleasant host who appears to understand the mat-trans systems extremely well.

Seeing signs that local inhabitants have been used as guinea pigs for the scientist's ruthless experiments, the group realizes that they have to stop this line of research before it goes too far....

James Axler

OUTLANDERS™

ICEBLOOD

Kane and his companions race to find a piece of the Chintamanti Stone, which they believe to have power over the collective mind of the evil Archons. Their journey sees them foiled by a Russian mystic named Zakat in Manhattan, and there is another dangerous encounter waiting for them in the Kun Lun mountains of China.

One man's quest for power unleashes a cataclysm in America's wastelands.

GOUT7